Jenny

Starborn

Diana Yvonne Walter

Also by Diana Walter

IN THE FIRE FLIGHT SERIES

Book I

An Unusual Beauty / Fire Flight

www.createspace.com/3924949

Book II

StarFire / Bricca Down West

www.createspace.com/4310563

Other Books by Diana Walter

Vulcan and the Golden Teachings

Angels and Body Fat

See Amazon.com

Dedicated to

My Nieces

Allison, Beth, Cassandra

Kitty, Laurel and Sarah

❧

With gratitude

For

The Future they Bring

One

৭

Jennifer Bridger-Mead pulled her suit jacket down and snugged up the zipper on her pencil skirt as she turned around in the full-length mirror to make sure there weren't any wrinkles in the lemon colored linen. Her stripped white and navy blue blouse had a simple cowl neck so she had opted for a tiny deep blue sapphire on a thin, almost invisible chain. Sweeping her long gold hair into a loose knot she applied the barest minimum of makeup. With brown eyes, dark eyebrows and smooth olive skin all she needed was a little bit of shiny nude lip-gloss. Slipping on a pair of deep blue high-heeled shoes she studied the effect.

I look edible, she smiled to herself. Perfect for the presentation she was making to the foundation board members.

Her cell phone rang and Jennifer grabbed it off of her dresser hitting FaceTime so that she could see her mom and dad on the screen.

"Hey Jenny Rabbit, are you all ready for the big interview?" her dad, Jace asked. Jenny saw that he was wearing his cowboy hat and canvas jacket so he must have just come in from feeding the cattle.

"As ready as I can be. I've prepared each board member with a packet of information and I'm bringing samples and a power point presentation on my proposal."

"Sounds pretty fancy. You'll knock them dead."

Jennifer's mom, Lily piped in. "Don't forget that Judd Barron's daughter has one of my champion jumpers in her stable out of Brave Day. Sometimes stuff like that helps when you are trying to win support."

"Thanks for the heads up. I had forgotten about that. Do you think I look professional enough or too young?"

"You look perfect. Professional but not too stiff," Lily said.

Jace piped in. "Well you *are young* baby, those folks will appreciate your youth. Just enjoy it while you can. And be careful taking the El into the city. Is someone going with you? Hey, when are you coming home?"

"I've taken the transit plenty of times by myself and Grandpa Barry is meeting me for a late lunch at Holly Oak Bistro. Hopefully it will be to celebrate!"

"Well, give him and Sophie a kiss from me," Lily said. "Also your brother says to 'give 'em hell.'"

"I love you guys," Jennifer said, as usual getting a little homesick after seeing her folks. "Give Bern a squeeze from me."

"We love you too, Jenny Rabbit Bo-Peep," Jace said. Jenny could see that he was tickling her mom who was laughing and pushing him away while she tried to hold onto the phone.

Jennifer hung up with a teary feeling of nostalgia. Her mom and dad were always goofing around, hugging and teasing each other. Why had it been so hard for *her* to find the right guy?

Grabbing a little purse and her briefcase she checked to make sure her laptop was there and counted again to ensure that she had six packets for the board. Slipping her shoes into a bag she put on some white tennis shoes, locked the door to her flat and trotted down the stairs waving at the doorman.

From here it was a brisk walk through the residential housing area of the campus to the transit station. Tall trees lined the road and overgrown lawns sloped down to the sidewalk with messy gardens and scraggly flowering bushes. Kids skipped down the sidewalk beside moms pushing strollers and dragging reluctant dogs who were anxious to get off the leash and find a yard to sniff around in. Jennifer saw some students walking towards campus and she smiled.

She had just graduated with a BA in Business Management. She was twenty-one years old and free as a bird but nervous about that freedom. It was time to try to follow her dreams and see where it took her.

Jennifer had been preparing for this moment for most of her life. It had started for her when she was only four years old. She remembered asking her mom if she could count her money for her into piles and get a quarter for doing it. Her mom had laughed and said, "Instead I'll give you a quarter as an allowance if you will feed the dog every day." Jenny had taken her job seriously. She loved feeding their golden retriever, Bodhi. Half of the time her own supper would end up as a snack for him under the table when her mom wasn't looking.

The retired neighbors Betsy and Shortie Hall had taken her under her wing as a surrogate granddaughter. Betsy grew a large garden, canned vegetables and made currant and huckleberry jams. Betsy also knitted and made soaps and candles. They had chickens for eggs and goats for fresh goat cheese. Betsy had helped her come up with recipes for animal treats and helped her cook them at their little homestead cabin at Spotted Horse Draw. Betsy knew how to sew and taught Jenny how to put the thread through the needle and make small blind stiches that you couldn't see.

First Jenny had become fascinated with making dog treats out of ingredients like peanut butter and oatmeal. Then she had stitched doggie daypacks so that dogs could carry their own food when going on long day hikes. She had experimented with horse and goat treats and even spent a summer designing unusual animal feeders. On everything that she made she would put her adopted Dad's brand for the M Rocking B Ranch. The Brand looked like a half moon lying on its side with an M above and a B below. The Bridger-Mead cattle ranch was one of the largest working cattle ranches in Montana. Her Dad's wranglers still summered the cattle on ranges high up on Snow Mountain and Mount Anne above Paradise Valley. The brand carried the historical weight of four generation of settlers who had homesteaded and founded White Cloud, Montana.

Sometimes Jenny packaged her treats in her mom's canning jars with colorful gingham clothes that Betsy provided under the lids. She and Betsy had spent many hours by the fire during the long mountain winter months cutting circles with pinking shears and knitting warm neck gators for her dog and the kittens, Jacqueline and Jillian (Jack and Jill).

Jenny had had a gift for inventing things at an early age and had been a business tycoon ever since she first discovered money. Her family knew it and made a habit out of making her birthday and Christmas gifts fit the theme. She had a collection of piggy banks; all full by the time she was seven. She had been given gold nuggets, money trees and an antique silver dollar. They all went on her shelf or in treasure boxes. She decided at nine she needed her own small business.

At age eleven her Aunt Bricca had helped her put her logo on a computer so she could print flyers and try to sell her horse and dog treats in town. In order to get supplies for her business she had begged her dad to let her have an afterschool job inputting the invoices for his ranch bookkeeping. Jace had agreed as long as she promised not to work more then 1/2 hour a day. They had had plenty of fights where he had tried to shoo her out of the office to go and play. Jenny loved writing the numbers in neat columns and had a knack for understanding the bottom line and reconciling books to the penny.

Aunt Bricca had helped her put a Photoshop sketch of her beloved golden retriever Bodhi behind the brand. Even though Bodhi had gone to dog heaven when she was eight, now he was immortalized. She called her dog treats Bodhi Bones and the name had caught on. It had been easy to have 500 labels made over the Internet. She had tied each brown paper bag with a twine bow and sold horse and dog treats for $12.00 a bag. The local feed store and grocery store agreed to carry Bodhi Bones and she marketed them in nearby towns too. By age twelve she had needed to open a savings account for all of her cash. It had been sad breaking the piggy banks, but her whole family had made it a ceremony. Her mom had even made a cake that said 'Jenny Rabbit gets Rich' for the occasion.

Jenny had perfected her recipes for the last sixteen years. Being a cautious young woman she had protected her unique formulas and unusual ingredients with copyrights. She had also handwritten each recipe on cards that her Granny had given her and put them into the old green tin recipe box that was a family heirloom. Grandma Sophia Barry had given her mother's recipe box to Lily when Lily and Jace had married. It was stuffed with recipes that were Nebraska church potluck favorites. Tucked among them were original poems, quotes, creative crafts ideas and noteworthy magazine clippings. At her college graduation Lily had gifted the recipe box to Jenny. Jenny had promptly scanned all the recipes and memorabilia onto a computer and printed books so everyone in the family could have a copy. She had titled the family book *Home in the Heartland* and made the cover sepia of her grandmother, Sophia Rose Wildner as a little girl being pushed on an old wooden swing under an immense cottonwood. Sophie's mother was pushing the swing looking young and carefree in a white short-sleeved blouse and gathered skirt. Sometimes just knowing that her great grandparents had once been that young would make Jenny feel sentimental and tearful. Now Jenny held the recipe box and prayed, thinking of it as her 'good luck box.' It carried the power of generations of strong women from both sides of her family.

Jenny was used to seeing women excel. Her mom, Lily, had been a professional equestrian who had through sheer determination built Bricca Down West, a successful horse-breeding farm in White Cloud, Montana. Lily had a champion stud named Bricca Down Thunder and eight champion broodmares. Her grandmother Sophia Rose Wildner was an acclaimed author of books that were now considered classics. Her Great Grandmother Charlotte Stanford had built Stanford Farms in Virginia. Her Aunt Bricca had been talented dancer, a creative teacher, a rodeo star and a champion in the international circuit before raising a large family. Aunt Bricca could sometimes see the future. She and Jenny shared that odd psychic ability.

It is a lot to live up to, Jenny thought as she sped up a little just to make sure there was no chance of missing her connection into the city.

Once on the train Jenny tried to relax but couldn't quite stop her heart from beating too fast. The day was getting muggy and she slipped off her jacket so she wouldn't perspire in it. Her tight skirt kept twisting and she wiggled around on her seat trying to get comfortable. She noticed a man who looked down on his luck was watching her. His straggly beard bushed out in all directions from a grey stocking cap pulled low over his aging face. Grey work pants held a layer of grease and Jenny could smell him across the aisle. In front of her was a young black mother with a toddler who had a long line of snot running down her cheek. Behind her were two teenage girls with black eye liner, tattoos and eight nose rings among them laughing over a magazine. Jenny immediately put her head down so they wouldn't make eye contact. It was a lot different living in the city than in a small mountain town. She would have never been so rude in White Cloud. Here being too friendly made you a target, especially when you were young, preppy and blond. Jenny had learned the hard way that the transit wasn't a place to strike up a conversation.

Everything about the city had been an exciting and sometimes scary adventure. She had grown up in a town of 200 living on a ranch that was 15 miles down a dirt road and snugged up into the mountains. There had been 22 kids in her high school and she had had the same best friend her whole life. Leaving home to attend a huge university had been daunting. But Jenny had never been one to turn down a challenge. Her mom had originally been from Chicago and she, her grandparents and her mom's old nanny, Sheila, still lived here. Sheila and Max had had two kids, Alex and Nina that were only three and four years older than her mother. Jenny thought of them as a surrogate Aunt and Uncle. Having family to support her in Chicago made being in a big city less frightening.

For the first two years at Chicago University she had lived in the dorm, visiting her grandparents on weekends when she wasn't working for her advisor trying to earn her tuition. Then she had found roommates and a flat. While it had been harder to study living off campus she had managed to remove herself from her roommate's late night parties. Jenny didn't like to feel out of control. When everyone else was drunk or high Jenny would put on earphones and listen to music or sketch out her business plans. She had excelled in her program and been granted a Dean's fellowship. Two of her professors had sponsored her for the business grant.

Now her flat mates had moved out and soon she would have to decide on where she was going to live. The flat was too expense for her to cover the rent by herself. In ninety days she would need to start paying back her student loans and she needed to get a job soon. Creating a portfolio for starting her own business had been either a brave or foolish thing to do. Most people would have seen her as too young and suggested she needed to get more experience in business working for others. Jenny had had other plans all along.

Getting the business degree had seemed like a formality. It was a way to pass the time so that she could grow up and get on with things. Her classes had been easy for her so she spent a lot of time doodling or daydreaming. In her dreams she saw herself at a desk with a big window that looked over a beautiful city. In front of her was a neat stack of papers for her to sign and a pad with her calendar on it. She was wearing a deep blue dress with a bold scarf and had her hair twisted in a sophisticated knot. Her secretary was a young man who was polite, friendly and efficient. She was working on the ad campaign for a new product line and was buzzing with excitement at an idea that was starting to take shape.

Then the professor would ask her a question startling her out of her revere. She would spend the rest of class wondering why there was never a photograph of her husband or children on her desk in those flashes of the future.

Jenny checked her watch as the transit took on more passengers. Only 10 more minutes. She took the opportunity to study the portfolio of the five men and the woman she would be talking to. It was the woman who seemed most interesting because her name was Sandra Tavery. Jenny's real father had died when she was only four years old. His name had been Ned Tavery and he had been an investor for a stock market company in Chicago. There was some mystery around his death and Jenny's memories about it were fuzzy and traumatic. She remembered a gunshot, screams and blood but nothing else. For some reason Jenny had always been afraid to ask her mother to fill in all of the details. She didn't want the memories to surface. Jenny had been adopted when Lily had married her dad Jace. Her last name had been changed to Bridger-Mead and that was that. They never talked about her real dad again.

Sandra Tavery looked to be in her mid-fifties. *Could she be related to my dad?* Jenny wondered. *She's the right age for them to be brother and sister.* Sandra owned a real estate firm and her dress and picture looked mature, polished and successful.

Jenny scanned the other board member descriptions. Judd Barron was a lawyer who was partners in a large firm. The two bankers sported blue suits and ties. George Bueve looked dashing in a cable knit sweater and was pictured in front of his well-known restaurant, Bon La Bon. The last gentleman wore bright colors and a scarf with a curled lock of hair over his forehead. He owned a popular faddish men's store in downtown Chicago. All of the board members were members of the Brinton Foundation, a philanthropic foundation with anonymous donors that gave worthy businesses start-up grants.

Jenny had already passed two grueling rounds to get to the interview. She had submitted her grant proposal, budget and idea in detail in the first step. Two hundred applicants had been narrowed to 25. In the next step she had done financial projections and written a business plan. She had shown them some ideas for branding and marketing and videotaped client testimonials of her product and service. With glowing recommendations from her professors she had progressed to the final interviews. Ten people were being interviewed. Only five would receive grants. The most worthy project would receive the 'Golden Grant' and an opportunity to meet other interested investors.

Suddenly Jenny wished she had worn a dark blue power suit. She probably looked ridiculous wearing such a summery outfit, like Princess Diana on an outing.

When the train stopped Jenny carefully dismounted trying not to rub against the greasy poles with her lemon yellow skirt. She was immediately aware of the chill as they lost the sun to high-rise buildings with cool wide sidewalks and glass fronts.

Jenny was early, which she always preferred. The tall modern front of the Brinton building was only one block away. The interior of the lobby was marble and modern with potted ferns and silk covered chairs. A fountain in the center replaced piped-in music and a smooth curve shaped reception desk dominated one corner of the space.

Jenny checked in at the desk and found her name was on a list. She was politely asked to wait until someone came to show her up to the conference room.

The wait was terrifying. Jenny hated this part. In high school she had never been good at waiting. If she had to give a speech in front of the class she would always volunteer to go first so that she could get it over with.

Today Jenny took the extra time to change her shoes, check her lip-gloss and make sure again that her laptop was charged. She asked at the desk that they send down a tech person to talk to her about her PowerPoint presentation. Jenny hoped everything would go well. She had followed all of their technical instructions exactly. The young tech, Rich, was a handsome young man who was only a few years older than herself. He brought a thumb drive with him and promised her everything would be loaded and checked before she began. Jenny smiled with appreciation and Rich flashed his own dimples back.

Twenty minutes later Jenny's name was called and she stepped on the elevator noticing that her leg was shaking slightly and she felt a bit clumsy. The adrenaline amped up even higher when she saw the glass windows with the long conference table and large leather chairs. Each board member had a leather notebook and silver pen that was stamped with the Fleur di leis logo of the Brinton Foundation. A silver tea service nearby held croissants, cheese and fruit. There was a screen in the front of the room and a small podium.

Jenny bravely decided to stand in front of the podium so she could walk around the room as she spoke. The board members were visiting among themselves so Jenny took time to give each board member a packet, animal treats and a greeting or handshake. She made sure to mention to Judd Barron that her mother wanted her to say hello. When she got to Sandra Tavery, Jenny felt a bit undone. The woman had very light blue eyes that seemed cold and distant. Sandra barely looked up as the packet was put in front of her. She was deep in conversation with somebody by text and Jenny felt oddly 'put in her place' by the exchange.

Jenny began to notice things as she looked around the room. Most of her life she had had the ability to see small patterns and understand people through careful analysis. Something shifted in her and she began to feel her confidence coming back. Judd was clearly a proud father. The banker looked like a kind-hearted grandfather. The owner of the clothing store was gay and had a small white dog that had left hair on his suit. They were all volunteering to be on this board. Sandra was the only person in the room who seemed unsupportive.

Jennifer cleared her throat and the room became quiet as all eyes turned toward her. With a little rush she remembered how much she liked rallying people to her causes. Jennifer had been the president of her middle school and high school. She was a good leader and this moment wasn't any different.

Jenny started off by warmly and genuinely thanking them for taking their free time to do such an important job. Immediately the men smiled and sat forward enjoying her enthusiasm and charisma. She changed her presentation as she spoke to fit the room asking if anyone had a dog or a horse that they especially loved. Now a few of the men were ready to tell stories describing just how special their animal was. Jennifer went on to show them statistics that even in times of economic decline people were willing to spend money to buy their animals special treats and toys.

Throwing in a little bit of her history she showed them her first successful products and how they had been received, then started the videotape of testimonials that featured happy families, excited dogs, cats and horses and cheerful music. When she turned the tape off she asked each person to open their packet to see her financial projections.

The men seemed won over by her optimistic confidence while Sandra frowned. When Jennifer was done Sandra said with a formal voice. "You'll be notified once we make a decision."

However Judd Barron interrupted Sandra. "Wait in the lobby and we will meet for a few minutes to see if anyone has any other questions and then let you know our decision."

Sandra looked annoyed at being usurped but Jennifer smiled cheerfully gathering all of her things. She felt buzzed and happy. She had done her best. The interview had gone better than she had expected. If they took a vote she was sure she had won at least five of the board members.

Jennifer waited in the lobby her limbs warm and heavy with exhaustion. When the phone rang at the reception desk her name was called and she was escorted back to the elevator.

This time the room felt familiar and Jennifer was genuinely happy to see each face in front of her.

Judd Barron asked her to sit down and took the floor.

"I have been leading this selection committee for ten years. Let me first congratulate you. I have never seen a better presentation than you gave today. If you are as good at marketing your product you will certainly be a success."

"We feel especially fortunate when we can offer a grant to a business graduate from Chicago University. Your professors speak highly of you and based on their recommendations and the work you have already done it is easy for us to award you our 'Golden Grant' by a vote of five to one. The other grant recipients are being notified now. We would ask that you be available for the next two days for interviews with the Chicago Tribune and for photographs with the board. A photographer is coming up now to get a few preliminary shots while we are all here together. Once again, congratulations and good luck!"

Jenny found she was smiling and trying not to cry at the same time. The board members stood up to shake her hand. A few of them even gave her a little hug.

Sandra Tavery quietly slipped out of the room.

Two

❧

Lunch

Jennifer was floating when she left the Brinton Building. Her cheeks felt sore from smiling and her feet were killing her from standing on stiletto heals for photo after photo. She had just received $100,000 to start her business, build a brand, manufacture her product and begin to sell it on the market place. She had also been given a chance to meet with a group of investors who often supported the Brinton Foundation winner. Jenny's mind was buzzing with the steps she needed to take.

The money had no strings attached to it other than a requirement that she incorporate her business, show proof of her business license and give them a progress report at the end of a year. She also needed to give interviews when asked and remember to acknowledge the Brinton Foundation on all of her first year's advertising.

Jenny put out her hand for a taxi and checked her watch. She was just in time to meet her grandfather at 2:30. He would be so proud of her. Jenny got into the cab with a sigh and put her head back. For a moment she slipped into an exhausted sleep as all of the adrenaline drained away leaving her empty.

Jenny knew everyone at home was waiting for a text or call but she was still in a fog of disbelief. The cabbie stopped and leaned back expectantly as Jenny fished for the fare. He looked surprised to be given a large tip. Jenny said. "I've had the *best* day, you wouldn't *believe* my good fortune." She checked to make sure she had all her bags and then got out and looked around.

The Holly Oak Bistro was built next to Lake Michigan. The building featured an indoor/outdoor restaurant on the top floor that was cantilevered over the water. The décor included metal artwork and modern art with square blocky furniture and art deco chandeliers hanging low over the tables. The menu was varied and pricey. Jenny smiled with excitement at getting go to a new place and seeing her beloved grandfather.

Drew Barry stood up as she came into the room. Always the old world gentleman, he helped her out of her jacket and held a chair for her. Jenny took a good look at his tall slightly stooped frame. At 86 he still looked like he was in his mid-70s. He had always been a jogger and now a healthy lifestyle was paying off. He and Sophie had been retired for 15 years and spent most of their time gardening and going for walks around the lake. Drew had been writing poetry for the last decade that was being published by his company Chicago Heron Publishing. When asked about it he always demurred about his talent saying he'd only been published because he owned the company.

Jennifer thought Drew's sensitivity was amazing. Most of his poetry was a commentary on man's relationship to nature. His work had a soulfulness that held a strong appeal for the ecologically aware and enlightened. Drew's wife and Jenny's step-grandmother Sophie was an award-winning author who had written four novels about growing up in the Heartland. Her books had become classics.

Drew wanted to meet with Jenny today to talk about the inheritance her great grandmother Charlotte had left for her at her death seven years before. Charlotte had originally been the daughter of a confederate family called the Applewhites from Georgia. Amelia Applewhite had passed her possessions to Jenny's grandmother Lizbeth. Lizbeth had left the entire household to Jenny's mom Lily. Lily had sold everything to get a start in Montana. The inventory had been impressive including Victorian furniture, a 1900 Steinway and valuable oil paintings. But Charlotte also had important pieces from her childhood. Charlotte had protected the antiques in her will for Jenny. Sophia and Drew had stored the items in order to give Jenny time to grow up. Charlotte had wanted Jenny to know where she came from, the rich tapestry of generations of both joy and sorrow.

"How did it go," Drew asked when they had ordered large ice teas and deep-fried breaded vegetables for an appetizer.

"I won! Out of 200 people I made the final cut to get an interview. My presentation was well received. They narrowed it down to five recipients who will each receive $25,000 and awarded me the 100K Golden Grant. I've been taking photographs for the Chicago Tribune for the last hour. I'm still in shock!"

Drew patted her back and beamed, "I knew you could do it. You've always had that special spark your grandma Lizbeth had. She could make anyone fall in love with her ideas. You are special! I still remember how at 3 you decided you needed to be the president of the club you had formed with Nanny Sheila's grandkids. They were 5 and 7 but you insisted that I help you make a sign that said, 'Jenny for President.' Then you all voted. Of course you each voted for your own self. It was a three-way tie for President. Sheila insisted that all three of you share the presidency."

"I did that?"

"Yes, it was the summer that Sophia discovered that your mom had a sister named Bricca that we hadn't known about. You moved that year to Montana and that fall was when Bricca came to stay with you guys to help your mom start Bricca Down West, her horse breeding operation. Just before Lily and Jace got married.

Jenny said, "I just remember how big Jace was. I think I fell in love with that cowboy the very first time he picked me up."

"Well, you've been lucky. You couldn't have asked for a nicer life for you and your brother Bern. You've had all of us wrapped around your finger from the time you were knee high with all of your unusual business ideas." Drew chuckled as he remembered. "Once you made a special carrier so that Bodhi could carry the kittens on walks. Another time you invented a plastic bag with dog food in it that would dribble out just a little bit at a time so that Bodhi would follow you around the ranch." Drew laughed and sat back steepling his fingers. "And now look at you. You've talked that fancy board into giving you $100,000 to start a company!"

"Well I talked five of them into it. There was one lady there who didn't seem to like me at all. It was odd. She was pretty creepy. Her name was Sandra Tavery.

Jenny looked sideways to see how her grandfather reacted to Sandra's name and caught the way that he tightened around the mouth and gripped his napkin before he visibly made himself relax.

"Well, the important thing is you wowed everyone else."

Just then the waitress came with a big plate of fried cauliflower, asparagus, onion and broccoli saying, "Your shrimp and spaghetti will be up in a few moments. Would you like some garlic bread?"

Starved, Jenny dug in, forgetting the mystery woman.

After a desert of crème brule and berries Jenny sat back sighing with satisfaction. "I can't wait to call home and tell everyone the good news."

Drew looked surprised. "I thought you would have already done that by now."

"I was so beat I couldn't even talk. I feel more normal now that I've sucked up a huge meal. I wish Max were here for me to tell. I miss him. I can't believe that he is gone. Sheila must be so lonely."

"Well, she has the kids. Nina just moved next door so there are grandkids in and out all day. Max was ten years older than Sheila so we all knew he would go first. It's hard though when you see friends pass. Every day it seems like I see someone I know in the obituaries. It makes me grateful for all of the time Sophie and I have been given to watch you kids grow up."

Jenny reached out a squeezed he grandfather's hand and smiled. "This seems like a morose topic. Let's start planning how I'm going to spend all my money in order to make more money."

"About money," Drew said. "I need to talk to you about the antiques that belong to you. They are quite valuable now. You could sell them or keep them, whichever you choose, but a few of the things have a lot of family history and I think you'll want to do a bit of research before you let them go."

"Family history? Like what?" Jenny sat forward.

"Like an old French Renaissance writing desk that has a secret drawer. In it we found a pack of letters written during the Civil War from your great, great, great grandmother Gwenn Anne to a confederate soldier. They were obviously in love but Gwenn Anne married a Yankee instead and was one of the few southern bells that was able to keep her plantation intact. It might be interesting to know if her confederate soldier died before she made that decision or if Yankees had invaded her town ready to burn everything to the ground."

"Wow, that sounds like the makings of a book for Sophie to write."

"I've thought so too. To bad *you* don't have the writing bug."

"Only if I'm writing a business plan. I'm more like Nanna Charlotte that way."

"Well, she would have been proud of you today."

Drew and Jenny sat together silently in a companionable way.

"Maybe I'm more like you. You've always been a business man until recently."

"Well, I like that idea too."

"Grandpa?"

"Yes, Bunny."

Jenny smiled at his old nickname for her. Jenny had had a stuffed rabbit as a kid that went everywhere she went. Even when it had lost all of its filling and been chewed up by Bodhi she had carried a little piece of it in her pocket. Now she had the last tiny piece of it glued into a special locket. The rabbit had earned her a lot of nicknames growing up that she had always liked.

"I need to know about my real dad, Ned Tavery. I haven't wanted to ask mom because I know it will upset her. Seeing Sandra today got me thinking that she and Ned might be related. If his family is here in Chicago I might see them when I go the next leg for my business by looking for investors. I feel like I'm operating in the dark. I want to know, but another part of me doesn't want to know."

Drew got a pained look on his face and took Jenny's hand across the table.

"I'm not sure it is my place to talk about any of this."

"Well if not you, then who? It has *got* to be you."

"Now?"

"No, not now. Today we are celebrating, but soon.

"Do you mind if I talk to your mom about it first?"

"I guess not. Just stress that I'm a big girl now and I can take whatever the truth is.

"Okay, Bunny."

Drew changed the subject. "Now what is you first step in getting your business going?"

"To find a good bookkeeper who can file papers to make my business an S Corp. But first I have to decide where I'm going to live. I need to move out of my flat in two weeks. I've been thinking about going back home for a week to see everyone and decide whether or not I should start my business in Montana or Chicago. The investors are more likely to be here but I can always travel to meet with them and renting a manufacturing facility is going to be cheaper in Montana or Wyoming. In Wyoming there is no sales tax."

"You are welcome to stay with us."

"I know, gramps, but I need something more permanent."

"Let's get your jacket and then go break the good news to Sophie and Sheila. They are at our house today separating iris bulbs. I managed to avoid the task. Then you can call home."

Jenny laughed with delight.

21

"I'll drive."

"No problem. My eyesight isn't what it used to be."

As they stood up to walk from the table an elderly woman looked up from her menu. With a frown she quickly picked the menu up higher until it was hiding her face.

What was the chance? It seemed impossible. In all these years she had never run into Drew in public. Now she was seeing him with Jenny when Sandra had just called her to say that Jenny had been awarded the Brinton Foundation Golden Grant. A little bubble of rage almost made her stand up and call out to them. The rage didn't care that she would embarrass herself in front of all of the other diners. It was primitive mother-rage that had no qualms about killing to defend it's young. She felt like a wild cat with claws and sharp teeth, looking for a throat to crush. She had never gotten blood for blood. And now the little 'nothing' was being rewarded and pampered. Nedra bit her tongue. There was a lot at stake and now wasn't the time to blow it.

Jenny took the freeway to her grandparent's home. It was 45-minutes drive to Winnetka, Illinois, a satellite suburban city near Chicago. Once there she wound through stoplights and gated communities getting closer and closer to the lake where Sophie and Drew's little cottage was. The Hansel and Gretel look of it seemed incongruous with the large estates surrounding it. There were flowers spilling out of every corner of the lawn. Walking through the open living room Jenny pulled open the sliding door into the back yard where she could hear Sophie and Sheila laughing. Drew immediately withdrew to the quiet of his study leaving the women to visit in peace. After Jenny's announcement there were screams of delight. It seemed all was right with the world.

Three

Going Home

Jenny's Aunt Bricca was there to pick her up at the Missoula airport.

Once again Jenny was struck by how beautiful Bricca was. Her shiny auburn hair cascaded down her back in thick curls that hadn't been tamed for a while and she was wearing a typical Bricca outfit that was orange, pink and purple with a pair of spring green tights and lace-up sandals over toes that were painted deep blue. Bricca let out a whoop when she saw Jenny and ran across the gate, not caring what anyone thought about her exuberance.

"My, aren't you a sight for sore eyes," Bricca said. Her natural Atlanta southern accent slipped out in moments like this.

Brown eyes sparkling she made Jenny turn around. "Let's see, your tall, blond, gorgeous and dressed perfectly. How do you manage to match shades of violet with grey? Standing next to you I look color blind."

Jenny laughed and Bricca gave her another squeeze.

"How are the family and Starfire doing?" Jenny asked.

"Well Starfire just turned seventeen which isn't all that old for a horse. He is still standing stud and loving it. Lizzy has started to ride in competition and he has been her training mount. It doesn't really get better than Starfire unless you count his dad, Thunder. The family is all doing great. Lizzy just turned 12, Paddy is 10, Tonka is eight and Charlotte is six. I can't believe I had them all two years apart. I must have been crazy. But now that Charlotte is in 2nd grade things have gotten a lot easier. I'm a woman with a lot of time on my hands and nothing to do. I've been doing a bit of writing again."

"You've got to be kidding. You have four kids and a horse breeding business and you have some time on your hands?"

Bricca just laughed and pulled Jenny to baggage claim.

"Now I want to hear every detail of how you wowed them in order to get this 'Golden Grant.' What did you say? What did you wear? How impressed *were* they?"

Jenny and Bricca were deep in conversation by the time the bags had cleared and they were loading everything into Bricca's Toyota Sienna.

"Jenny looked around the van that was filled with coloring books, soccer balls and horse tack. "Geez, Bricca. You should let me clean your car for you."

"No, you'd make me pay you like you used to in middle school. Plus I don't want anyone in here with a Q-tip and Amoral. It would give me some kind of anxiety attack."

Jenny laughed but pulled her purse a little closer. In it she had a little package of Q-tips, Kleenexes and hand lotion. She had her purse organized so that there was a pocket for everything. It helped when you needed to find something quickly. She had spent a little bit of time hand sewing some of those pockets herself. If the animal treat company went bust she could always design bags for different uses. Something she had always been interested in.

Jenny looked over at Bricca. "Remember how Sophie called you 'The Young Woman in Red' when she wrote about meeting you for the first time? You still look like that. How old are you now?

"I'm not tellin'"

"Come on."

"Well I just turned 39. I guess that is young now but would have been old in the 1600s."

Jenny laughed again. "I have a great idea for a book for you if you want to write it. Grandpa Barry just gave me some letters written by our great, great, great grandmother to a confederate soldier that were love letters. The kicker is she married a Yankee in order to save the plantation. It would need a lot of research, but it sounds scorching."

Bricca almost pulled the car over to think about it but made herself keep driving.

"Well what do you know 'bout that! I'm sure I could write about the south, being from there myself. I'm the perfect person to write this! Did you ask Sophie if she was interested?"

"Yes, but she is still retired and totally focused on her garden. She and Sheila have also started some kind of women's group in Chicago for empowerment of women over eighty. You should see them."

Bricca smiled. "Sophie and your grandmother Lizbeth had a women's group too called Women Exploring Beyond the Beyond. They set a whole town on their ear in the 1970s with their creative radicalism. When I first met Sophie I even wrote a piece for the club. I think I'd really like to write about these love letters!"

"Do you mean it when you say you have time on your hands?"

Bricca frowned. "I'm alone a lot. But enough about me. How long do you get to stay?"

After a bit more chatter Bricca focused on driving and Jenny threw her head back and for the first time since Monday let herself really relax. She was asleep within minutes.

Jenny woke up just as they were driving through White Cloud.

It looked like nothing had changed. There were still only a few buildings strung along the highway: a diner, saloon and hotel and a church. The turn off for the M Rocking B ranch came up quickly and Jenny unrolled the window to listen to the birds and frogs enjoying the cool, sweet mountain air.

"I've missed this," Jenny said.

"We've missed you!" Bricca replied. "Bern has grown up into a little man without you. It just isn't the same with you gone." Bricca continued as she drove down the long dirt road toward the ranch skillfully avoiding potholes and keeping her speed just under the danger of sliding. "Chance still stops by to visit your mom and dad sometimes. He seems lonely for you."

Jenny felt her pulse speed up.

"I thought he might be married or something by now."

"Chance? You've got to be kidding. It was always you. I'm sure he'll be over as soon as he finds out that your home. You'll have to take the horses up into the mountains on one of his days off. He's been working construction with his dad, Judd and caretaking some wealthy older woman's second house. Della is over there bringing food regularly as you can imagine."

Jenny felt a little frisson of discomfort. It almost sounded like Chance hadn't grown up at all. She had left, changed and experienced new things. What about Chance? He hadn't seen any of the world or tried to make it on his own yet? It didn't bode well for their relationship.

"How is Ellie Bell?" Ellie Bell had been Jenny's best friend since she was three. They had done everything together and cried buckets when they separated to go to universities in different states.

"Ellie hasn't been home much either, maybe Della can give you an update," Bricca said. "Frankly, I'm plum pissed that neither of you have come home in four years. Your momma feels the same way though she'd never say anything to you about it. To spend your whole summer working and taking summer classes seems like a waste of youth. Although Ellie's reasons for staying in New York are different. I hear Ellie has been modeling a line of clothes and doing swimsuit ads. She's knock down gorgeous!"

Jenny winced at Bricca's forthrightness. "I guess I have been being a bit selfish."

"A bit? Well, the important thing is your home now."

They had just come up to the end of the fifteen-mile long dirt road that led to the Bridger-Mead ranch, which was tucked up under the Snow Mountains. The dirt road ended at a T. Ahead was Bricca Down West where Bricca and Will lived with their large family. To the left was Spotted Horse Draw where Betsy and Shortie had once lived. The cabin now stood empty after they had passed away five years ago within a month of each other. Jenny was surprised the Hall family hadn't sold the land yet. Maybe the kids were using it as a vacation cabin. To the right was the turn-off for the M Rocking B ranch, the sign with their brand swinging in the breeze. Jenny sat up and started to smile. She could see her dad, cantering across the field riding down to greet them. He looked strong and fit as ever, grey hair making him seem even more handsome. He was riding a big red roan and as usual looked like he was one with the horse. Bricca stopped the car on the road and suddenly Jace was there picking Jenny up and swinging her in a circle while his horse grazed nearby.

"Welcome home Jenny Rabbit!" He grinned. "Your mom has been cookin' all day."

The homestead still looked the same. Only the garden had changed. The lilac bushes were huge and flowers were bursting out of the small bed between them. Lily came running out of the house with an apron on and her hair in a long braid. She wasn't wearing any make-up, which brought out the freckles across her nose. With her short, compact frame she looked like a young girl. Jenny felt like she was towering over her when they hugged.

"Oh, my God," Lily said. "I think you are taller. Jace, look at her standing next to Bricca; they *both* look like ballerinas. We need to take a picture of the three of us together for my website to let everyone know your home for a visit."

Jenny smiled and looked around. "Where's Bern?"

"Football practice. He is the quarterback this year and reveling in all the attention he gets from the cheerleaders. Jace has to keep him on a short leash so he doesn't end up getting in trouble. Fortunately we are still a working ranch so there are plenty of chores to do."

Jenny tried to imagine her fifteen-year old brother being old enough to get in trouble and couldn't quite picture it.

A little brown furry dog was dancing around both of their feet, wiggling and twisting his body as he jumped up on his hind feet. His long hair mopped over big brown eyes and he had what looked like a permanent smile from two crooked front teeth.

"Who is this?" Jenny asked scooping him up on her hip while he tried to lick her chin.

"Tootsie, Your dad found him abandoned down the road. He was laying on a piece of cardboard and Jace almost passed him by thinking it was a dead fox or raccoon. Then he stuck his little head up. We've been nursing him back to health for months. He was skin and bones and covered with sores and stickers.

Lily stepped forward and stroked Tootsie's nose. "Poor little baby. But now he's king of the couch and part of the family. You must be exhausted after traveling all day. What do you need? Lemonade, a nap, a walk, a back rub? We are here to please."

Jenny grinned and thought about it. She put Tootsie down but he followed at her heel as they walked into the house. "I'd love to go up to my room and throw myself on the bed and then take a shower. Then I'm starved. Dad said you've been cooking."

Lily swatted Jace who was tugging her braid. "Well I made my slow-cooked BBQ beef for sandwiches, corn on the cob, coleslaw and some chocolate chip cookies for dessert. How does that sound?"

"Amazing," Jenny said as she turned to give Bricca a little hug and then started to get her suitcase out of the van. Jace stopped her.

"I'll have one of the guys bring it in. Bricca is staying for supper. Will is joining us and the kids will all be here for a picnic. We are going to make some homemade ice cream and Chance is bringing inner tubes so the kids can float around in the pond. It has been hot here for the past couple of weeks."

Chance was coming by too? Suddenly Jenny felt too tired to socialize. "I'll just go lay down for a while," she said.

As she walked into the cool log cabin she heard Bricca say to Lily, "Isn't it a bit soon to throw Chance at her?" Jenny waited for the reply, which came from Jace.

"I saw him today in town. Della already knew she was comin' home. You know how the gossip is around here. Chance offered to bring something out for the kids to play with."

Lily patted Jace on the arm. "It is no biggy. They were bound to see each other soon anyhow. Come on Bricca, let's go pick some rhubarb and I'll cook some to serve with our vanilla ice cream tonight."

Jenny stopped to look at the large living room. The dark logs and colorful wool Indian blankets made it all look cozy. There was a picture on the mantel of Jace on his horse Midnight with his dad standing next to them. In another photo Jace was holding Jenny while Lily looked up at them. The picture had been taken before Jace had proposed to Lily. Jenny couldn't believe how young they both looked. She was just turning to walk up the stairs when she heard a sound behind her.

It was Reese bringing in her bag. He must be almost fifty now Jenny thought. Reese had worked for her dad his whole life, never marrying and becoming Jace's horse trainer when Dusty had passed away.

"Hi Reese," Jenny smiled. "I was just admiring this picture of daddy on Midnight. How's Midnight doing?"

"Well, he went to horse heaven last year. Died real peacefully during the night on a day when the grass was deep and the night cool. I've always thought that is the way I would like to go."

Jenny blinked back tears. "It all passes too fast. Time that is."

Reese looked a little surprised at the sudden intimacy of their conversation. "You know Dusty once told me that he blinked and he was old. But then at a certain age he found he could blink and he was young again. He said it's all connected. Each memory that we have is never lost. He used to spend hours with Honey, Dotty and all the old horses. He said that they were the best ones in the pasture. They had the biggest hearts."

"Well, Honey Bee Bear sure did," Jenny smiled and squeezed Reese's arm and reached for her bag. "Thanks, Reese. I'll carry it up."

Jenny slept hard and woke up tired, not really remembering where she was until she heard the sound of kids yelling outside her window.

Tootsie was snuggled next to her on the bed. As she woke up Tootsie jumped down and brought her a sock, ready to play. Jenny rolled it up and tossed it across the room amazed at how acrobatic and nimble Tootsie was as she slid across the floor and then shook the sock fiercely before bringing it back.

Jenny staggered into the shower and took her time running out all the hot water out before dressing in a pair of jeans and a white halter-top. Picking her hair off her neck she tied it in a loose knot and put on a little lip-gloss. Some boots and she was good to go.

As she walked downstairs with Tootsie trailing behind her she heard an argument going on.

Tonka was standing over Charlotte pulling at a toy dinosaur that she was clutching. "You can't have my stegosaurus." Tonka said. "He doesn't like being hauled around by a girl."

Charlotte clutched the toy tighter and kicked out one foot connecting to Tonka's shin.

Tonka yelled, "Mommmm, she kicked me."

Bricca came strutting in hands on her hips and assessed the situation. "Charlotte, give me Stevie the Stegosaurus. You know he doesn't like picnics. He might end up in the pond, what would Tonka do then?"

Charlotte put her head down. "He wanted to come mommy."

Bricca smiled. "Did he tell you that?"

"No, but my Bear Bear told me he would feel lefted behind if he didn't come."

Bricca took Stevie the Stegosaurus from Charlotte and noticed how Tonka was trying not to look like he cared.

"Charlotte," Bricca said. "You know that Stevie belongs to Tonka just like Bear Bear belongs to you. Tonka, take Stevie and put him somewhere safe so he won't get hurt."

Tonka grabbed his toy and ran from the room while Charlotte put her thumb in her mouth.

Bricca scooped her up and tickled her. "Now, how about some supper?"

Watching the little interlude Jenny was amazed at what a good mom Bricca was. She seemed to just 'get' kids. Jenny remembered that she had felt that way about Bricca the whole time she had been growing up. Bricca was an amazing teacher who was loved by all her students. She just had a 'way' about her. She could see things the way that kids saw them.

Jenny wondered if she would ever be like that. She had always been uber-organized and obsessive-compulsive about control. Her mom had once had her talk to the school counselor because she had started to scream uncontrollably when another student had broken her pencil. The teacher had been alarmed and suggested the counseling session.

"I think Jenny is suffering from some deep-seated fears and might need someone to talk to about it," the teacher had said to her mom not even noticing that Jenny was in the room listening to every word.

The session with the counselor had been a bust. She had really wanted to ask some questions but the counselor had just asked her to draw pictures of her mom and dad. It had all been pretty stupid.

Jenny paused at the door to take a deep breath and went out to join the group at the picnic table in the side yard. Paddy was in the pond paddling around and Bricca was holding tight to the little kids.

"You can't go in without me. That is our rule and we aren't breaking it tonight. But I promise I'll go in the water with you after a little while. Why don't you play fetch with Tootsie." Charlotte and Tonka seemed mollified and ran off to play together while the bigger kids splashed.

Jenny could that Lizzy and Paddy could both stand up all the way across the pond. She could see now why Bricca had set a height limit.

The kids yelled out a "hello" to Jenny and kept splashing around. Chance had his back to her talking to Jace but now he slowly turned around.

Jenny's knees went a little weak. In four years Chance had gone from being a muscled gangly boy to a man with a square jaw and the shadow of a beard. He was medium height but broad and big like his Norwegian father. He had inherited green eyes, a square face and a row of straight shiny teeth from Della. His hands and feet were huge just like his biceps and shoulders. Chance had always had a quiet way about him. His unusual eyes were assessing as he took Jenny in noticing her tight jeans, halter and the little tattoo she had gotten on her upper arm of some kind of Celtic symbol. Her hair was still waste-length and golden but everything else in her had filled out and now she looked like a woman instead of a girl.

Both of them felt like they were seeing a stranger even though they had been best friends then boyfriend and girlfriend for most of their life.

Jenny decided to play it extra cool by keeping her distance and said politely, "Hi Chance. It's nice you could stop by tonight. How is your family doing?"

Chance looked confused for a moment, not really understanding her formal tone. He looked away and swallowed then planted his feet, not willing to pretend with her.

"I've got to get going. I just wanted to drop these inner tubes off for the kids. Nice seeing you all." He addressed the whole crowd.

There was a little awkward silence before Lily rushed up to him.

"At least take a sandwich with you. You're probably half starved after working all day."

"I had something earlier," Chance said. "But thanks!"

Without saying another word to Jenny he just walked to his pickup truck, got in and drove away.

Jenny felt crushed. *He was her best friend and he had just left like that. No hug, nothing.* Then she remembered she had been dreading seeing him, had already told herself why he couldn't be her boyfriend, and had greeted him like they were strangers.

Jace didn't get any of the nuances of what had just happened. He just pulled Jenny towards the table. But Lily and Bricca exchanged a meaningful look and Lily was looking sad for Jenny thinking. *It is just like a man to act like a jerk. Couldn't he have just agreed to get to know her again instead of making everything so black and white?* Lily realized she really wanted this to work between Jenny and Chance. She had an ulterior motive. It meant that Jenny would settle closer to home and start her business in Montana. Lily was tired of being in a household with two men and no daughter. She and Jenny had always been extra close. It had been only them together before she met Jace. There was something about having a daughter that nothing else could replace.

Lily walked up behind Jenny and gave her a little extra squeeze to let her know she understood then went in the house to bring out the BBQ meat.

It was dark before Will, Bricca's husband and Jace's brother arrived with his bigger than life smile and movie star good looks.

Bricca looked at her watch.

"What happened this time?"

"Had a colicky horse. He came out of it but we almost had to put him down."

Bricca nodded but stepped aside a bit when he walked over to hug her and Will went for a beer instead. Only Jenny seemed to notice that something wasn't right between them. But when Will picked up one sleeping child and Bricca took another they seemed like the happy family that Jenny had remembered from before.

She went to bed that night listening to the crickets and counting the stars out her window. Her window opened onto the roof and a trellis. Chance had often climbed up the side of the house to that very window when they were in high school. They would sneak a horse out of the pasture and ride bareback in the moonlight, or skip stones in the creek. Once they had stayed up all night and watched the sun come up before sneaking back. Chance had gotten away with it only because he was supposed to be spending the night with a friend. Jenny couldn't believe they had never been caught.

Jenny heard an owl call out and the immediate response from another owl. Restless she realized she was waiting for him. Waiting for Chance to hit her window with a pebble and hoot. It was their signal, and he wasn't here. Tootsie seemed to sense her loneliness and gently licked her hand and tried to snuggle closer.

Jenny woke up while it was still dark and slipped on her jeans and boots. Tootsie followed her downstairs, her little toe nails clicking on the wood floor. As Jenny grabbed a jacket she heard her father call out. "Don't take Buttercup, she has a stone bruise."

Jenny walked into the living room and saw him sipping coffee in his favorite chair by the fireplace.

"Why are you up early?"

"Same reason as you. But it's work. I've got to take that red roan you saw yesterday, Taliesin, and help round-up a few cattle that we need to move. I'm a man short. I wanted to be back by mid-morning so we are leaving early."

"Do you need help?"

"Not this time baby. Your momma will skin me if I keep you away all morning. She sure has missed you."

"Well, I've missed her too," Jenny said. "So who should I take?"

"We have a new mount that Reese has trained named River. He is a beautiful horse and very calm and even-tempered. He's already in the small pen so you can ride him. It seems Tootsie has taken a liking to you. He will insist on going too. We usually carry him in one of the saddlebags so he doesn't have to run so hard to keep up.

"Thanks dad for planning this for me."

"Okay, baby. Were you happy living in Chicago?"

"Yes, it was all a really good experience for me. I learned a lot and now I have to take everything I've learned and do something with it."

"Well, I've been thinking. If you want some privacy and feel like starting your business in White Cloud you could move into the cabin on the south fork. Just thinking. It has electricity, gas, and a wood stove. Dusty was the last one to live there so it has been empty for a while."

"I'll think about it dad. Isn't that supposed to be for Reese now? Besides, I might need to be closer to my office and manufacturing plant. It would be hard to drive 15 miles on a dirt road into town every day."

"Well, I also have a couple of rentals in town. Just saying, mind you. You probably need some time to think about it all."

Jenny tugged on Jace's boot and gave him a kiss on the cheek.

"Thanks dad. Then she turned around and walked out into the early morning darkness.

The dawn was a thin line in the east by the time Jenny had River saddled. He looked excited about their little outing. Jenny was sure he didn't like being cooped up in a small pen away from his pasture mates and decided she would let him go into the big pasture after their ride.

Tootsie kept begging to be picked up, so Jenny put a saddlebag on River and loaded him into it. He was the perfect size to sit in the bag with his head sticking out. They took off at a slow walk then trot to warm up and then Jenny let him have his head. River raced down the two-track, headed for the mountains, occasionally popping his butt up with excitement.

Jenny laughed and pulled the rubber band out of her hair so it was flying behind her.

That was the way that Dirk first saw her. He was simply having a smoke by the back corral and she came flying by, her waist long hair whipping out behind her while she laughed. It was archetypal goddess stuff and Dirk fell in love at first sight. To bad she was the boss's daughter. He'd never had a woman this young before. But they all fell when he turned on the charm. The lonely wives, the virginal school marms, the lawyers and doctors.

Dirk put his hand over his crotch for a little comfort. Yes they *all* eventually fell.

Lily woke up to an empty house and rolled over to look at the clock. It was only seven and everyone was gone already? She groaned and pulled the pillow over her head. There was a groomsman now who fed, groomed and mucked out stalls down at her pastures so she didn't have to do it every day like she had in the beginning. Bricca lived right by the corrals and kept an eye on all of the horses. Lily's job was keeping the website and blog going, training horses every day, organizing and teaching clinics and selling colts and fillies from her bloodlines. After sixteen years her operation ran so smoothly it was always in the black. Bricca had her own side business going getting stud fees for Starfire and they split the profits on Bricca Down West 60/40. Bricca got free use of the house and property for her horses as a perk. That made the profit split more even. Bricca and Will had added another bedroom to the house as her family had expanded. Will's veterinary offices and large animal hospital was just outside of White Cloud on a piece of property that belonged to the Bridger-Meads.

Lily grabbed a robe and wandered down to the kitchen. Where was Bern? He ought to be here begging for breakfast. Oh, that's right, he was at a football tournament in Livingston today. The bus had left early and he gotten picked up at 6:00.

Lily poured some orange juice and checked her supplies in the refrigerator. She wouldn't need to go to town for a few days. Just then her cell rang and she did a double take. It was her dad calling from Chicago. He never called early and suddenly Lily felt worried.

"Dad?" Lily answered.

"Hi Lollipop. Called early to catch you before you're out on the range." Lily smiled at his endearment and bit of sarcasm.

"What's up?" Lily asked.

Drew hesitated then got right to the point. "Jenny has asked me to tell her the whole story about her dad. She said to tell you she is a big girl now and can hear all the details. She met Ned's sister in Chicago and is worried she might have to work with investors who knew Ned since he owned an investment company. I told her I'd call you to let you know and then that I would tell her everything."

"Dad, do you really think she is ready to hear the worst of it?"

"Yes, I do. I actually think you should have told her about this years ago. Jenny has always been kind of keyed up and afraid of things. Her fears have made her compulsive. I think it would have helped for her to talk about everything earlier."

Lily felt a little flare of temper. "You didn't set the best example of that. I'm sure you remember that you didn't tell me *anything* about my mom, Lizbeth. It took Sophie writing a book for

40

the whole truth to come out. If she hadn't done that I might have never found Bricca."

"I know. And I'm not proud of it. That's why I want you to face this with Jenny."

Lily squared her shoulders.

"If anyone should talk to her, it should be me. I've been rehearsing the whole thing in my head for years now anyway," Lily said.

"Do you promise to tell her soon?" Drew said knowing that Lily had a way of putting off things she wasn't comfortable with.

"I'll tell her today!" Lily said.

Drew sighed. "I wish this was easier for you."

"Believe me I do too. But I don't want her finding out from people who could hurt or manipulate her. You are right. I can't believe I waited this long."

Drew hesitated then said firmly. "I'll call you tonight to see how it went," and then he hung up.

Lily looked at the phone with a bit of shock. Could the day have started any worse than this?

When Jenny sauntered into the kitchen a half an hour later she was looking rosy cheeked and radiant from her morning ride.
Lily smiled at her dreamy look and laid a plate of eggs and bacon in front of her.

"We are alone," Lily said. "Bern has a tournament and daddy won't be back until eleven."

"I know I talked to him this morning as I was leaving for my ride."

"You left at 5:00?" Lily questioned. "I don't remember you ever being an early bird."

"Chicago changed me. My first class was usually 8:00 and it took an hour to get there. If I wanted any exercise before sitting all day long and then grading papers for my advisor I had to take it in the morning. It was always muggy and hot later anyway. I got use to jogging a 5:00 in the morning like clockwork. It really is the best time of the day once you get used to it. This dog is hysterical. He really likes riding in the saddlebag."

"I know. It makes me wonder if he originally belonged to a cowboy. His last owner taught him all sorts of tricks. He can beg, play dead, and even knows a few words like 'beer.' We advertised and called the animal shelter but nobody responded."

Lily poured herself another cup of coffee and took a little bite of an egg. Her stomach was grumbling with nervousness. Finally she just jumped in.

"Grandpa Barry called this morning."

Jenny flushed.

"He told me you want to know all the details about your dad. I promised him I'd tell you myself. He is calling back to check on me tonight so I don't chicken out."

Jenny took a good look at her mom then noticed her hand was shaking on the coffee cup.

"Is it that bad?" Jenny cringed.

"I'm afraid so bunny. Some of it you may remember, but my guess is you've blocked it all out. It was pretty ugly."

Jenny sat her plate aside and prepared to listen as Lily told the story.

"Your dad loved you, Jenny and you had nothing to do with what happened. That said he wasn't always a very nice man. I found out soon after we were married that he had a terrible temper. I kept trying to work it out but our fights got more and more abusive until he broke my arm during one of his rages. I moved out overnight and filed for divorce but we had to stay for a while with grandpa and grandma and then find a place that Ned didn't know about to live. I didn't accept any child support because I didn't want to have to interact with him. I was afraid Ned might steal you from school so I always told you not to get in a car with him.

"We were very poor, living on almost nothing. I'm sure you suffered for it because you only had a few toys, we could never buy good food and all of your clothes were from thrift stores. It was a miracle when I was deeded this land in Montana because of Great Uncle Donald's will.

"There are a lot of secrets in our family. One of them is that Uncle Donald had molested your grandma Lizbeth when she was a little girl. That is why she left home and gave me up as a baby when she got sick. Her only way to cope with things was to separate from everyone. Uncle Donald tried to make up for his sins in his last days by giving me this property and I took it gladly. It was my chance to make a clean break from Ned.

"The day before we left to move to Montana Ned found out where we were living and came over. That is why we left so fast and you didn't get to say goodbye to any of your friends or to Alexander or Nina. After we moved here he found out where we were again.

"He came to Montana and he saw me out riding. In a rage he shot me in the leg, winged my horse and hit Bodhi on the head."

Lily saw Jenny cringe but steadfastly went on.

"You were only three but you were scared too. I always told you not to get in the car with him and sometimes you would question me about it and cry. You missed him because he had always treated you special. But you had witnessed some of our fights and you were afraid of him.

"The day that he came to Montana I rushed you away from school and had you stay with Della. That night when we picked you up you noticed that Bodhi had been hurt and you asked Jace to protect us.

"That night Ned tried to set fire to my property and Jace and some of his men caught him and he was arrested.

"I decided to press charges instead of accepting a plea bargain of $200,000 because Ned couldn't control his rage when we met even in front of other lawyers and police officers. He yelled that he was going to take a contract out on me and give me the punishment I deserved.

"Jace hired a private investigator to look into Ned's finances and contact the police in Chicago. He found out that Ned had mob connections and that the police were going to offer him a plea bargain and put him in witness protection program if he gave them information on the mob's illegal activities.

"Ned was killed by a sniper gun when he was exercising in the outdoor courtyard at the Livingston prison. On the same day someone with a sniper gun killed two people that were hiding in our barn with the intent of killing Jace and me. The police believe that the two people killed on the ranch had been hired by Ned. They were part of the mob family. Because Ned was becoming an informant, the mob not only took him down, but also took down the two people Ned had been associating with. Ned was up to his ears in trouble.

"You were out on the grass with me when the sniper shot the two people in our backyard. I covered your eyes and carried you inside but you still saw their bloody bodies.

"For months after that you had nightmares and kept asking if you could call Jace daddy. You wanted to know if he could protect you.

"That Christmas, only 2 months later Jace asked me to marry him. We put it all behind us and never spoke about any of it again. Jace adopted you immediately and we changed your name so your would have nothing to do with the Tavery family."

Lily paused. "That is the whole story. Do you have any questions?"

"Do I have another grandmother or other relatives in Chicago?"

"Yes, you grandmother's name is Nedra and Ned's sister is named Sandra. I was never close to them. Nedra was the head of the family business and Sandra let me know that she didn't like me. They thought I had stolen Ned away from the family because he was set to inherit money. I couldn't have cared less about money."

Jenny searched her memory.

"Did dad ever hurt me?"

"He gripped your arm too hard and left a bruise. When I was pregnant with you he ran into my car because of fight. My water broke early and we did an emergency C-section. You were born one month early."

"I was born premature?"

"Yes, but you had all your fingers and toes and your lungs were strong. You gained weight quickly and were always a healthy baby."

"Did dad fight to share custody?"

"Yes he did. In fact I always worried that what had broken him was me taking you away from him. That is why I almost didn't have him prosecuted when he shot me and tried to set fire to my property. He said that he loved you and I believe that he did."

Jenny hung her head again. "Did he ever scream at me for no reason?"

"Yes. Frequently. Once it was because you accidently broke one of his pencils. I was outside and rushed in and grabbed you. We left for the day so he could cool down."

"Do you think I have mental problems because of him or that I'm anything like him? You know being so compulsive about everything?"

"No, honey. You're nothing like him at all. You take after your Grandpa Barry and Grandma Charlotte. I think you would have always been an organized business woman with or without your Dad."

"But what about the part of me that is over-compulsive and frightened?"

"I'm hoping our talk will help that part of you. Ned is gone, he can't ever hurt you again."

"Oh yeah? Sandra was on the board that decided on the grant. She voted against me."

"What!"

"Yeah, I couldn't understand why she was being so cold."

Lily felt her temper rise. "I can talk to her."

"No, don't you dare. However, I'm glad I know the whole story because I'm sure I'll be seeing her again. She has connections with every investor in Chicago.

Lily put her head in her hands.

"I'm so sorry, honey."

"You don't have anything to be sorry for. It is all him. He is the one that was spoiled and mean. I'm starting to remember things. He burned my first bunny didn't he?

Lily gasped. "You were only two."

"I still remember. He told me if I was going to whine he needed to take Bobby Bun Bun away. I suppose that's why I tried not to complain later, so nobody would take Cindy Bun Bun away and burn her too." Jenny started to cry. First softly and then with heaving sobs. Lily just held her quietly.

Afterwards Jenny blew her nose and smiled. "I think I have been secretly terrified most of my life."

Lily shook her head sadly. "I should have told you earlier."

Jenny shrugged. "Maybe so, maybe not. This is the first time that I've insisted on knowing. I always knew the story would be ugly. I already knew the story because I watched it happen. I just wasn't ready until now to hear it out loud.

Lily smiled tremulously. "Forgiven?"

"There is nothing to forgive," Jenny replied. "You sound like a brave woman who was doing your best. The point is you got away, moved us here and started a new life that gave me a dad who Ned could never have measured up to."

Four

ॐ

Bricca looked at the pile of dishes in the sink and put her head down on the table. To get the kids to the bus by 7:00 meant that everyone was up at 6:00, breakfast was served at 6:15, and Will had the kids in the car and was ready to go to work at 6:40. Leaving usually meant a few runs back and forth to the car for boots, lunch boxes and books that someone had forgotten. After the car headed down the drive the silence was deafening.

Bricca could hear birds again outside the open window and the horses nickering to each other. She heard Musty out watering the horses and talking to the them in the singsong way that he did while he curried them or cleaned out their stalls.

Bricca set her coffee cup in the sink and grabbed a jean jacket off the hall rack going in mudroom. She didn't bother to tame her wild hair, just slipped on worn riding boots over her tights. Starfire was waiting for a treat and a little ride before the day got too hot.

Starfire greeted her with a nicker and a little rub of his head. Still strong and beautiful he gathered under her as she mounted and immediately started to prance. Bricca grinned.

"At least I know *you* love me," she whispered as she patted his neck. "Let's go boy," she said and broke into a canter.

Musty set his pitchfork down for a moment to watch. It was a beautiful sight.

He was lucky to have this job, doing something that he loved. Frankly, after getting so close to ruining his life with drinking and gambling he couldn't believe that Bricca and given him this chance.

The whole town knew that he'd left a wife and spent most nights at the saloon. But when he had started going to AA and tried to make amends Bricca had been the only one who saw how important it was that he occupy himself with meaningful work.

"Musty," she had said one day when she had met him out on the boardwalk in front of the grocery store. "I seem to remember that your Daddy is a VanDyke.

"Yes'm" Musty replied politely wondering why she was striking up a conversation with him when most people around White Cloud ignored him.

"So you must *know* horses?"

"More than most I suppose," Musty said.

"Do you love them?" Bricca asked.

Musty took a minute to think about that. He had grown up on a horse. Been taught to train horses by his dad. Competed in rodeos as a teenager and cried when his mount had died of old age.

"I do."

Bricca had offered him the job then. It had included room and board and a chance to ride some of the best horseflesh in Montana. Musty had been working at Bricca Down West now for ten years and it had been the most fulfilling years of his life. In his colorful past he had done things he wasn't proud of. But Bricca had believed in him and given him a way to begin again. Over the years he'd gotten pretty protective of Bricca and the kids too. He didn't understand how Will could leave a woman like Bricca alone all day, all night and most weekends. Why, she was still young and beautiful. The fact of the matter was that Musty had always had a little bit of a crush on her. He'd loved watching her during her pregnancies. She had been beautiful, laughing with joy and pleasure at life. He'd loved seeing how much passion she gave to her kids and her horses. Musty was about the same age as her and they spent every day together working with the horses, feeding, riding, and training. But Bricca had never even once been anything other than friendly. And that was the kicker. Will was a damn fool, because she was *loyal* too.

Musty heard a truck pulling up and Musty walked out to greet it. It was Dirk dropping off some feed that Lily had purchased with Jace.

"I have ten bags of Gro-Strong here. Where should I unload them?"

Musty led him into the barn and the large storeroom next to the tack room. "You can just stack them there," he pointed.

Dirk leaned against the wall and ran his hand through hair styled to look windblown. He was aiming to look like the Marlboro man. His face was chiseled and masculine. He sported a three-day shadow. He had a low voice, big hands and faded jeans with a chambray shirt. Dirk reached into a worn pocket for his crumbled pack of cigarettes and shook out an unfiltered cigarette. Out of his jean pocket he pulled a flask and handed it to Russ.

Musty quickly handed it back. "Too early for me."

"What do ya mean, it's never to early for Jack."

"Well, me 'n Jack aren't friends anymore."

Dirk laughed. "I forgot. You spend your Wednesday nights at AA."

Musty flushed under the collar but tried to hold his temper. "Please don't smoke in the barn. We are very firm about that. If Bricca sees you, we will both lose our jobs."

Dirk huffed and took a few steps out of the barn to stand by the truck where he lit up and leaned back.

"Where's the beauty queen now?"

Musty felt his muscles bunching up. He'd love to wipe the ground with Dirk but it didn't do to make enemies in a place as small as White Cloud.

"I'll leave you to unloading. I've got some gates to open and some horses to move."

Dirk took a good look at Musty. He saw what other people probably didn't see. He saw someone who was would never own anything. Someone who would always be working with other people's horses but treating them like they were his own. He saw someone who would be like a loyal husband to Bricca but would never be a husband. He saw himself before he'd gotten disillusioned with seeing how some people would always be rich and the rest would be poor.

Dirk looked away from Musty with disgust. At least *he* had a plan. He'd make his way out of this shithole of manure and hay and into the big house someday. Musty wouldn't.

After talking with her mom about Ned, Jenny felt like she needed to get away by herself for a while to think.

"Mom, I think I need to drive into town this morning and look around a bit. Dad said he had some rentals I should look at and I want to check things out to see if there are any buildings I could put my manufacturing plant in. It looked like The Feed Store was empty and had a "For Rent" sign on it.

Lily felt a little shiver of excitement. This was the first time that Jenny had mentioned the possibility of living close to home.

"Yes, they couldn't compete with the prices in Livingston."

"I'm going to take a truck."

"Do you want some company?"

"No, I think I'll have lunch, visit with Della a bit and also take some time alone to think about Ned Tavery. I still need to think it all through."

"Sure Bun, We won't plan on lunch but I'll make a nice supper. It will be good for you to have a little time alone to process everything."

"I love you, Mom." Jenny said. Her eyes tearing up for a minute with how well her mom seemed to know her.

Tootsie tried to follow her out of the kitchen but Jenny told him that he was going to stay. He seemed to understand immediately because he lay down with his head on his paws and looked at her imploringly. "No, I mean it, the truck will be too hot. Go find your mama, maybe she'll have a treat for you."

Tootsie seemed to understand because he immediately trotted over to Lily and begged. Lily and Jenny both laughed. "I think he actually understood everything I just said," Jenny commented.

After a quick hug, Jenny climbed into the tall diesel ranch truck and started it. It felt good to be in a truck sitting way up over the road. The diesel was powerful and it gave her a little lift from feeling so helpless earlier as she had cried about her dad burning a stuffed rabbit.

She wasn't that little girl anymore but it felt like that sometimes.

Hearing the truth this morning had been like finally seeing how all the puzzle pieces of her life fit together. She had had nightmares for years growing up. A recurring one was that she couldn't find her stuffed rabbit Cindy Bun Bun anywhere. Then she would see her bunny in the hand of a woman lying on the grass. There was blood coming out of the woman's mouth and pooling beneath her. She would wake up screaming.

She remembered wetting her pants when she was looking out the window of her preschool. She had seen her Daddy's car and mommy had told her to never never get into his car and to tell a teacher if she saw it. Jenny had disobeyed and not told the teacher. She didn't want Daddy to get in trouble again. He's only gotten mad because she had been such a bad girl. She had spilled her milk. That was why he'd yelled at mommy that night and hit her. She had to be very careful and not do stupid things, like breaking pencils or making messes.

Jenny remembered seeing Bodhi with a cut on his head. His fur had all been shaved off and the stiches had looked very painful. He had tried to itch it and needed to wear a cone on his head for a while and Jenny and been miserable with him.

Mostly Jenny just remembered this underlying feeling of fear that something could happen at any minute. You can lose the people you love in an instant. There was nothing about life that was secure.

Jenny found herself crying again and she slowed the truck down and pulled over at the side of the road. Then she got nervous again, this was the creek where Ned had shot her mother. How could she possibly have had a father that would shoot someone else? Did she have some of that badness in her too?

Suddenly all Jenny could think about was Chance and how mean she had been to him. More than that, she really needed him now. He was the one who had always made her feel safe as a kid. He was quiet and calm and solid. He had always been there and now he wasn't because she had been a jerk. It was time to go talk to his mom Della.

When Jenny pulled into town she was struck again with how small every building in town was, like a miniature toy town next to Chicago.

The restaurant was open and they had just switched to the lunch menu. A young girl with an apron, dreamy eyes and pale skin was waiting tables. Jenny searched her mind but didn't know whom she was seeing.

"Is Della here?"

"Yeah, she's back in the office doing payroll or ordering. Should I go get her?"

"No, I'll go back."

The girl got interested in rolling forks and knives in napkins and seemed to have lost interest as Jenny made her way through the kitchen to the little office in the back.

"Hey, Della?"

"Why I'll be gaddummed if it isn't little Jenny Cowgirl all grown up," Della said and stood up to envelope Jenny in a huge hug.

"I wish Ellie Bell were here to see you!"

Jenny looked at the big mess on Della's desk that seemed to flow over into piles on the floor and cringed. "You look as if you could use some help."

"I just need to do some filing or something and get rid of some of these papers. You're not looking for a job are you?"

Jenny laughed and sat down on one of the chairs in front of the desk. She picked up a receipt and saw it was dated 3 years earlier and put it in a pile. "I'll just help you sort some of this out while we talk." Jenny said while Della laughed with delight.

"You haven't changed at all, and I hear you got a big grant for your business. We are so proud of you. I called Ellie Bell about it and she said to give you a thumbs up. Of course she's so busy all of the time it is amazing I reached her at all. We talk on the phone with FaceTime sometimes and I'll tell you I worry about her. She is so skinny she looks gaunt to me but she says she has to be like that for the camera. She makes plenty of money but comes home exhausted from all-day shoots. They're making her the face of some new skin care product and it seems like it is going to get worse before it gets better. I was hoping you could talk some sense into her. Maybe fly out there and do an intervention or something!"

Jenny just nodded. She had gotten engrossed in checking dates on receipts and had found three empty file folder boxes to sort things in. A corner of the desk was already showing.

"Are you even listening to me, child?" Della asked.

Jenny nodded. "Yes, You want her to come home."

"Well, I guess that's about it, I do."

"It sounds like this is an amazing opportunity for her."

"Maybe, but maybe not. You know how she always thought she was gangly and homely. Then she just turned into a swan overnight. I'm not sure she knows how to handle it. You know though that what she really wanted to do is be a clothing designer. She got all the way through two years before that big wig in New York saw her and talked her into modeling. He stole my little girl and I'm not sure she really knows who she is anymore."

Jenny nodded sympathetically. "What is her phone number? I'll call her and maybe we can rendezvous somewhere and see each other. But I wouldn't bet on her coming home if she is sinking her teeth into this. You know how stubborn Ellie Bell can be, almost as stubborn as you are."

Della stood up and swatted Jenny then gave her a little hug from the back as she looked over her shoulder at her chaotic desk. "I've missed you, cowgirl."

Jenny smiled. "Well I haven't missed seeing the messes you can make. How did you do Judd's books all of those years."

"Truth tell, I don't know. I don't know."

"Do you know who dad has in his rentals right now?"

"Well both of them are nice people. One's a young mother trying to make ends meet on her own with a little girl named Clementine. Her name is Amy. The other rental is occupied by a friend of Mustys that he met in AA at Livingston. The guy seems to be making a clean start. I haven't seen him at the saloon, least-ways. He's a pretty good mason so Judd just hired him to do the fireplace on a job that he's been working on."

Jenny had her answer. While her dad was offering her his rentals they were already taken and the ranch house should be for Reese. If Jenny stayed in White Cloud she would need to figure out something else that would work. She didn't want to move back and kick someone out of his or her home just because she was the Boss' daughter. Jenny had always tried to pay her own way, including working and getting student loans for school. She figured her parents worked hard enough and deserved every penny they made for a nice retirement.

"What's the 'special' today?" Jenny asked.

"Same as always on a Tuesday. Some good hot chili and meatloaf and mashed potatoes. But we've added salads to the menu now for the faint at heart."

Jenny's eyes lit up. "An arugula and chicken salad with almonds and cranberries and honey/sesame dressing?"

Della swatted Jenny and said.

"You've got to be kidding. But I *do* think I have those ingredients in the kitchen, so I'll just make you one."

Jenny smiled. Della always had been a push over when it came to food. Jenny stacked the three boxes she had used to separate receipts and looked at the cleared spot with some satisfaction.

Jenny had just started to dig into her delicious salad when the bell to the restaurant tinkled and in walked Chance with a pretty girl. The girl had straight black hair and very white skin. She looked like the thin and nervous type. Her translucent skin made her look frail and her posture looked like someone who was shy. The girl gave the waitress a hug and Jenny saw that they had the same face and pale blue eyes. They were obviously sisters.

Chance was escorting her with his hand on the girl's back and she seemed to be enjoying the attention.

Just then he looked up and saw Jenny and the moment became incredibly tense and awkward. Jenny did the first thing that made sense. She stood up and greeted him politely.

"Hi Chance. Good to see you again. I've just been visiting with your mother and she spoiled me with a special salad."

Jenny looked expectantly at Chances friend waiting for an introduction.

"Hi Jenny. This is Kiera Paige. She and her family just moved into the valley this year. Her parents live in Livingston and they have an uncle who is a wrangler at the Lazy Joker up at Crystal Mountain. Your waitress is her sister, Osha."

Jenny politely put out her hand and squeezed Kiera's limp hand a little too boisterously.

"Well, good to meet you and welcome to White Cloud."

Kiera responded softly, keeping her head down.

Jenny sat back down and with determination picked up her fork but now her food tasted like dust. She ended up asking for a 'to go' container from Osha and escaping from the restaurant as quickly as she could. As she left she snuck a peak at Chance's table. Chance looked miserable too.

After putting her salad in the truck cooler Jenny took a little walk around town. The first stop was the empty feed store.

A "For Lease" sign stood in the empty window and the front wood deck looked empty and forlorn. Jenny tried the door, locked, so she just looked in the windows. It was a big open room fronted by windows facing west towards Snow Peak. There was a long counter where the cash register had been. Jenny walked to a side door and peeked into the warehouse room behind the retail area. It was spacious with a tall ceiling and cement floors. She tried the door and it opened.

Heart beating with excitement Jenny let herself in and began to look around. There were plenty of outlets, a little kitchenette and a handicap accessible bathroom. The back of the space held two rooms with doors into small rooms that looked like they had been used as an office and copy room. The entire place was around 3,000 square feet.

Jenny got out her phone and starting snapping pictures.

She was so engrossed she didn't hear someone come in until she heard the sound of a man coughing.

"Well dammit, little girl. You plumb scared me," a low gruff voice said when she jumped.

"Dabey Jenkins, Is that you?" Jenny asked

"Jenny, Is that you? Dabey replied.

They both laughed.

"Sorry I let myself in but the door was unlocked and I'm looking for a place to rent for a business I'm starting."

"Is that so, what kind of business."

"I'm going to manufacture horse and dog treats and sell them over the Internet. I'll be shipping them out to various markets.

"You have to have some kind of special kitchen for that I suppose and permission from the FDA."

Jenny's eyebrows went up. "Yes. It has to be an inspected, licensed commercial grade kitchen. If I rented this space I'd have a lot of work to do to make it work."

"Can't beat the price though," Dabey said with a twinkle.

"Well that depends on what the price is," Jenny said.

Dabey gave a ridiculously low price and Jenny had to keep her face still so she wouldn't show her hand.

"That much?"

"Well, the owner might be willing to go down a little bit seein' as how the building has been empty for six months or more. I can talk to them and see what they are willing to do."

It was then that Jenny really looked at Dabey. He looked old and tired. His suit looked worn and practically threadbare. His attempt at being the dapper businessman seemed pitiful.

"So how is the real estate market these days?" Jenny asked.

"About the same as always," Dabey answered, which meant next to nothing.

Suddenly Jenny couldn't help being a bit of Santa Claus. Clouds parted and she could see the road ahead of her. First of all there was no way she wanted to live in Chicago everyday knowing that Ned's family would be there following her every move and perhaps working against her. Secondly she could see that White Cloud really needed a business that could provide work for people and put some income into the town economy. Her little business could make a big difference to some of the families living here. Thirdly, she wasn't giving up on the possibility that she and Chance could be close again. Not being able to have him right now was making her feel stubborn and determined to let him know that she was here and he couldn't ignore her.

Jenny went for broke. "You're a real estate agent, right?"

Dabey just nodded his head not sure where she was going with her question.

"Ask the owners of The Feed Store if they would be willing to sell and what that price might be or whether-or-not they are willing to do a lease to buy. Would you feel comfortable representing both of us when you talk to them?"

Dabey's face creased with a huge smile.

"Also," Jenny continued, "I'm looking for a place to live. Do you know if anything is empty right now?"

"By gum, I might know just the thing. A great opportunity just came up. I'm trying to help one of my clients find a caretaker. They have a separate cabin for the caretaker and are only at the big house a couple of months a year. The duties are pretty light. No animals. Just watering some plants and making sure the place is kept up."

Now Jenny smiled broadly. "Dabey, you're a wonderful man."

"Well, Jenny Cowgirl, the same goes for you."

"Do you know how big this lot is and whether or not anything can be built onto the building?"

Dabey took out a little notebook to jot notes. "I'll find out for you."

Jenny decided to play her cards close to her body. She didn't want Dabey to know about the grant yet.

"Talk to them tonight and give me a call to see what the possibilities are."

Jenny's mind was racing. If she could buy cheaply enough the monthly mortgage would be a tax write off but she would be gaining some equity for her business. Jenny like the idea of White Cloud, Montana being her home manufacturing base. It sounded clean, pure and connected to nature. (Something to go on her marketing and packaging.) Jenny took a good look at the little town again through different eyes. Suddenly she was seeing the "new and improved" White Cloud. They could fix the boardwalk and paint it. Some colorful planters and a park bench would be nice. The little area between the diner and the saloon looked like a perfect spot for an outdoor garden. Why, a little sprucing up and they almost had a downtown.

If the City Council could hear her now they would be running for the hills. Currently the town fathers consisted of three men that were avid fly fishermen. Meetings were cancelled when the water looked clear and the sky was blue. In fact there hadn't been a meeting for a while because there wasn't all that much to talk about. They had no idea that Jenny was a girl who had always needed to be President. And she was moving to White Cloud!

Five

≈

When Jenny broke the news to her Dad and Mom at supper her dad let out a huge whoop and her mom got a little dizzy and had to sit down.

"Wow, that was fast," Lily said with a huge smile.

"I do better making big decisions when I just trust my instinct. Things will be inexpensive here and perfect for an Internet business. White Cloud needs a pick me up. And I needed to decide something quickly in order to move out of my flat. It all makes sense. Besides I don't want to be in Chicago now that I know Ned's family would be watching everything I do. Jace raised his eyebrows at that statement but Lily gave him a steely look that said, "Shut up."

Jace got the silently conveyed message and asked an innocuous question. "Who are the people that need a caretaker?"

"Dabey says their name is Bettina and Thomas Princeton. Do you know them?"

"No, seems like there are more and more folk moving here for second homes that are pretty much complete strangers. Hopefully they will be nice, reasonable people. But if for some reason you don't like them you can always live in one of my rentals."

"But daddy that would mean kicking someone out of his or her home. I'm sure this will work just fine, " Jenny replied.

Jace beamed again. "I can't believe our good fortune. Bern will be thrilled he will have a sister in town. He's been running with the wrong kids and I'm worried about him. You will be a good influence. Maybe he can even work for you if he doesn't want to work on the ranch."

Jenny closed her eyes as she felt a little headache coming on. "Dad, I can't hire anyone underage when I'm manufacturing. But I can hang out with him and be a buddy to him."

Lily shooed Jace away from Jenny and said loudly enough to him so that Jenny could hear. "Jace, Jenny is a grown-up with a lot of business sense and a plan. You can't tell her what to do now."

Jace crossed his arms. "I tell everyone what to do, that's my job."

Lily just laughed and Jenny found herself joining in.

It was almost 8:00 when the front door slammed and Jenny got the first glimpse of her brother Bern. Tootsie jumped up from her bed in the kitchen and ran to greet Bern almost turning inside out with pleasure as he twisted his little body this way and that. Bern picked up Tootsie and set him on one of his broad shoulders.

Bern had Lily's golden brown hair but Jace's grey eyes and tall muscular body. Like all of the Bridger-Mead men he had a commanding presence even as a teenager. He was wearing a letter jacket and a pair of faded jeans. Jenny took another look and saw that his eyes were dilated. He was stoned. She suddenly hoped her mom and dad wouldn't see the signs and innocently they didn't.

Bern set down Tootsie to give Jenny a big hug and she realized he was already two inches taller than her and she was a tall girl.

Flexing his muscles he picked her up and swung her around to show off.

Jenny laughed and squeezed him back. "I've missed you, you slug," she said.

"Well, I'll have to think about whether I've missed you," Bern replied teasingly.

Under the guise of getting hot chocolate for everyone Jenny pulled Bern into the kitchen with her and whispered. "You're stoned! I'll cover for you and you go to bed. We'll talk about it tomorrow."

Bern sighed with relief. "Thanks, it was stupid to come home this way. The guys were toking up on the bus and the weed was a lot stronger than I thought it would be. I was paranoid the entire ride home that I wouldn't be able to act normal."

Jenny sighed. "Go to bed."

When Jenny brought hot chocolate back out for her parents she made Bern's excuses. "Bern was beat from two days of tournaments so I sent him up to bed and said I'd say good night for him."

Lily accepted her cocoa gratefully. "He's quite the looker, isn't he." This year girls were asking *him* to the prom and he had to turn them down. In three months he gets his driver's license. I just hope it doesn't all go to his head."

Jenny rolled her eyes but looked down at her drink so her mom wouldn't see her expression. It had *already* had gone to his head.

That night Jenny couldn't stop thinking about her business plan. Finally she got up in the middle of the night to jot down ideas in her notebook. A couple of hours later she had filled her notebook with ideas: possible new names for her business, packaging, marketing ideas and a rough plan for how to remodel the big room at The Feed Store. Hmmm, everyone called it "The Feed Store." What a good name for her business. "The Feed Store" made you a picture a small agricultural store in farm and ranch country. Since her marketing audience would be pet owners in large cities the idea of an old-fashioned Feed Store would be an appealing twist in her brand. They would see a photo of Snow Mountain and the quaint front porch of The Feed Store in White Cloud, Montana. She'd keep her dad's brand and then sell treats for every kind of animal with a sketch of each animal behind the brand. That would make her store unique. She already had recipes for various flavored Bodhi Bones for dogs and Honey Bee Biscuits for Horses, Jack and Jill Snacks for Cats. What would be a good treat for a guinea pig, an iguana, a parakeet, or a goat? She should have an organic line.

Jenny went to sleep buzzing with even more ideas for innovative products and woke up exhausted from not getting a good nights sleep. Now that she was home it didn't seem as easy to get up at 5:00 in the morning.

Bern was at the breakfast table eating three eggs, toast; four slices of bacon, some oatmeal, and ½ a grapefruit and a large glass of orange juice. Lily was busy packing a huge lunch for him. Jenny poured herself some coffee and watched him suck down the food.

"Do you need some steak and gravy too?"

"Huh," Bern said and looked down at his almost empty plate. "Do we have any?" His look was hopeful and Jenny couldn't believe he was serious.

"What do you do with all of this food?" Jenny asked.

"I have football practice for an hour from 7-8. Then I don't get to eat until noon and I have another hour of track practice after school before I get to have supper. I'm starving to death. I've been loosing weight."

Jenny smiled and left him to his meal and went and sat in her dad's leather chair in the living room. There was a nice fire taking the morning chill off the room. Jace came out nursing his coffee cup.

"Mine!"

Jenny moved onto the couch, stretching out on the warm blanket. Tootsie came over and looked at her appealingly. Jenny could just hear her say it. "Mine!"

"Oh, all right," Jenny grumpily complained and moved to sit in front of the fire. Soon she found herself lying on the rug, curled up as the fire warmed her back. Lily came out with a blanket to put over her and a pillow and went to curl up with Jace in his huge armchair.

When Bern rushed out the door at 6:00 they had all fallen asleep again lying around the living room.

Jenny was the first to wake.

"Since when do you guys sleep in?"

Lily smiled. "Since we got a good groomsman for my horses, and since Jace realized he has wranglers so he can spend more time with me, and since Bern started to wear us out. Sleeping in in the morning is our one concession to retirement."

Jenny lay on her back and did a few yoga twists, getting the kinks out.

"Dad, I need a car. It might be a while before my business is up and I'm making money. Can I borrow the old ranch truck?"

Jace waved his hand magnanimously. "You can *have* the old truck and trade it in when you're ready to buy a car. Consider it a graduation present."

Jenny whooped. "Thank you *so* much!!"

"Anything else?"

"I need some help moving into the caretaker cabin. Grandpa Barry is shipping out all of Charlotte's antiques for me. Some of them will go to furnish The Feed Store and the rest will go into my cabin. Also, if there is too much can I store a few things in the barn?"

"Not the barn, but you can use the basement here in the house if you want. And I'll send a couple of guys to help you move the furniture. I think Reese and Dirk could help."

"Yippee," Jenny said.

Anything else? Jace asked.

"Hmmm, I should think of something. You're saying yes to everything."

"That's because we have missed you and we are thrilled you're going to be settling nearby," Lily said

"I'm going to go shower." Jenny said.

Jace jumped up. "Well that's a No. Let me go first. You used all the hot water last time."

At 8:00 exactly the phone rang with Dabey on the line. "Hope I didn't wake you?"

"We've been up for a while."

"Well, I've got good news for you. Jed and Mary want to sell. They're planning to move to Helena to help out with their grandkids and permanently retire. They were thrilled that you might be interested and would prefer that to a lease to buy. However, they'll go either way depending on what you need to do."

Jenny crossed her fingers and squeezed her eyes shut. "How much do they want?"

When Dabey told her she felt a little whoosh of dizziness.

"Are you sure they are firm on that and won't be looking for other buyers?"

Dabey sounded surprised. "What, here..in White Cloud?"

"Okay give me a little while to do some calculations and I'll call you back."

Jenny hung up the phone and started pacing the floor. Maybe she needed a bag to breathe in, she seemed to be hyperventilating.

Lily immediately looked alarmed.

"Did something happen? Are you okay?"

Jenny just grabbed her in a tight hug. "Jed and Mary want to sell and their asking price is $65,000.00. I thought it could be something like $650,000. The monthly payment on $65,000 over 15 years is only $550.00. I could even go for a five-year mortgage so I wouldn't be paying as much interest. This is completely within my means! It leaves me some money for the remodel. I could finance the remodel when I buy the building. I'll be up and operating in my own building for under 100K!"

Lily looked a little alarmed. "That still seems like a big investment when you haven't started your business yet. Doesn't it take some time to get regular clientele and make sure you'll have the sales to afford this?"

Jenny considered. "Possibly, but if this is all a bust I can always sell The Feed Store or live in it. The most important thing is to believe in what I'm doing and go forward. I have the grant money as start-up and if I need to do it I'll get an investor. Part of the Golden Grant was an opportunity to meet with interested Investors. While I'd rather not do that at all, it is always a possibility if I need to. Grandpa Barry said some of the antiques he is sending are also very valuable. I could sell them."

Lily smiled. "I remember how I felt when your great uncle willed me his horses and my land. It came out of the blue. We were living on nothing without enough money for food or gas. I was substitute teaching at an elementary school. I almost fainted when I heard the news and then I was nervous for weeks while I planned my move. I'd been given a chance to remake our life and I didn't want to blow it. Your grandma Charlotte was a big help then. She gave me an early inheritance and sold Lizbeth's antiques for me.

"Suddenly I had enough to build a house, barn and hay barn and put fencing up around 270 acres. But I also needed a truck, tractor and 37 tons of hay. The money kept leaking out: transporting eight horses, vet bills, $800.00 a month in property taxes. Bricca saved me. She believed in what we were doing and used her energy and enthusiasm to start marketing for me. She bought us a fancy Apple computer, found a place for our first eventing workshop and then went on the circuit with Thunder winning blue ribbons and getting reservations for our foals. By the first year we had a waiting list for our broodmares and they had dropped the first six babies. I sold them for $10,000 each and made another $28,000 teaching workshops. We were on our way. Your Dad and Betsy and Shorty were a great support, but in my mind it all came down to Bricca. I feel like I owe her everything because she had courage and faith."

"Well, momma, from what I see you had the stubbornness to do the hard work that made it happen too," Jenny squeezed her.

"But, now it's your turn and here I am warning you about possible pitfalls. You need to go talk to your Aunt Bricca. She's good at shooting for the stars."

Jenny went outside and walked around the house, still burning inside with excitement and fear. Her mind was buzzing with possibilities and worries. She took a deep breath and tried to look outside of her frantic mind. Zen meditation had become a necessary technique to learn so she could make it through the stress of college. You paid full attention to whatever was directly in front of you. Jenny made herself breathe and look. The elm tree beside the house was immense and the grass green. The flowers tucked in corners had been begun to bloom: Peonies looked ready to pop from the tight red buds, columbines in all colors danced in the breeze, bleeding hearts leaned gracefully over the fence. The daisies hadn't opened yet but held promise and the lilacs were sending a heady scent on the breeze. The rhubarb looked healthy next to lemon balm and other herbs that were already going to seed. Everything was quiet and lazy. Tootsie was rolling in the grass. The robins were sitting on their nests and the horses were laying down in the early morning sunshine. There was a swift darting movement and Jenny saw there was a new barn kitten. The bunkhouse already looked empty as the men were out working in the cool of the morning.

Jenny wondered behind the barn and saw the old green Ford parked there. The key was on the dash and there was a mess of old tools, gloves and bailing twine in the back seat. The mats were mud covered and a large crack ran the full length of the windshield. Jenny put the key in and cranked the engine. After one falter it started but sounded like it needed a muffler. Jenny got out and checked the tires, pretty good, and the odometer, 220,000. She pulled the seat forward and gripped the wheel.

"Let's go baby."

She pulled the Ford in front of the barn and began to unload it and went back inside the house for a rag and Windex. When she came back Tootsie was already sitting in the front seat ready to go. Detailing the old Ford was making her feel calm again. Soon she was working on cleaning out the thick line of dust in the air-conditioning vents, removing grease from the steering wheel and giving the seats a washing down. The mats had been scrubbed and the windows washed when Jace rode into the yard on Taliesin.

"Wow, that looks so good I probably should keep it." He said startling Jenny who had her face down scrubbing the floor of the back seat."

Jenny bumped her head coming out. "You scared me. Yeah, she's starting to get her groove back."

Jace ground-tied his horse on the lawn and came back to look through the pile of junk on the ground. Grabbing an old rag he asked Jenny to pop the hood.

"I'll check the oil and the fluids but you should have Bob look at the brakes. I think we had them done when we got new tires a couple of years ago. My insurance will fix this windshield. If you want to take it down we'll fix it on my insurance before I sign the title over to you."

Jenny smiled. "About that, are you sure? I'm starting to see that this old truck might still be pretty valuable to you. How about I just drive it for a while and give it back when I get a car."

"Are you kidding? It is already yours. Don't look a gift truck in the mouth, babe."

Jenny laughed and got excited again. "I'm thinking about naming her."

"I don't think this is a 'her'."

"That's because she was never really clean enough for you to see. I think Bertha is a good name since she is old and dependable."

Jace just grunted. Now that he had his head under the hood he might as well change the oil filter.

As they worked Jenny told her Dad about the possibility of buying The Feed Store and asked his opinion.

"I'd do it, if I were you. Maybe I'm old fashioned but I would much rather buy something than throw my money away on rent. No matter how things go your always getting equity. Do you need a co-signer on the mortgage?"

Jenny hadn't even thought about that. "I don't know. I would have to show them I have enough with my savings and the Golden Grant to back my business. I think I could qualify on my own. I've always had a credit card that is current and have paid off a few cars in my time. I'm going to try for it alone."

Jace didn't answer. He was taking a good look at the fan belt. It needed replacing and he had another one in the barn.

After lunch Jenny decided to drive Bertha to Bricca's and get her take on the good news. This time Bertha started right away and seemed to appreciate being spotlessly clean. Jenny let Tootsie go along for the ride. However, on the first bump Jenny's head hit the roof and she had to reach out and hold onto Tootsie to keep her from flying onto the floorboard. "Shocks, Bertha, you could use some shocks." Jenny patted the dashboard lovingly. "Don't worry, I won't get a new car soon." She was already attached.

When she drove into the turn around at Bricca's she saw Bricca on her knees planting violets around her and Lily's little pond. Jenny wished she had a picture to capture the scene. She looked like some wood nymph or fairy queen with her red hair cascading down her back and violets in her basket.

Bricca sat back when she heard the truck and shaded her eyes calling out, "Well if it isn't Jenny Rabbit Bo-Peep my favorite niece and Toot Toot Tootsie."

"Your *only* niece."

"Not so, I have twelve more back in Atlanta all wanting to come west to visit me."

"I didn't realize that."

"You didn't know that my dad Paddy is the youngest of 10 kids?"

"No."

"Hmmm, I've plenty of relatives but I'm the only one that lives way out here all by myself."

"You sounded lonely when you said that."

Bricca grimaced then took a good look at Jenny. "What is your news? You're beaming."

"I am?"

"Practically shiny."

"I'm staying in White Cloud and I have an opportunity to buy The Feed Store for my business."

Bricca jumped up and did a little shimmy around the lawn while Tootsie jumped around too, getting excited because of the show of enthusiasm. "Way to go, girl."

"I just found out I can buy the store and I'm am freaking out a little."

"It is just because it is new. After you make the first payment you'll settle down and it will feel normal. Everything new feels like that."

"I think I'll feel better once I start to clean out the store and work on a remodel for it."

"Is it a done deal yet?" Bricca asked putting on a straw hat.

"No, I wanted to talk to you first."

"Me? Well, let's go get some lemonade and bring it out into the sunshine. I'm going to put on a pair of shorts. Do you want a pair?" Jenny looked down at her jeans and then tested the warmth of the sun.

"Sure, but my legs are pale and white."

"We'll put on a little sunscreen then. Just enough so you don't burn."

"Do you ever worry about skin cancer?" Jenny said as they walked in the house.

"I think about it sometimes since that's how my mom died. I have pale skin like she did. But I see my dermatologist regularly and have never had any problems. I see no reason to live in fear. And now they know Vitamin D prevents cancer, so go figure."

Jenny slipped on the shorts that Bricca gave her and the little sun top.

"Actually," Bricca said, "If Musty weren't around I'd sunbathe nude. I love that feeling."

Jenny grabbed her glass of lemonade and the blanket that Bricca pulled out of the linen closet.

Bricca continued, "Sunbathing reminds me of growing up on lime fizzies with flip flops and a swimming pool in the south. I was a sun bug."

Jenny lay on her stomach and soon felt herself getting drowsy.

"So, do you think it is a good idea to buy the store? I have a choice. I could ask for a lease."

Bricca rolled over on her back. "Definitely buy! Commitment is important to make something succeed. You have to give it everything to see the rewards."

"Will you help me a bit with my marketing like you did Mom when she began?"

"Sure, baby. It will give me something to do. I'm wasting away down here at the end of the road."

"You don't really mean that do you?" Jenny asked as she turned over and shielded her eyes from the sun.

"Yes, honey I do. Will works nonstop. The kids are in school. Musty does all the chores. And the horses just eat and sleep. I still have some life to give the world. I don't need money or to work as an employee, but I'd love to come in and work with you a couple of days a week. Believe me, you'll be saving *me* by letting me do that."

Jenny felt a huge sense of relief. "Wow, would I love that. I can't even tell you. There is so much to do and so many decisions to make."

Bricca laughed. "Tell me all about it tomorrow. Right this moment, let's make like a bug on a rug."

Jenny giggled and rolled onto her stomach and promptly fell asleep.

She was woken by Bricca who wanted her to get out of the sun. "We've been out here an hour. That's probably enough for the first time," Bricca said as she began to gather up the blanket.

She waved Jenny off and told her to bring back the shorts and halter later. "I'll call you and we'll work out a schedule for work," Bricca said. Jenny called Tootsie out of the shade by a tree and loaded her up and went home.

Jenny looked at her forearm and midriff as she drove the truck back. She had already turned a light gold brown. She had always tanned easily, almost never burning. In the summer her hair would streak and her skin would get dark. The sun had made her feel tired and comfortable. It was an incredible relief knowing that Bricca was willing to help her out for a while. Everything seemed to be working out perfectly. She'd call the bank first and then call Dabey back this afternoon.

When she pulled into the yard the men were back for lunch.

Reese greeted her with a tip of his hat. Another man stood up from the porch and came out with a swagger. For some reason Tootsie didn't like him because she growled and showed her teeth. Dirk pushed Tootsie aside with his boot as he came forward and Jenny took an immediate dislike to him because of it.

Jenny almost giggled. He was a Marlboro man look-a-like and seemed to know that he was handsome.

"I'm Dirk, nice to meet you." Dirk held out his hand so that Jenny was forced to step towards him a take it. He held it a little bit too long then turned a little sideways so that Jenny got his profile. *Yep,* she thought, *He looks even more rugged that way if it's possible and he knows it.*

"Nice to meet you, too." Jenny said politely and turned to talk to Reese.

Dirk took that moment to check out her bare back in the tank top and the top of her long legs in short, shorts.

She was definitely a looker, he thought, feeling a little irritation that she was talking to Reese now instead of him.

Dirk interrupted. "You need me park the Ford back behind the barn for you?"

Jenny kept smiling up at Reese and only gave him a perfunctory glance. "Thanks, but no. Dad gave me the truck and I'm driving it into town today."

Dirk continued to wait but Jenny wasn't responding and he began to feel a little foolish.

When he stomped away he didn't see Reese smile. Reese was pleased that Jenny could see right through Dirk with one handshake.

Dirk however was fuming inside. *Well, there are lots of ways to get a woman to cooperate,* he thought with a nasty smile, remembering his last 'date' in Livingston. *That had been a fine night and the bitch hadn't had a clue.*

The bank officer in Livingston suggested that they meet in person and said he had time this afternoon. Jenny put on a pantsuit and got her briefcase. She had already prepared a resume so she brought that with her as well as her grant promise and her bank account statement. Better to be prepared, she thought.

The drive to Livingston was pleasant and an hour later Jenny was sitting in a chair in front of a man in a small cubicle. His desk seemed to barely fit the space and he was twice as large as his chair. Jenny tried to move her chair back and hit the wall.

Mr. Hugo Clark not only had a big body, he also had a booming voice. Jenny was sure her news would be all over the bank as soon as he started questioning her.

"Do you mind if we shut the door for some privacy?" She asked.

"Of course not." He tried to pull himself up and Jenny waved him back down.

"I can get it. I would like this meeting to be confidential. I don't want anyone else to know that this business property is for sale. I'm sure you can hold that confidence for me, but maybe someone else in the bank wouldn't."

Mr. Hugo Clark gave her a wink and then pretended to whisper. "You can count on that," leaving Jenny wondering if he meant, 'count on everyone finding out', or 'count on confidentiality.' The meeting was short but satisfactory. Mr. Clark felt the bank could guarantee that she could qualify for the loan based on the assets in her savings account and the liquid cash that she had. He was also impressed with her credit score, resume and business plan. When he figured the payments Jenny had him calculate the loan as a fifteen-year loan and was pleased that interest rates had stayed low for the past five years.

After leaving the bank Jenny gave Dabey a call. "I'd like to meet you at the property and check out The Feed Store again." Dabey was glad to meet her and an hour later they were walking through the rooms together.

"How is this heated and what do the heating bills run in the winter?" Dabey had been doing his homework and pulled out a file. "It has baseboard heat in both rooms. There is also a wood stove in the front retail area. I don't think they heated the back because they used it mainly for storage of feedbags. The highest bill was 215.00 in December. The lowest bill was $34.00 in July. There is no air-conditioning system and the water is city water. There is a monthly fee to the city of $25.00 for the water. There is a phone line put in by AT&T that includes Wi-Fi and LTE Internet service."

"Any problems with the roof or plumbing? Should I get an inspector?"

"Well, I don't know about any of that or an inspector, but you could just call Ray Potts, he does all of the plumbing round here and Judd can give an eye to the structure of the building and the roof. I don't seem to remember Jed and Mary every saying they had trouble."

"Did you get the survey of the plat?"

"Yes, it's right here. It looks like this is a city lot and a half. The line for the property actually runs down the hill to the creek. The sides of the lot already are built out to the setbacks but the back isn't. If you ever wanted to expand, that would be the way to do it."

Jenny was pleasantly surprised. "Does that mean I can have use of the creek?"

"I'm not sure, I'd have to ask the city planners about that. But for sure you can do anything you want right up to its shore."

Jenny had a flash of making the back a park connecting the two buildings next to her with pathways to the creek. She could see a little bike pathway by the creek that would run all the way through town.

Jenny swallowed hard and then got her courage to speak. "Tell them I'm willing to give them 60,000 pending an inspection by Judd and Ray Potts. I've been prequalified by the bank."

Dabey looked a bit uncomfortable. "Now I need to speak a bit on their behalf. They could probably get a lot more on the market if they were willing to wait to sell. But Mary has a new grandbaby on the way next month and they are anxious to be there to help. If I were you, I'd just take their price so no one else ends up in a bidding war with you. If you offer $60 they will counter and things might get a little complicated. It might end up costing you more than the 5k."

Jenny appreciated Dabey's candor. She had forgotten how things were done in small towns after spending time in Chicago.

"Okay, I trust you Dabey. Tell them I'll give them their asking price pending the inspection and getting the mortgage that I've pre-qualified for."

Dabey looked relieved and handed her a key. "They don't mind you having a key so you can get in with Judd to check things out or make plans. Oh, and I called the Princeton's. They are trusting my recommendation. You've got the caretaker position if you want it. The sooner you move in the better. I'm keeping my eye on their place for them now."

Jenny couldn't help it. She grabbed Dabey and gave him a big hug. "You are amazing!"

Dabey turned a little red and sweat broke out on his brow. "Well, this is the fastest sale I've ever made and it certainly has made my day."

Six

❧

Back in Chicago

Jenny had only been back in Chicago for a few days but she was already missing Montana. She had just finished packing the last box from her flat. Taking a break she went to sit on the back porch that overlooked a small fenced yard. The birds in the trees were making a cheerful racket and she could hear kids playing next door. She was going to miss her little flat. It had been her first home away from her parents and she had made a real effort to decorate it and make it cozy. She needed to find someone to give her seed starts to and her little window herb garden. Perhaps Sophie could take them. There was no way they could make the trip back to Montana. However, her huge palm and well-loved houseplants would probably look nice in the front room of The Feed Store.

The flat had been furnished with the basics but over the last two years Jenny had gone to yard sales and picked up cool finds like a paned window that had a mirror behind it and dressers that she had stripped and painted with milk paint. She had kept most of the furniture white and covered pillows with silk fabric in bright jewel colors. There were two tiny rooms and one big room so she had claimed the larger room and paid ½ of the rent. Her two roommates had been close friends that spent a lot of their time gone and together.

Jenny hadn't minded. She liked her space to be pristinely neat and they were always a mess when they were around.

Jenny heard the doorbell ring and ran back inside opening it to her ex-boyfriend, Kelly. He looked around rather stunned to see everything in boxes.

"You're leaving?"

"Things have been moving pretty fast, I'm headed back to Montana in a few days. I'm driving my stuff and some antiques out in a U-Haul. I'm buying a building in White Cloud for my business and have a position as a caretaker there for a place to live."

"Buying a building?" Kelly sounded dubious. "Just like that."

"I haven't talked to you for a while. I won the Brinton Golden Grant and they have given me start-up funds for the animal treat business I've always wanted to start."

"You're kidding, right. Nobody just starts a business and succeeds right away. It takes a lot more money than a grant to make that happen. And isn't White Cloud just a dot on the map with 200 people living there.

"I think the census is now 156." Jenny said her eyes getting sad and the hard. "Did you just come over the rain on my parade."

"No, I came to ask you to go get some pizza with me."

"Kelly, you *know* it was never right between us, and now it *really* isn't going to be right. I have plans with my family tonight and then I leave tomorrow."

Kelly slipped his hands into his pockets and looked down. "I really blew it with you, didn't I."

"I don't sleep with guys who have multiple sleep partners. You should have told me you were seeing other girls. I feel like you tricked me."

Kelly ran a hand through his thick red hair. "Nobody else mattered. But it's too late for that now. Do you need any help?"

"Actually," Jenny smiled "I would love a little help. I have to get all of these boxes into the front of the U-Haul parked at the bottom of the front steps."

Kelly sighed but tucked his shirt in, ready to lift. "You wouldn't happen to have any pizza here would you?" he asked hopefully.

Jenny grinned. "I'll order a large to be delivered. What do you want?"

With Kelly helping the apartment emptied out fast. He loaded her plants on the seat and floor of the truck and even helped Jenny clean. They ended up in the backyard munching a large pizza with everything on it.

"I don't know, Jen, I think we make a good team." Kelly said as he reached for another slice.

Jenny felt a little well of sadness. "Probably, but look where my life has taken me. You would never have been happy in White Cloud."

"I came to bring you some good news and to celebrate too.

"About what?" Jenny looked up surprised.

"I got a job working for a big real estate company in town. I'm going to be an assistant to start. Then hopefully I can move up to business contracts."

"Kelly, that's wonderful! You'll be wonderful at it. What firm?"

"Tavery, Swift and Roberts"

Jenny felt a little frisson of fear. "Have you heard the rumors that they might have ties to the Chicago mafia?"

"Now look at whose raining on someone's parade. All of those rumors are just crap. Everyone in Chicago is rumored to at one time or the other had connections to the family. This firm is incredibly professional and successful. I couldn't believe the salary that they offered me."

"Did you have to interview with anyone?"

"Yeah, Samuel Swift. A really nice man who took the time to read my resume and asked me some good questions. He told me that I would be Sandra Tavery's assistant."

Jenny shivered and considered telling Kelly about her father but then held back. That had happened sixteen years ago. The real estate firm hadn't even existed then. Ned had been a stockbroker and investment broker. There wasn't any reason to think that Sandra knew that she and Kelly had ever dated.

Sandra was cleaning out drawers when she found the journal she had started as a teenager and kept until the day that Ned died. The last entry had sounded cheerful and innocent. Then the writing had just stopped. Sandra remembered what it had felt like that day, seeing her mother wail with grief, knowing that no matter what she did, she could never replace her revered brother. Sandra had helplessly dropped the journal in her bottom drawer and never picked it up again.

The day that she had been dreading was here. Sandra called her driver and put on a hat and gloves. This afternoon was the reading of Ned's will. He had specified it to be read within 90 days of his daughter Jenny's twenty-first birthday. They couldn't put it off any longer. Today was day ninety.

When the driver opened the sedan door for her in front of her mother's huge estate home a butler was there to take her hat and gloves. Sandra was ushered into the foyer and then to the library where her mother, Sandra's husband, Edward, and the lawyer were waiting.

Dale Pincer, the lawyer looked nervous. He kept taking off his glasses and wiping sweat out of his eyes. It irritated and disgusted Sandra. Her brother had hired the fop when he and Lily first married. Ned hadn't been willing to listen to Nedra and use the family estate lawyer. It was another little way Ned had rebelled against being controlled. Like marrying someone like Lily. Nedra had hated her on site. But the family had tried to accept her graciously. Look where *that* had gotten them.

The lawyer cleared his throat and nodded at Sandra. "Now that you're here we can begin. This is the final will and testament of Nedrow Theodore Tavery dated December 10, 2003.

"What," Nedra said sitting forward. "This is his will from right after Jenny was born? He didn't change it after he and Lily divorced?"

The lawyer turned bright red. "No. Now if you don't mind I'll simply read its contents."

Sandra was sitting on the edge of her seat too. This was a nightmare. Why hadn't the lawyer let on, even a little bit what to expect. She would certainly see that he never got a client in this city again.

When Jenny got to Sophie's house she was relieved to have made it through the freeway traffic and already be on the first leg of her journey out of Chicago. Tomorrow she would stop by Grandpa Barry's storage shed to load the antiques and then the open road was calling. Everyone stopped to greet her as she joined in the cheerful conversation around Sophie's kitchen counter. They were grilling kabobs for supper. Sheila, Alex, Nina, their spouses and kids, Grandpa Barry and a next-door neighbor were laughing and talking boisterously.

Jenny felt a sudden premonition. This was one of those special moments that needed to be frozen in time. Within years everything would change. But today her grandparents were happy and healthy. Sheila was laughing and swinging her great grand child Maximus around in circles. Jenny wished that Lily were here. Grandma and grandpa couldn't travel like they used to.

Sophie got up to accept the herb garden that Jenny was carrying and her little flat of starter seeds. "Well, I'll be. Just what I needed. I have the perfect spot for those herbs." Sophie looked genuinely pleased and it made Jenny feel warm inside.

Jenny let the group fold her in and forgot that there were greedy people in the world who lived with the ugly seed of bitterness every day. Instead she saw the tears in Kelly's eyes when they had hugged goodbye for the last time and now the tears in in her grandfather's eyes when he laughed too hard at little Max's antics. She breathed in gratitude and catching Sophie's eye knew that she was feeling nostalgic too.

Seven

✌

Going home

The trip home to Montana stretched across miles and miles of open country that ended at the foot of the Rocky Mountains. The plains held a fascinating beauty. You could watch a thunderstorm coming for ten miles and it would still miss you. There were vignettes that sometimes took your breath away of wildflowers crowding the sides of the highway and a lone antelope standing on a barren hill. But the closer Jenny got to home the more she noticed the green. The world changed from a pale spring green to a deep emerald green with blue green sage and dark green pines. As she traveled she listened to books on tape. Her favorite was a philosopher who held that everything is connected. Everything makes up everything else. He had now written over 20 textbooks on the subject in all fields and his integral theory was gaining weight in universities and schools.

Even White Cloud had begun recycling and promoting higher consciousness and green activities. People were encouraged to ride bicycles and there was an electric recharging station now at the gas station since the majority of cars on the road were electric. If you drove an old beat up truck like her Ford you were likely to get a few dirty looks these days. The public had shifted their view of animals. The mainstream idea now was that they shared the planet with us and we did not have dominion over them, that they had the right to live free of pain in the environment that best suited them. Jenny had always been a lover of dogs and cats. But she was also a fierce animal rights activist for elephants, wolves and cougar. She had watched first hand the way her dad had found a way to live on the land without competing with the animals and she knew it was possible. She was determined her new business would get a green stamp and would also encourage small farmers and the growing of organic foods and humane treatment of animals.

When they got big enough Jenny would like to direct some of the profit of her business to the causes that she believed in. She wondered if she should just decide to do that now. It was like tithing. When you did something good she believed that the universe rewarded that.

On her next phone call home she got Lily. She was on the last leg of the trip and was enjoying the Beartooth Mountains. Because the road was narrow she pulled over to talk, rolling up the windows to keep from getting eaten by mosquitoes.

Lily sounded a little worried. "You got an overnight fed ex package today from Pincer and Pincer Estate lawyers in Chicago."

"What?"

"Do you want me to open it for you or wait until you get home? We had to sign for it."

"Definitely open it."

Lily opened the four-page typed document and began to scan it. "Oh, my God."

"What Mom. Here, take a picture of each page and send it to me so I can see what you are looking at."

Lily did and the Jenny saw what was so upsetting.

"It's Ned's will?" Jenny said open-mouthed with astonishment.

"Yes, Honey."

"Did you know about this?"

"I only know I wouldn't accept any kind of support from your dad because I didn't want to deal with him. It looks like he just invested his money for you in stock market accounts and then had the profits deposited regularly in a trust account."

"There is a deposit here for $200,000 close to the time that he offered that during the plea bargain. Then the sell of his business and house after he died and those profits were put in the trust for you too."

"On top of that he owned 33% of the Tavery Family Estate and was a 33% shareholder in the family business. He transferred all of this to you when you reached the age of twenty-one in the event of his death."

"Are you kidding me," Jenny said in shock.

"No, you are wealthy. It looks like all of that money over the course of sixteen years has grown into millions of dollars."

Jenny felt her heart start to race and couldn't breathe again. "Mom, I think I'm having an anxiety attack."

"Just get out of the truck and walk down the road a bit. You are going to want to give this some time to let it sink in, there are a lot of ramifications."

"Yeah, like I don't want any of his blood money. What if it all came from dirty dealings with the mafia? How am I going to be a shareholder in a corporation with a family that hates me? I don't want any of this!"

"Take more time to think about it bunny. You've always wanted to do something good in the world. You have strong principles and vision. Maybe this is your chance to turn this around to give your Dad some good karma. That is what happened with your Great Uncle Donald. I built the farm on his blood money. He gave me the land because he felt guilty about Lizbeth. But I have done something good with it and done something that I think would have been healing for Lizbeth. You need to wait and see how much contact you would need to have with the Tavery family before you decide to just throw your dad's gift away."

Suddenly the beautiful day and the amazing view felt ruined to Jenny. Even her vision for her own business felt like it had fallen flat. Perhaps what she had always wanted was the challenge, to know that she had built her company with sheer determination and talent. Getting an inheritance was oddly disempowering.

Jenny spent the rest of the ride home thinking about charities that could really use the money and feeling a bit foolish that she was so afraid of that much money at the same time. After all, she had a degree in Business Management and had been working with money in some form or the other her whole life. She had just hit Park Place on the monopoly board and now needed to rethink things.

Just inside of Yellowstone Park Jenny stopped again in the Lamar basin and read through the will slowly looking for something personal from her Dad to her. The money felt completely impersonal. No special objects of sentimentality had been willed to her. There was no mention of her mother. Then in the last paragraph she found the line she was looking for: It was a second signing of the will made only weeks before he died. He must have been in prison at the time. Under his signature he had handwritten the following: "I sign this will knowing my imperfections can only erased by what is perfect. She lights my way home."

That is when Jenny started to cry for her father in deep sobs with the sorrow that she had never allowed before. She remembered missing him as a little girl when her parents had separated. How she had always been his "special girl." She remembered clinging to him when he got home from work and how he had let her suck on his knuckles and stroked her hair. Jenny remembered that her Dad had loved her and it shook her to the core. Now she was being burdened with his money. It was a responsibility and also a special challenge. Those last few handwritten words were directly from him to her. He was asking her to take his gift and heal something that he couldn't heal. And she had his nasty family to deal with. What could be more of a challenge than that?

Jenny squared her shoulders and focused on the road again. She needed to get home and see her mother and Jace. She needed to hug her brother and take Tootsie out for a ride. She needed to tell Chance that she had always loved him. Soon, before it was too late.

By the time she had reached Livingston there was another message from her mother. Ned's family had sent another federal express message. They were contesting the will.

Jenny decided to just pretend for now the whole idea of the will wasn't out there. She didn't want to tell anyone about it or change her plans. She would go forward just as she had originally planned, hoping that the loan would go through from the bank, and hoping her new caretaking position would work out.

When she drove into White Cloud she looked around with a little sense of pride. She saw the town spruced up in her mind now. It was just a matter of time before she got everyone on board for the project. She saw the Diner and smiled, maybe Chance was there. Then she saw the school bus and groaned. It was time to talk to her brother.

Bern looked thrilled to see her. He hated riding the bus with all the little kids and couldn't wait until he finally had his own car. Jenny looked beat sitting in the tall U-Haul truck cab after three days of driving.

"Hey, I'll drive home," Bern said as he climbed up. "Geez it's a jungle in here. Where did you get all of these plants?"

"They are from my flat in Chicago. And *you* drive? You've got to be kidding. Do mom and dad let you drive?"

"I've driven the tractor and dad has let me drive his truck down the dirt road." Bern insisted.

"Well, this thing isn't a tractor. How did school go today?"

Bern was searching through Jenny's munchies on the seat and had already filled his mouth. It was fine but I got creamed in practice and my shoulder and back are killing me. Being quarterback is like being a bull's-eye. Our defense stinks right now and I'm always getting beaten up."

Jenny noticed he had a bruise on his check. "Did you get that bruise at practice too."

"Naw, got creamed again, but this time in a fight. It wasn't a good day."

"How is it you are fighting at school?"

"Wasn't at school. There are some real tough creeps that hang out just outside of school grounds. One of the creeps came onto a girl in my class and I socked him and then got jumped. I'm definitely on their shit list now."

"Your teachers don't know any of this is happening?"

"They are clueless."

"Why don't you tell someone?"

"I'd get ostracized as a nark by the other kids. That would be even worse, believe me. At least now I'm kind of a hero for standing up to that jerk."

"Do these guys sell you pot? Who buys the pot for your friends?"

Bern took a good look at his sister. "I'm not going to talk to you if you're grilling me so you can talk to mom and dad. There is a code. Are you being trustworthy?"

Jenny shook her head yes knowing that was the only way that she could help her brother.

"Only one of the kids in school makes the deal. We all get our pot from him and he puts a hefty mark-up on it for himself."

"Have you bought pot too?" Jenny asked searching his face.

Bern looked a little guilty. "Only once. Most of the time I just borrow from friends. There always seems enough to go around."

"How has being stoned affected your games or school?"

"I only smoke on the weekend or when we are hanging out after school. I'm not stupid," Bern said and then he looked a little frustrated. "Hey, lets change the subject. Mom and Dad said you're staying and buying The Feed Store. Cool!"

It was clear to Jenny that her mom and dad were keeping her inheritance quiet like they had agreed.

"Yeah," Jenny said, grabbing Bern's shoulder and squeezing. "You have to put up with me. I'm here to stay. We'll talk more about this later. You're not going to get off this easy with me!"

Eight

When Jenny and Bern got home there was a feast waiting. Lily and Jace had invited company. Della and Judd were there along with their younger son Joel. Bricca had come with her boys Tonka and Paddy. They were running around the yard and Tootsie was chasing after them. Bricca said that the girls Charlotte and Lizzy were at a sleepover. Reese had been invited and surprisingly he had brought a date, a shy woman named Janet. Musty was there by himself looking kind of awkward. Jenny immediately rescued him by striking up a conversation and soon everyone had warmed up and was feeling comfortable.

Della was someone who always said what was on her mind, and to her way of thinking everyone at the BBQ was family.

"So how are Sophie and Drew doing? They are in their mid-80s now aren't they?

"Amazing well, considering. Neither of them has been sick or infirmed in any way and they still have family around them because of Sheila and her kids. I just felt for a moment though that everything is poised to start a slow decline and I was seeing some of their last really good moments. It made me sad even though I really had no reason to feel that way."

Lily looked a little bit guilty. "I need to go visit more. I haven't been out to Chicago in three years and I know that they can't come here any more. It's a long trip."

"Well, Drew is still spry as ever and Sophie's garden is beautiful. You still have time."

"What kind of antiques do you have in that there U-Haul?" Della asked.

"Do you want to see?" Jenny offered.

"Well, sure if your offering."

Jenny opened the back of the truck and everyone wondered over to see the jumble of furniture as they took a swig of their beers.

Lily's eyes opened a bit wider. "That is a almost a whole house load of stuff."

"Yep," Jenny smiled. "And I'm afraid I'm already a bit attached to it all. That French desk has a hidden drawer that held confederate love letters. The credenza came with Amelia Applewhite's family when they emigrated from England. That chair with the ornate legs used to be in Grandma Stanford parlor. I remember sitting on it when my legs couldn't reach the floor. I think it would look beautiful re-covered. The bed canopy has a painting of Mary Magdalene on the bedpost. It is by some unknown Italian artist. I think it would bring good luck to whoever slept on it."

Reese just whistled. "We're moving all of this stuff tomorrow?"

Unfortunately it will all have to be unloaded and some of it moved again. I won't own The Feed Store for 15 days yet when the loan and title papers clear. Jenny grimaced and then looked over at

Joel. "Hey you're a big brawny guy. Why don't you talk to Chance and you guys both come along. I'll feed everyone."

Joel nodded without commenting and Judd and Della gave each other a look.

Judd said quietly, "Chance has been working out-of-town. He got a job in Livingston and he's been staying there for the last couple of weeks."

Jenny looked away so her disappointment wouldn't show. "Well, Joel I guess that leaves you, me, Dirk and Reese."

"I can help tomorrow," Musty pitched in. "Unless you need me for something else?" He looked over at Bricca who gave him a big smile.

"You're a free man Musty. But before you close the truck I'd love to get my hands on those love letters, Jenny. I can't wait to get started on researching them a little bit."

Jenny handed Bricca a shoebox that was near the desk and Bricca grinned.

Lily looked confused as Jenny filled her in. "Bricca wants to write a book about our great, great, great grandmother who lived on a southern plantation. She has also agreed to come work with me a couple of days in my business."

Lily looked over at Bricca. "You're going to have time for all that?"

Bricca scoffed. "*All* I have is time," she said and took a long swig of her beer. Everyone sensed it at the same time. Things were not right in Bricca's family. It was the first time that Jace had gotten wind of trouble and immediately he wanted to start asking questions.

Lily shushed him with signal and everyone made their way back to the picnic table. Before long the joking had begun and the little moment of revelation was gone.

However, when Lily and Jace went to bed that night Lily took her time unraveling her braid so she could contemplate the unthinkable. Jace came to sit behind her and began running his fingers through her silky hair, unloosening it and then kissing her neck softly.

"You are as beautiful as the day that I married you," Jace said.

"I'm lucky too," Lily said. "Every day in some little way you show me that you love me. I'm worried about Bricca and Will. He wasn't here again. Now that I think about it I haven't seen him for more then 20 minutes for six months. He even missed Christmas this year. Bricca is starting to look really sad. I'm afraid their marriage could fall apart if he doesn't get his priorities straight. And they have four kids." Lily was on the verge of tears when she said that.

Jace stroked her arm to comfort her. "I'll talk to him about it. He probably doesn't even know something is wrong."

Lily wrapped her arms around Jace and suddenly the fire heated up between them. Jace began to kiss her passionately. Pulling off her blouse he kissed the column of her throat, nibbling his way down to her breast and unclasping her bra with one flick of his wrist. Lily moaned. "You just undo me, Jace. Somewhere inside there is a little knot and when you touch it, I fly apart and into pieces."

Jace laughed and lets his hands work their magic. He had always wanted to lose himself in Lily. There had to be some way that it was possible. It felt the same every time they made love. She was everything pure and sweet that his mother had been and he couldn't figure out what he had done to deserve her.

The next morning Jenny got up early again to ride River. Tootsie was waiting at the door ready to go too. Jenny went out into the pasture to catch River and he seemed to recognize her in the half dark.

"Here baby, I've brought you a carrot. I couldn't think of anything better. I don't have any of my Honey Bee Biscuits made yet. How about a nice ride and a little run down to the creek?"

She was walking River back in the half dark When Tootsie growled and began to bark. A shadow stepped out from beside the barn spooking her horse and scaring her. Jenny picked up Tootsie to calm her down.

"Mornin', Jenny." Dirk said, the red tip of his cigarette just visible under his hat. "Just stepped out for my early morning smoke and thought I was seeing a vision. You look great."

Jenny felt a little wiggle of discomfort at his blatant flirting and did what she had always done when one of her dad's wrangler flirted, ignored it.

"See you later. I'm saddling up River for a ride. It looks like we have a little crew for unloading furniture set for around 10:00 a.m."

Dirk replied a little too forcefully, "Well, I won't mind seeing *you* later. You're like an oasis in a desert."

Jenny felt a little spurt of anger and decided it was time to nip his flirting in the bud. "Actually, I think we have enough people to help this morning. Daddy said he needs you here." Jenny would pass that word on to Jace when she got back from her ride.

Dirk put out his cigarette and stamped it under his heel. This time he ground it out hard. It was time to do a little research on this girl. There had to be some way to get to her and make her see him in a different light.

When 10:00 a.m. came Musty was waiting and Joel and Reese were in the living room visiting. Jenny threw her still wet hair into a braid and tugged on clean jeans and a tank top. She had ended up going for a longer ride than she had expected and gotten back with only a half an hour to eat and shower.

Joel said casually. "Chance came home for the weekend and he's gonna help too. We're picking him up in town."

Jenny's heart started to pound hard and she wished she had taken more time to dry her hair and put on a little makeup. But you never kept ranch men waiting. They were always early and they had a lot more to do before the day was out.

Jenny threw the U-Haul keys to Reese and motioned to Joel. I'll take Bertha. Joel you can ride with me. Reese you and Musty can bring the U-Haul. We'll pick Chance up in town and meet you there. Do you know where the Princeton house is?"

"Is it that big new fancy log one up by Eagle Rock?"

"That's the one. There is no one there but I have the code for the gate."

Reese scrunched up his face. "They have an electric gate?"

"Yep," Jenny said. "And all the latest in burglar alarms. We don't want to set it off."

Out in the yard Joel looked around and saw his beat up Toyota. "I ought to drive my car in and park it somewhere in town to save another trip."

"Okay," Sophie said, "I'll meet you in front of the Diner. Where will Chance be?"

"Same place," Joel said. "He's probably letting mom stuff him with a big breakfast now."

Jenny pulled her car way back in line to keep from getting grit and dust on her newly washed truck. Now that she had replaced the window she didn't want a rock to chip it and she was trying to baby the muffler a bit so it didn't fall off if she hit a bump too hard.

Jenny checked herself in the mirror and groaned, fishing around in her little purse for her makeup bag and putting on a little lip-gloss. The she let out half her braid and loosened the rest of it letting her long hair dry in the wind coming through the window. At the last second she tucked her tank top into her jeans, which pulled the top down to show the barest amount of cleavage. Jenny laughed with excitement. She was going to get to see Chance.

When she pulled Bertha up to the curb her heart was beating hard. She slid out of the truck and saw him through the Diner window. He waved and Jenny lit up, all smile and dimples. She saw Chance choke on whatever he was eating and then pound his chest as he picked his cowboy hat off the seat and adjusted it on his head.

When he walked out of the Diner Jenny did what she hadn't done two weeks ago. She made a run for him and he picked her up just like they had done it in the old days. Chance was looking a little dazed when he set her down.

"I guess I haven't let you know that I've missed you." Jenny said.

Chance suddenly seemed quiet and serious. "It didn't seem like that two weeks ago, why suddenly now?"

"I don't know. I was just being nervous or foolish or something. You didn't have to just walk out of the BBQ the first night we saw each other again."

Chance took his hat off and rubbed it, then put his fingers on his forehead like his head was hurting. "Well the thing is. I'm dating someone now. We just started but I'm not really free unless I call it off."

Jenny's mouth fell open. There had never been anyone for Chance but her and she had never really had anyone but Chance. She tried to keep tears from brimming up and in the end had to look away.

Joel saved the day by arriving in his Toyota and Jenny said briskly. "Why don't you two ride together and follow me."

Jenny used the ride up to Eagle Rock to pull herself together. She dug the code for the gate out of her little zip pocket with her floor plan for the caretaker cabin. She had already measured and decided where she wanted everything to go.

When the guys started to unload there was a lot of good-natured ribbing and it allowed Jenny to not have to see Chance alone.

The furniture for the store went in her garage and the boxes inside the house. When they were done, Jenny pulled sandwiches out of her cooler that her mom had made and a big jug of lemonade and cookies. She busied herself with walking around looking at the furniture and moving some of the smaller pieces as the guys ate.

The men had wolfed down lunch in ten minutes and were ready to get on with their day so Jenny cheerful waved everyone off with an effusive thank you. As Chance and Joel started to walk out Chance motioned Joel off and came back alone.

"Don't miss your ride, Chance." Jenny said.

"I thought you could drive me back, I want to talk a bit."

"Well, I don't want to talk to you."

"It's too late now. He's already gone."

"I have stuff to do."

"Then I'll help you. Do you need to put together that bed?"

Jenny threw her hands up and stalked into the bedroom with her hands on her hips. "Yes."

Chance just picked up a screwdriver a started quietly figuring out how it all went together while Jenny unpacked some boxes in the kitchen. It took only a half-an-hour before he called her in.

"Jenny help me drag this mattress in here. It's heavy so don't even try to lift it."

Jenny pushed, pulled and kicked it but the huge king size mattress bent in the middle and seemed to be stuck in the door.

She put all of her weight into it while Chance pulled and suddenly it popped into the room and practically sprang onto the bed.

Jenny ended up thrown into the middle of the bed on her back. She started to laugh. Chance was pinned between the mattress and the frame.

Slowly he climbed out ending up in the middle of the bed with her and then there was no way to stop the inevitable.

They were kissing passionately, Chance pulling her tank top over her head and kicking off his boots. Jenny immediately felt the sweet pain of exquisite longing. She was hanging on the edge of an orgasm before Chance could pull her Jeans down and push himself up into her. They had always fit so well together. Chance was strong and muscular. Jenny was able to flow around him and when he filled her she bit her lip so she wouldn't scream but she did anyway. With one hard push Chance was groaning, trying to hold himself back, to make things last but unable to.

Jenny found that there were tears on her cheeks. This was what she wanted: his smell, his skin, and the quietness in his eyes, his kindness and his intensity. Chance looked shaken and lifted himself off of her gently.

"Did I hurt you? That was a bit out of control."

Jenny just groaned and rolled onto her side, snugging him up next to her. "Again." She said with the luxurious smile of a cat licking cream. And this time Chance began with a long slow lick up her spine then down to the small of her back. Jenny was shaking with anticipation by the time he took her with his tongue and then his hand and then his whole body."

When they were done Jenny looked around the room a bit stunned. Their clothing was flung everywhere. There was no sheet on the bed and they had been lying on Chance's shirt.

Light was streaming into the room and they were totally exposed to each other in bright daylight.

She couldn't have asked for anything better.

"Chance," Jenny said. "It has always been you and me. You've got to break up with this girl, whoever she is. I can't stand thinking about you being with another woman."

Chance wrapped his hands around Jenny's braid and pulled just a little bit. Enough to hurt and enough to turn her on.

"Okay. But it makes me feel bad to do it. She's pretty fragile."

Jenny closed her eyes. "Don't tell me anything about her. I can't stand to hear it. But you should remember that this is better for her too. She is better off not being with you unless you love her. Do you love her?"

"No, I think she needs help. It's nothing like what we've always had."

"Okay. I'm sorry I was such a jerk when I first came home. Please forgive me."

For an answer Chance just gripped her hair and pulled her head back exposing her throat. At first just smelling her skin and then carefully nipping. Jenny shot up as heat poured through her and melted her insides. "Chance, it has always been you. Always."

Nine

Dirk spent part of the morning on the Internet searching for dirt. He remembered hearing that Jenny's father had been some kind of low life. When he found what he was looking for he whistled. This was better then he thought. The guy had been murdered with a sniper gun and had tried to kill both Lily and Jace. Not only that he was from some bigwig family in Chicago. An investor. He must have had tons of money stashed away somewhere.

Dirk did a search on obituaries in Chicago and hit the Jackpot. Sandra Tavery. He googled her and found out she had a real estate firm and served on the board for Brintons. Wasn't that where Jenny had gotten her grant? Maybe the whole thing had been rigged. Had the other board members known that the two of them were related?

Dirk thought about what to do. A phone call to the right people might be valuable. Or a threat to Sandra and she'd see she ought to help him win Jenny over.

Dirk had no idea he was disturbing a nest of deadly water moccasins when he picked up the phone.

In the meantime Jace had taken the morning off to go to Will's vet clinic and see what was going on. When he walked in the door he saw two clients waiting. An older lady was gripping her small dog looking upset and frightened. Another lady was holding her hands over her ears as her cat howled from its cage.

The receptionist was someone Jace hadn't met before. She looked young and intelligent, like a university student, which proved to be true.

"You must be Jace, I'm Julianne, Will's assistant trainee. I'm doing my internship here which is split between office work and getting to see clients."

Julianne's smile was generous and warm. She seemed comfortable and familiar as she went to get Will, pulling him in by the arm as he kept talking to the woman who was questioning him about her horse.

"Sometimes I have to be forceful. Everyone wants a little piece of Will and if I don't protect him, they'll eat him all up."

Julianne said that with a southern accent and Jace raised his eyebrows. Will just smiled and waved to his clients. "Julianne, I think you could see these two for me. Mrs. Ross just wants her worming medicine for Bitsey and the cat needs a rabies shot. You might want to sedate him first and give him a check-up, make sure to check his teeth too. He doesn't sound like a very happy cat.

Will walked with Jace back into his office and shut the door pulling off his gloves. "Whew, it's been a long morning. He sat on the edge of the desk. What brought you all the way here?"

Jace got right to the point knowing it was going to piss Will off but jumping in anyway.

"Okay, I know you're not going to like what I'm going to say, but what are big brothers for if it's not to tell it like it is. Lily and I are worried about Bricca. She seems unhappy and lonely. She is starting a book and planning to work for Jenny. Did you know that?"

"No, but good for her. She's been bored just hanging out at the ranch."

"It's more than that. She seems disillusioned and sad. You are never home."

Will felt his temper rising. "I have four kids to feed."

"I repeat. You are *never* home. Not for Christmas, not on the weekends, not in the evenings. You don't do the little things that show her you love her anymore."

"Did she tell you that?" Will was boiling now.

"No. I can *see* that with my own two eyes. *Anyone* watching can see that. You have a gorgeous, talented wife who is passionate and personable and you don't seem to want to spend any time with her."

Will blew up. "*You* try having a veterinarian practice where every one in town wants a little piece of you. My fridge here is filled with apple pies and casseroles. I'm invited to lunch every day. I'm constantly questioned and stopped even if I'm just getting groceries. It is like being fucking Elvis Presley or something. I don't even get one minute to myself and you want me to turn on the charm when I'm at home, at the only place where I can relax and be myself!"

"Isn't being charming something you *want* to do with Bricca."

"Not when there are four kids screaming or whining around me every fucking minute. You said Bricca isn't happy. Well I'm not either. I love my family but I'm overworked, overtired and running on empty. Yesterday my twenty-year old assistant tried to come on to me and I couldn't even respond to *that*. I just felt used by her too."

Will looked a little grey as he said that and suddenly Jace saw what he must feel like.

"How about a vacation?"

"What's that? Are you ready to take care of our whole brood? Who would take my practice and oversee my sick animals?"

Jace straightened his shoulders. "Yes, I'll keep your kids. We can call Dr. Duncan out of retirement for a month and you can take a sabbatical for a month with Bricca."

Will put his head in his hands. "That might work. I've been worried about Bricca. She has seemed so despondent. In the past the only way I could keep up this grueling schedule was because she would give me energy and strength when I got home. Now she just ignores me. Won't even accept a kiss and a hug and half the time won't talk to me. It's driving me crazy."

"I'll have Lily talk to her and we'll make a plan for some kind of intervention with you guys. A vacation might be all that you need."

Jace left the clinic feeling exhausted. How was it that he hadn't even seen what had been going on until yesterday. This was his kid brother and Lily's kid sister. He should have been taking better care of them.

When he stepped off the curb to get in his truck he noticed Bricca's car driving by. He was about to wave when he saw there was a man in the Van with her talking animatedly and gesturing effusively with his hands. Bricca was laughing at something he had said.

Jace's gut tightened. Hopefully she hadn't already met someone else.

Bricca hadn't had such fun in a long time. Her companion was the gay brother of one of her old dance students. He had come home to visit and Bricca had struck up a conversation with him at the Diner. Before she knew it she was driving him home to the north side of the valley so he wouldn't have to take a cab and they had started laughing and laughing and laughing. Justin had a knack at telling stories and being able to switch into different accents. He did a great southern drawl. Before she knew it Bricca was telling him about the book she wanted to write and telling him how she used to write for the Atlanta Sun as a ghostwriter in a column about birds. Justin took that piece of information and ran with it soon offering funny scenarios about her new book.

"Maybe Gwenn Anne had both men on the line. Her Confederate and her Yankee. She liked playing them against each other. Scarlet starting her own little civil war."

Bricca laughed until her sides hurt.

"Justin, you are a bad boy. If you ever want to have coffee call me. I'll fill you in on where the book is going."

Bricca felt a sense of relief driving home that day that there was someone new in her world that could be her friend. She needed a confidant right now that she wasn't related to or who didn't know everyone else in town.

Minutes later her cell rang.

It was Lily asking if she could stop by on her way home.

Immediately Bricca wondered if she had been reported riding in a car with a man. The White Cloud gossip train was immediate and vicious. It made Bricca want to move back to Atlanta. For the first time she considered it. Will wouldn't care. The kids would get to see their other side of the family. Lily didn't need her anymore.

Starfire could come along. It might be one way to get out of the miserable place she had found herself in.

When she pulled into the yard she found Lily had set a little table for them in the backyard with a bottle of wine and two glasses. There were chocolates and strawberries on the table as well as some bright colored fingernail polish.

Oh, Oh, Bricca thought. *Someone* did *tell on me.*

Lily gave Bricca a hug and led her to the table.

"Do you see this feast before us?" Lily said playfully.

Bricca laughed.

"Well as you know already it is an intervention."

"I thought as much," Bricca groaned, but she sat down and let a piece of dark rich chocolate melt in her mouth and than reached for a strawberry.

"What are you intervening in?"

"Your love life. Jace went down and had a talk with Will today." Lily put her hand up to keep Bricca from interrupting. "Will told him that he was exhausted and worn out from work and from never seeing you. He told Jace that he was worried that you had become sad and unhappy. He said he was unhappy too and didn't know what to do to change all of the pressure that he felt to work constantly."

"They hatched a plan together. Will is asking Dr. Duncan to take his practice for a month. Jace and I are taking your kids. You guys are going to take off and go on a long vacation together, just the two of you. That is the plan. Than Jace saw you in a car with another man and panicked thinking maybe this had all come to late and you've met someone else."

Bricca was crying now, great big tears of gratitude and sadness all mixed together. "I've been so lonely and felt so unloved. For years I just hung on believing I had enough love to hold us together. Will would work late every night and I would fix a big dinner and cheer him up if he was sad or rub his feet if he was tired."

"Than after Charlotte was born I just didn't have the ability to do that anymore. The four kids took everything and I had nothing left to give him. He hadn't been even trying to give anything to me for years. I lost myself in my kids and than they grew up and went to school and I was left with nothing."

Bricca went on tearfully, "Will and I are probably finished. Today I was thinking about leaving him and moving back home to the Atlanta. He wouldn't really miss me; we never see each other anymore. We haven't made love in months."

Bricca continued, "The man I was with today is a new friend. It was nice to talk to someone who isn't family or part of this gossip mongering community. He's gay and I need a friend. I'll probably still call him and hang out no matter what anyone thinks!"

Bricca went on as Lily listened sympathetically. "If Will really does this, agrees to take off for a month, I'll be surprised. I think he's addicted to his work and the movie star quality of being like God to so many people. Did Jace meet his cute young assistant? You can bet your ass she's been coming on to him. Will always attracts women. They flock around him with their kittens and puppies and look at him adoringly. He loves it."

Lily broke in. "Well, he told Jace he was sick of just that and all he wanted was things back with you the way they used to be. I think he's going to want to go on this trip."

Bricca took a sip of her wine. "Are you sure you want to take my kids. They can be quite a handful. They each eat different things and have a host of allergies and bedtime quirks." Bricca was looking a little worried. "I've never been away from them for that long."

Lily just smiled. "I can handle it and Jace will be helping. We have Jenny here also to lend a hand and Bern to watch them too."

"Well, if I were you I'd be *watching Bern* a little better. I think he looked stoned the other day at the picnic."

"Stoned? He doesn't smoke. We've asked him point-blank."

"Well, than he lied," Bricca said.

Lily poured herself an oversized glass of wine and took a big gulp. "I think I'm going to need this too." Bricca just groaned and picked up the fingernail polish. "What colors did you get?"

"Aqua with silver stars in it and purple with rainbow glitter."

"Totally cool."

By the time Jenny got home from unpacking and making love all afternoon with Chance her mother and Bricca were drunk and laughing their heads off. Tootsie ran to greet her and Jenny walked over to the table to say Hi. Jenny had never seen them act so foolish and she wanted in on the fun but didn't know how to break into their little twosome.

Bricca broke the ice. "You naughty girl. I recognize this look about you. You have been well and truly canoodled."

Jenny gasped but Bricca just laughed loudly and Lily snorted.

"Chance by Chance?" Bricca said, handing Jenny the bottle.

Lily patted a seat. "Have some chocolate and a strawberry but don't tell me anything about it. I don't want to think of my baby daughter making love all afternoon while *we* just painted our fingernails."

Bricca held up her hand and Jenny saw she had alternated colors.

That night when Will came home Bricca wasn't home yet. A rush of cold fear went through him and he ran upstairs to make sure she hadn't left him, than sat down at the kitchen table and put his head in his hands to wait.

When Bricca did come in the door he could see that she was weaving and completely soused.

"Where have you been?" Will asked tightly.

"Drinking with my best buddy." Bricca slurred as she stumbled to the couch.

"Barb Finn said she saw you in a car with some man, laughing."

"She did, did she? Well Barb Finn needs to get laid. She has a mouth like a p…per..simmon." Bricca drawled the words trying to pronounce persimmon even though her mouth didn't seem to work right.

"Bricca, what's going on? Are you seeing somebody else?"

"Do you mean, am I being *seen*? Today I was *seen*…twice."

With that she passed out on the couch leaving Will to wonder if that meant she'd made love to somebody else twice. Thank goodness the kids were camping out with the church group this weekend. He needed to fight this out with Bricca. By God, no wife of his was going to make a fool of him.

The next morning Bricca woke up holding her head and groaning. She was sleeping on the couch in her clothes and Will was asleep on a chair in the living room. Bricca checked the time. Saturday at 8:00 am. Will should already be gone on his rounds.

Will woke up too and looked at her out of slitted eyes, checking to see if he could still move his neck.

Will started the argument. "You were completely drunk last night and admitted you had slept with someone else, twice."

"What! You've got to be crazy! I couldn't have said that."

"Well you did."

"I did not."

"How do you know what you admitted to, you were falling down drunk?" Will looked miserable. His face was grey and there was hopelessness in voice.

"I know I didn't say that because I've never done that. What did I actually say, word for word?"

"That you'd been seen by a buddy…twice."

"I met and had a great conversation with a gay guy that I think really got me and who could be a good friend and I got drunk with Lily, ate chocolates and painted my nails with her. I finally told her how I've been feeling lately and she understood."

Will sighed and rubbed his head. "Shit, Bricca. Last night was a nightmare for me."

"Well, to be frank, the last four years have been a nightmare for me. I've been thinking about leaving."

Will looked shocked. "When did you think about that?"

Bricca laughed. "The first time was yesterday. But before that I was miserable every day. Will, you *don't* want me to think about leaving because I'm not afraid to do it. I'll just be gone one day and you'll have to travel to see your kids."

"That sounds like a threat."

"No, just the truth. You aren't happy either. I thought you wouldn't care."

"How could you think that? You're everything to me. I have been working day and night for you and the kids."

"Oh, be honest for once!!" Bricca shook her head with disgust. "You work because you enjoy being everyone's best friend and the local movie star. I know what motivates you!"

"Than you don't know me at all! I fucking hate it! I've been hating my work, resenting everyone's demands and attention, disgusted with my assistant who keeps trying to come on to me. I've been miserable too."

Bricca really looked at Will and saw the tears in his eyes. *Maybe there was still hope.*

Bricca sat forward feeling the first possibility that maybe this was fixable. "Lily was setting up an intervention for us. She said she would keep the kids and Dr. Duncan could take your practice for a month so we could get away together."

Will nodded in agreement. "Jace and I talked. I've already called Dr. Duncan and he is starting next week on Monday. In fact I asked him to be on call this weekend so we can pack and decide where we want to go. Do you still have a valid passport? I was thinking we could take the Europe trip you've always wanted to take."

Bricca's face lit up with excitement.

"Really, REALLY!"

Will walked over to Bricca and got down on the floor in front of her putting his head in her lap. "You scared me to death. I don't think I can start packing until we recuperate a little."

Bricca smiled. "Well, we can start with a nice hot bath with Epsom salts and than steak for breakfast. I'm calling Lily to see if she can really take the kids starting Monday. Do you think they'll be all right?"

"Yes, they are healthy, resilient and loved. They will be fine staying with their Aunt and Uncle for a month."

"Yes, they will won't they."

Will sounded a little whiney for a moment. "Will you scrub my back?"

Bricca smiled. "Only if you scrub mine."

The weekend flew by with too much to do and a new feeling of closeness. Bricca and Will picked the kids up together in Livingston Sunday night and took them to the Pizza Hut to break the news.

"They had expected tears and recrimination. Instead Paddy just said, "Cool. It will be fun hanging out with Tootsie. Why can't we get a dog?"

Charlotte was the one who seemed nervous. "Can I take Bear Bear?"

"Of course," Bricca said. She had practically written a manual for Lily about all of the kid's likes and dislikes. Lily and Jace were acting confident and Jenny had agreed to help babysit so Lily and Jace could have time off when they needed it.

Bricca thought, *Maybe that's what **we** need, a nanny or a helper who comes in two nights a week so I'm not stuck at the ranch all the time. Maybe what Will needs is a partner so he can cut his workload in half. Maybe I should let the kids have a dog.*

Charlotte began to cry when Bricca and Will brought them over to the M Rocking B Ranch. Bricca put her on her hip and let carried her like a baby. She always loved that. They were leaving for Missoula right away to catch a non-stop flight to La Guardia.

"Are you finally going to tell us where you are going?" Lily asked as Bricca transferred Charlotte into her arms.

Bricca smiled. "Europe. We are traveling through Ireland and Italy. I've always wanted to go to Ireland because of Paddy. I still have relatives there. The O'Briens are a big clan. Than we've rented a villa in Tuscany and we are going to tour Italy. I can't believe we will be gone four weeks. By the time we get back Bricca will have possession of The Feed Store and the kids will be out of school. Here is the key to our van if you need it and Musty has instructions on the feeding schedule and is checking the mares every day. I think Darling Dilly is getting close to dropping her foal."

"Dilly? Ready to foal?" It was the first moment that Lily wondered why she had agreed to this crazy plan. But seeing the love in Will's eyes again when he looked at Bricca was worth it. Even a weekend off had done wonders for him.

Charlotte clung to Lily crying and it was Tonka who pried her away.

"Here, you can play with Stevie the Stegosaurus if you stop crying. He doesn't like hearing people cry."

Charlotte promptly put her thumb in her mouth and took Stevie. Bricca gave Tonka a squeeze.

"You are the biggest, bravest boy in the world," she said, "And I love you." All four kids gathered for a group hug and than Will and Bricca were in his truck, driving away.

Lily and Jenny looked at each other and the four kids and got busy. Jenny tried to entertain them to cheer them up.

"Let's play hide and seek with Tootsie while Aunt Lily makes sandwiches."

Paddy spoke up. "No mayo on mine, please. "

Tonka raised his hand, "I don't like cheese unless it's the flat like the American cheese kind."

Charlotte nodded her head. "Me too, and no crust on my bread."

"And what about you, Lizzy?" Lily asked.

Lizzy just smiled. "I'll help you make them."

Jenny decided that her first night at the caretaker house would need to be tonight. There wasn't any room in the big house anyway with all the kids. Her bedroom and the guest rooms were taken. Tootsie had moved onto Tonka's bed. He seemed to know who needed him most.

It made her nervous that Eagle Rock was very isolated with no neighbors and she would be staying by herself. She considered calling Chance but he had one more week working on his painting job in Livingston.

Chance had called it off with Kiera Paige but she had been calling him nonstop, crying on the phone and talking about hurting herself.

Chance had been trying to be kind but wasn't sure what to do when he started receiving calls at 2:00 in the morning. Jenny wasn't sure what they should do either. She wondered if Kiera just needed a friend and if she should call her. She felt a little guilty about taking Chance away from her but Chance had been her boyfriend her whole life and Kiera had only known him for two weeks.

As she drove up to the house and got out to check the gate she noticed fresh tire tracks. Someone had been there today. The UPS truck? Who else even knew she was staying out here?

Everybody, that's who. Nothing was a secret in White Cloud.

Strangely the thought was comforting. Nothing is a secret in White Cloud. There wasn't any nefarious plot to harm her that the good people of White Cloud wouldn't find out about.

Jenny punched in the code and got back into the truck checking to make sure the gate shut behind her. She didn't see Dirk standing in the shadows watching with his binoculars as she punched in the code. After her headlights were gone he stepped forward and tried the code himself.

Damm, he'd gotten it wrong. It was a long walk in to the house in the dark. He'd wait and come back another night.

Jenny in the meantime had already called Chance.

"Hi sweets," she said when she got the answering machine. "Just a bit spooked but not sure why. It's my first night staying at the caretaking cabin. Let me know if you're in town and can come out."

She hung up not expecting an answer. Chance hated smartphones and was terrible at returning messages. As she walked through the house she congratulated herself on her lovely sense of style. The now polished antiques stood next to modern prints and her bright colored prints and pillows. It was an interesting combination that somehow worked. Jenny took a few pictures to send to Sophie and Drew and than lovingly ran her hands over the old desk thinking that the scratches on it must be hundreds of years old. On a whim she peaked underneath and saw names scratched in the bottom. GA loves BT it said with a heart around it. "Gwenn Anne loves Benjamin Thomas, the man in her letters. They must have grown up together just like she and Chance had because these scratchings were the marks of children.

That night Jenny tossed and turned in her huge bed. A few times she woke up and reached up to touch the painting of Mary Magdalene. The last time that she fell asleep she dreamed.

In her dream she saw a lovely woman with a tightly drawn waist and full skirt. When she turned around Jenny saw that they looked very much alike. The woman's blond hair was pinned up in an elaborate braid with small bows tied into it. She had Jenny's brown eyes but her skin looked whiter and her lips a bit thinner. The woman was primping in the mirror when she stopped for a second and whispered into the mirror. "Help me. He doesn't know. You've got to help me."

Jenny woke up than feeling spooked. The dream had had a numinous quality about it and Bricca wasn't here to talk to about it. Bricca would have understood. They were alike that way. Jenny suddenly knew she needed to read Gwenn Anne's letters. She hoped that Bricca had left them behind.

After tossing and turning for another hour Jenny fell into a restless sleep and woke exhausted. The furniture all around her seemed a bit oppressive and Jenny spontaneously decided she might need to do a bit of smudging. Maybe the pieces still held some residue from the past that needed cleared.

Showering and dressing quickly Jenny headed out the door. Today she got to meet with Judd to discuss the remodel of her new space. There were things she needed to do to get her business going and not much time to do it in. The closing for her property was next week. She wanted to be there ready to start the remodel on the day the loan closed. Also today Jenny had promised to relieve her mom with the kids and bring out some necessary groceries.

It all seemed worth it when she got a text from Bricca.

"We made it to New York and are ready for the next leg. By tomorrow we'll be in Ireland. I'm falling in love with Will again and him with me. Thanks for this honeymoon trip. Love, Bricca. P.S. Any problems with the kids? P.S.S. Try to pretend that I didn't ask that."

Jenny sent a text back, "Did you leave the Gwenn Anne letters? I'd like to read them. Had a dream about her last night."

An immediate text came back, "They are in the top of my closet. Did she look a lot like you in your dream? I've had a dream about her, too."

Jenny texted back. "Yes, only she had elaborate braids and a full skirt. She said to me, "Help me. He doesn't know. You've got to help me.""

Bricca thumbed back, "I read the first few letters. Benjamin's family emigrated from Ireland. I'm going to check out some of that while I'm here. Let's keep in touch. Love you. We are boarding now. P.S. I have a weird feeling of danger. Be cautious. "

When Dirk got home he had a mysterious email that was very cryptic. "Got your phone message. Call me on a throw away cell phone and I'll give you some information you might find helpful." The note was unsigned. Dirk felt a little leap of pleasure. He was hitting the right buttons. Maybe he didn't need to get the girl to get money. There were other ways to do that. He'd also heard that Chance had broken it off with Kiera and that she wasn't taking it well. She might be a way to get to Chance. Tomorrow he'd just take a little trip to Livingston for a visit with the poor thing.

Jace pulled his hat down and thought about earplugs. Had Jenny and Bern yelled all of the time like this when they were kids? He couldn't remember. Perhaps they had but because they were his kids, he'd somehow gotten immune to it. He hoped to hell that happened soon here because he didn't know how Will and Bricca had stood it. The kids seemed to fight all of the time. They were always calling on someone else to solve their spats for them and Jace was getting tired of the whining.

The next time Tonka screamed Jace called everyone into the room and brought Lily in as a witness.

"Okay, kids. We are having a family meeting. "No, and I mean NO screaming, tattle telling or whining is allowed at our house. If you scream for no reason you will go to bed. If you tattle when it's not necessary you'll have to wash dishes. If you whine when you're not hurt you will miss dessert. Do I make myself clear?

All of the kids nodded yes. It made Jace wonder if Will had ever helped Bricca parent them. Sometimes kids needed control and a strong father figure.

Within a half an hour they were at it again. Screaming tattling and whining. Jace started to hand out punishments and the kids looked shocked.

"My Daddy doesn't make me go to bed early!" Paddy stomped his foot.

"My mommy never makes me miss pie when everyone else is eating," Charlotte whined.

Jace sighed. "Well I'm not them. Tomorrow everyone gets a fresh start. But if you break the rules again you get punished."

"What are the rules again?" Tonka asked.

Jace wrote them down on a blackboard. "Scream, you go to bed early. Tattle you wash dishes, and whine and you miss dessert. If you have a good reason to do any of those things than that is okay. If someone falls in the pond or gets stomped by a horse, then scream. If someone's doing something where they could get hurt, tattle. If you're sick, whine. But you *have* to have a good reason."

The peace lasted all of one hour before the kids were at it again. Jace decided to stay firm. Sooner or later they would get it.

Meanwhile Lily spent most of her time trying to divert everyone to make them happy. By nighttime she was exhausted.

"Are we trying to undertake the impossible? Maybe it isn't our job to try to change their behavior. Bricca must have had a way around all this because I don't remember them being *this* bad.

Jace replied. "Maybe it is their way of acting out because they are mad their mom and dad are gone. Whatever it is I still think they will feel safer if they know that we are in charge."

When Jenny got to the ranch she ran over to Bricca's first to grab the box of Gwenn Anne's love letters and than hightailed it to the M Rocking B. Lily looked relieved to see her. "The kids are at school now but will be home in an hour. I'm just headed down to check Darling. Musty says she has milk and now we are in wait mode for the birth of her foal. I'll be there all evening. Jace should be home by 6:00 and can take the supper shift if you want to go home. I have no idea where Bern is. Here is my cell. Could you call him for me?" Lily was grabbing a sweater as she spoke and her muck boots and packing a cooler.

Jenny texted Bern right away and put him on FaceTime so she could see his eyes. "When are you coming home?" she asked.

"Jeremy wants me to go out to the lake with him."

Jenny heard Lily come up behind her to take the phone. "No, it's a school night. You need to come home and study."

Bern looked pissed off. "Everyone is going. I'll be the only one not there."

"Invite Jack to come home with you." Lily suggested.

"Jack and I aren't even friends anymore."

"I'm sorry Bern," Lily sighed, "But it is still a no. What are the other parents thinking? Is this another kegger?"

"They are all cool about it."

"Well than their kids don't have chores and the same responsibilities as you. Please Bern. Help out here. We've got four kids staying with us." Lily pleaded.

Bern huffed and hung up without really agreeing.

Jenny had a bad feeling about this. She'd never seen Bern be so disrespectful to their mom.

After Lily left Jenny put a chicken and some potatoes in the oven on a timer and than went to sit on the back deck anxious to read Gwenn Anne's first few letters.

The writing was small and perfect making it easy to read. Each letter was only a few paragraphs long and had a date on the top.

8/7/1873

Dear Benjamin Thomas,

The heat is suffocating now. Momma has been making us wring out wet cloths to put on the windows and we are forced to stay inside entertaining ourselves with the pianoforte. I'm still required to wear all five layers of petticoats even so and gloves if we go out. My dresses feel like they are dragging me down into a bog of heat and steam.

That's when I remember how you and I as kids would dive in the pond, leaches and all, wearing only bloomers to paddle around. And Miss Rose would always pack a whole watermelon for us to eat. It made the heat bearable. Do you remember the Little Sandy? Ray Tuttle has stocked it again with fish and pa brought home a big catfish last night.

I still can't believe that you are gone. The war doesn't feel real here. I am just waiting and wishing you'd come home.

Be safe for me and try to write if you can.

Love, Gwenn Anne

9/24/1873

Dear Benjamin Thomas

I've been hoping for a return letter from you and must face the fact that you are probably not getting these letters.

Just in case you are, though, I'll tell you the news.

We've started a Ladies Auxiliary to sew confederate uniforms. I've been there every day for a couple hours sewing and listening to the other women who have been getting a little bit of news from their relatives near the front lines.

It frightens me to think that you might be there in danger of your life. I still carry the locket that you gave me with your picture and I hope that you carry the locket that I gave you of my hair. That little spot is already growing in as we've been apart too long.

I've been taking good care of your horses. You have a new colt out of Down's Dandy. Momma says he's going to be the foundation of a whole line he's so special. We named him Heather Down for you.

I still treasure the promises that we made to each other.

I pray for you daily.

With love always,

Gwenn Anne

Jenny's eyes filled with tears. It must have been terrible sending off someone you loved to the war. Jenny wondered what it would have felt like to lose Chance. She did some fast calculations. Gwenn Anne was probably only seventeen when she wrote these letters. She and Benjamin were just kids.

That made her think of Bern and get a bit worried.

Jenny sent another text to FaceTime him and he picked up. Immediately Jenny could tell that something was wrong.

Bern looked not only stoned but also unsteady on his feet. "Jen, can you come pick me up. I'm in a little trouble."

"Sure," Jenny said immediately. "Where are you at?"

"I'm walking the railroad back from Clark's Lake."

"What? How did you get there?"

"It's a long story, but Jeremy and Billy got picked up by the police. I jumped out and hid. They didn't even see me slip away. Now I'm stuck in the middle of nowhere."

"The kids are going to be home in half an hour. I could send Reese."

"No, I don't want mom and dad to know."

"Bern, this is serious. I don't think I can cover for you on something this serious."

"Forget it, I'll find my own way home."

"No, I'm coming to get you. I'll figure out something else with the kids."

Jenny called Della. "Hey Della, I'm in a bind. Can the kids wait at the restaurant for me to pick them up? I'll be about a half hour late."

"Sure, no problem," Della said and rang off to go get them from the bus stop.

Jenny grabbed the keys to the van and loaded Tootsie in. At the last second left a note for her dad.

Went to get the kids, have Tootsie. Am picking up Bern too. There is a chicken in the oven set on a timer. See you for supper. Xo Jenny

Jenny rang Bern back. "Okay, I'm on my way. Has the railroad track crossed any roads?"

"I just got to the water tower road."

"Wait there. I'll be there in thirty minutes."

Bern looked miserable. "I'm sorry. I'm never doing this again."

Jenny just hung up and started driving as fast and carefully as she could.

When Jenny saw Bern sitting under the shade of the water tower she breathed a sigh of relief. He looked like he had just thrown up and his eyes were bleary.

"I'm sick."

"What were you drinking?"

"Some kind of cheap strawberry flavored wine. I've been puking my guts out. I'm seeing wavy lines in front of my eyes. You might need to stop the car on the way home. I think the pot must have been laced with something. I've never gotten so stoned that it made me sick."

"I can't believe this Bern. We've got to pick up the kids now and you're going to have to hold it together."

"You could drop me in town."

"Are you kidding? No way am I doing anything but taking you home. Here's a bag, use this as a barf bag if you need to."

Bern leaned against the window and held his hand over his eyes.

At Della's the kids were making a ruckus. Della handed them off gratefully.

"What a bunch of ruffians," Della said.

Jenny smiled and made them all buckle up into the two back seats of the Van. They were so engrossed in telling stories about school and teasing Tootsie that they didn't even notice that Bern looked sick. As soon as Jenny drove up to the ranch Bern slipped out and walked in the back door making it up to his room without having to greet his dad.

Jace was setting the table.

"What's this about you going to town to pick everyone up?"

Jenny decided it wasn't her place to tell.

"You can ask Bern about it later," she said.

Later never came. Bern didn't come down for supper and Jace was too busy with the kids to notice.

Before leaving Jenny slipped upstairs to see if Bern was all right. Bern was lying in a darkened room, totally miserable.

Jenny said, "Mom and Dad don't know. I think you should tell them in case the police recognized you or Jeremy or Billy tells them who the third person was in the car. Are you okay?"

Bern groaned. "If I get away with this I'm never drinking or smoking again until I'm out of high school. If coach finds out I won't be able to play football. If the police know, I'll have to go to court and drug classes for six months. I'm not a bad kid. I don't smoke and drink like most of these guys do. It will be easy for me to just stop. Please don't tell anyone. I promise you I've learned my lesson."

Jenny thought about it. "I agree, you have learned your lesson. I'll keep this quiet, but they might find out anyway and than you'll have to take your hard knocks. This could ruin you last year of high school and blow your chances for a college scholarship. I hope you are really serious about the promises that you are making me now.

Bern shook his head. "I've never been more serious. I've been a real jackass."

Jenny thumped him on the shoulder.

"I love you. You can always call me if you need to talk."

Jenny left wondering if this incident would turn out to be a blessing. Bern had a chance now to stop his downward slide before something *really* bad happened.

Jenny slipped out of the house leaving Jace to put the kids to bed. Tucking the box of letters under her arm she looked up at the half moon thinking about all of the moons that connected her to Gwenn Anne.

"We've looked at the same moon," Jenny thought. "We both loved boys we grew up with. Did you ever get drunk on your daddy's homemade whiskey? Did you get in trouble when you were a teenager and get a second chance to make it right?"

That night Darling Dilly had a colt that looked like Starfire. He had the conformation of a champion, and the intelligence and coloring of both of his sire Thunder and his grandsire Bricca Down. Spontaneously Lily decided she would keep this horse to continue her line. It would take her the next three years to train him and teach him to become the champion he had been breed be.

His birth was a portent of what was to come. Lily had been in the stable all night with Darling Dilly and had decided to get a little fresh air. It was 3:33 in the morning. The moon had set early and the sky was brilliant with stars that seem to hang from the sky. A spectacular bright meteor fell all the way across the sky at the same moment that Musty called out.

"He's here. And he is a beauty!"

Lily's started to cry when she saw him. "His name will be Starborn. Bricca Down Starborn."

Ten

❧
Chicago

Sandra Tavery checked her hair in the bathroom connected to her office. She had a full-length mirror in it as well as a closet with a couple of suits and changes of clothing. This afternoon Sandra would be meeting with Japanese investors who were interested in purchasing four factories in the manufacturing district. Their translator Quan Ho was waiting downstairs. Suddenly Sandra felt a need to change clothes. Her dark suit would be more dramatic with the crimson scarf that her husband Edward had given her. Besides, she was already wearing red shoes.

Sandra did a quick change and than looked at her self with satisfaction. Perfect.

She was just getting ready to go down to the lobby when her private line rang. It was the cowboy from Montana. Sandra checked her watch. Five minutes. Just long enough to see what he was up to.

Sandra sat at her desk to take the call, punching the button with a long, manicured red nail.

The first thing that caught her off guard was that the guy was drop-dead gorgeous and although she prided herself on not being susceptible, Sandra heart rate speed up a little.

"Sandra Tavery here," she purred. "What can I help you with?"

Dirk could see the little spark of interest in Sandra's eyes. If he knew anything, he knew women.

"It may be that I can help you," Dirk said.

Sandra fell just a little bit more. He had a wonderful deep voice and a square masculine jaw. "Just how do you mean," she asked a little breathlessly."

Dirk smiled. She was hooked. "I work for Jace and Lily Bridger-Mead. I understand Lily was married once to your brother Ned and they have a daughter, Jenny. She has been staying here at the ranch and just moved into a caretaker cottage."

Sandra tried to feign indifference. "Why do you think I'd be interested to knowing more about them?"

"I happened to see that she's gotten a grant from a foundation that you are a member of."

"What of it?" Sandra asked confused.

"I'm just wondering how you could have voted for her when she and Lily are the reason that Ned ended up dead."

"It's none of your business, but I voted against her getting the grant."

"Than I'm wondering if you might need some eyes and ears down here in Montana. I have my own grudge to settle with the Bridger-Meads and wouldn't mind helping you out."

"Are you asking for payment to spy for me?" Sandra got right to the point.

"Let's just say I'm asking for a little remuneration to help you out."

Sandra made a quick decision.

"I'll send you a check for $2,000. In exchange I'll need you to watch Jenny and report to me. I'll send you questions by email. This of course needs to be in strict confidence.

Dirk turned on the charm. "No problem. I hope that we can get an opportunity to meet personally sometime."

Sandra smiled and nervously played with her scarf. "Maybe that can be arranged. I have a meeting now. You can contact me on this private line but only if it is important. Always use a secure phone."

Dirk gave her his best smile. "I think we are going to have a very pleasurable partnership."

Sandra shivered and flushed. "I imagine that we are."

Dirk was already thinking that a little phone sex and she'd be addicted to him. He'd been right to go all the way to the top, where the power was. Already he was thinking about a way he could fly to Chicago.

Before she walked downstairs Sandra checked her calendar. Tomorrow she had an appointment with the lawyers Nedra had hired to contest Ned's will.

Sandra woke up remembering the call she had gotten late that night. She flushed with pleasure. She had gone downstairs so she didn't wake Edward. It had been Dirk telling her outrageous things about how she turned him on. He'd commented on her red scarf and gone from there to stripping off her skirt. Sandra had never had phone sex before and it had thrilled and scared her at the same time. Dirk had kept the phone call short and left her wanting more. Now she found herself checking her phone every few minutes.

The appointment at her lawyer's office was at 10:00 a.m.; she'd have to hurry to make it on time. Sandra looked over at Edward. Over the years he had lost his hair and had seemed to shrink. It felt like he was a foot shorter than her. When they went anywhere he always deferred to her. She didn't even want him to touch her anymore and last year had moved into separate beds. She was thinking about a separate room. Edward worked for her mother Nedra and Sandra wondered if sometimes he didn't spy on her for Nedra.

Sandra threw off her silk robe and put on a linen pantsuit with a white silk blouse and her pearls. Her hair went up in a chignon. Slipping into open-toed sandals she was ready. The purse looked wrong so at the last second she switched to one of her summer Gucci bags and called her driver.

There were three lawyers in the conference room. Two men and a woman all wearing dark ties and suits. They gave her some coffee and a tray of French pastries than put a file in front of her that everyone opened together.

Their news wasn't good.

Ned had signed his will twice: once before Lily and he divorced and than again when he was in custody in Montana. Both times the signing was notarized and legal. He'd left the original copy with Pincer and Pincer. There is no way to contest that the will wasn't legal. There were witnesses to the signing.

"What about the fact that he was acting irrationally at the time. That he had threatened Lily's life, almost started a wildfire, and put a contract out on Lily for her to be killed?"

"We might be able to make a case. We would need to call you and his mother to the stand. We would need to find people who worked with him who could attest to him having some kind of breakdown. We would need to get an expert witness who would describe his action as that of an irrational man. The whole thing will rest on whether or not we have the right jury and whether or not Jennifer Bridger-Mead fights us."

The lawyers continued, "There is a possibility she will just fold under pressure. You could offer her a settlement in lieu of contesting the will. Obviously you don't want her as a shareholder. You could give her the money her dad invested for her, plus the $200,000 he invested for her and take away her ownership in the family business. Chances are she doesn't want that anyway."

Sandra looked upset. She wasn't willing to give Jenny anything. "What if we proved Jenny is as crazy as her father was, that they shared the same genetic gene of mental instability. That her father would never have given the money to her had he known."

"Frankly," the lawyer said. "It would be a long shot as she isn't on trial here. However anything unsavory about the recipient of the monies can influence the jury who are deciding whether or not she should get the inheritance."

Sandra had an idea. She'd talk to Dirk. Maybe he could help her out.

As the meeting ended Sandra stood regally. "Frankly I'm a bit disappointed that you haven't been able to find some loop hole in how this will was written. I'd like you do some research into Pincer and Pincer. Everyone has skeletons in their closet. It may be that Dale Pincer shouldn't be practicing law at all. You should be ready to file a bar complaint."

The three lawyers looked at each other and grimaced. Sandra Tavery was a powerful force in Chicago. Right now they wished they hadn't taken the case.

When Sandra got back in her car she raised the window between her and the driver and called Dirk. From FaceTime she could see that he was out in a meadow with a mountain in the background. Dirk got off his horse and stood in front of it while he talked. Sandra got another look at how handsome he was wearing a cowboy hat and a jean jacket. The horse and background just added to the image.

Dirk smiled and Sandra felt her heart race again so that her voice was almost a whisper when she spoke. "I need something from you. I'll need the information on Jenny sooner than I thought. I would like to prove that she is mentally incompetent and as dangerous as her father was. I'm sure you can arrange that in some way."

Dirk thought about it. "I'll need $20,000."

Sandra gasped. "I just gave you $2,000."

"That was for information. I'll still give you that. The $20K is for sabotage. If you want her to look bad, I'll be taking some risks."

"Just don't get caught and never tell anyone we talked. This can never be tied to me."

"I'll call you tonight. What will you be wearing?"

Sandra flushed.

"Wear the silk robe you had on last night. No panties, no bra."

Sandra felt herself heat up.

"Until tonight," Dirk said and hung up.

Sandra was undone. She hadn't ever had an illicit love affair. All she had ever done is work to achieve success for her family. She was constantly under pressure to take Ned's place. Building the Tavery Empire had taken all her time and energy. She felt thrilled and nervous about having a lover. Besides now she needed Dirk. He was the only way they could win this battle.

Sandra's next stop was her mother's house. Nedra spend most of her time in the cavernous, dark parlor. Today she was dressed in grey up to her neck with her hair in a tight coronet. She looked like the bitter matriarch that she was. Sandra felt a little flush of irritation when Nedra snapped her fingers at her.

"Come here child where I can see you," Nedra commanded, "Now tell me about the meeting with the lawyers. How did it go?"

Sandra passed on the news and she could tell Nedra was getting more and more distraught.

"Mother, Lily is going to pay for Ned's death. I promise you that. I have already set something in motion that will prove that Jenny is mentally incompetent. If you hurt Jenny you've hurt Lily. A child for your child. As you always say blood for blood."

Nedra relaxed a little. "I should have known that you had the guts to see this through. I'll fund anything you need. My checkbook is in the top drawer. Take a couple of blank ones and write them when you need them."

Sandra felt a little sigh of relief. Taking $20,000 out of their joint account would have made Edward suspicious.

"And now" Nedra said, imperiously ringing a little bell.

"Let's have some tea."

CR

Sophie stretched her back and stood up for a moment looking out over her lush garden. She was getting too old for digging holes and today she ached more than normal. Sophie looked down at her long fingers and at the age spots that now seemed a normal part of her.

I'm eighty-one, she thought. That meant she had fifteen years at most left and maybe only five good ones. Recently she had started a club for women over 80, encouraging other women like her to live like they were still young. Sophie did that by talking to young people, keeping current on politics and science, using her mind as much as possible and eating healthy food. She supposed her best friend and partner, David, or as everyone else called him, Drew, Barry was the other reason every day felt fresh and new to her.

David was inside reading the manual on a tool he just purchased for his wood shop. He had been trying to make birdhouses. For now he gave them away to friends and family.

Sophie realized she was feeling more and more restless with the retired life they had been living. She had been talking everyone else into taking risks but she hadn't taken any recently. Now that Jenny was back in Montana they weren't needed in Chicago.

Sophie sauntered into the living room and then out into the garage and watched David work for a while, loving his long fingers and careful way of putting things together.

When he had put the last screw in he looked up.

"What is it?"

"I've been thinking."

"You've been thinking for weeks. I've been just waiting to hear what it is about."

"Let's go back to Europe."

"What?"

"I want to go back and write that last book that I started sixteen years ago. I want you to finish your next book of poetry. I think we should take a working vacation."

"But we don't work anymore," David shook his head.

"I know and I'm beginning to feel like that is a problem. I still have some things to say. Getting older didn't make me less observant, it made me more observant."

David straightened his back.

"You can't eat those rich foods."

"Well rent a cottage and buy stuff from a market."

"We'll be spending the last of our savings."

"That's not true. We haven't even touched your mom's inheritance to you."

"But that was for the kids."

"No, that is for us. They are all set up and doing fine."

"I guess I don't have any more excuses."

Sophie curled up against him for a hug. "The last time we went, I was the one who was resisting. Now you are. You have to admit I was a good sport about it and we ended up having a great time."

"How are we going to break it to everyone?"

"Who cares what they think. We already know everyone's reactions: Bricca will be thrilled, Lily will be concerned, Jenny will try to stop us, Sheila will help us pack, and Alexander will drive us to the airport.

David laughed and kissed Sophie while she giggled. "It's ten in the morning."

"So?" David said as he pulled her toward him. "Who cares what anyone thinks."

Eleven

❧

Home in Montana

Today Jenny was signing papers for the mortgage and title to The Feed Store. She had worn a skirt and bright coral lipstick for the occasion.

The Livingston title officer was a young woman with a big smile who seemed happy for her and patient with the fact that the loan papers were a half an inch thick. Jenny stopped listening after a while as the girl described what she was signing and why she was initializing each page. Instead she just noticed how their was a robin singing on the crabapple tree outside the window. He must have a nest there, Jenny thought.

The title officer gave her a polite handshake. "That's the last signature. The store is yours and the banks now. Let me go make a copy of this for you and you'll be ready to go. It will take about five minutes."

Jenny picked up her phone and texted Chance. "It's done."

No response. Of course, he wouldn't be looking. So she sent the same text to Lily and got an immediate response.

"Congratulations, Bunny!"

When Jenny walked out into the bright sunshine the world felt a little different. She owned something real and tangible. She had to get to work now and make her dreams come true.

To celebrate she stopped at a coffee shop that had an outdoor patio for a decaf mocha latte. It was a little shock when her waitress turned out to be Kiera Paige. Kiera still looked pale and nervous but she had a lift to her step that Jenny hadn't noticed before. It was almost pride. Kiera looked like she wanted to tell someone about her good fortune.

Jenny smiled and went out of her way to be friendly.

"Hi Kiera, it's great to see someone I know. What a cute coffee shop. You must love working here."

Kiera gave Jenny the menu and smiled shyly. "It's nice getting to know all the customers. I'm starting to like Livingston. It was hard at first leaving my friends but I've been adjusting."

Jenny felt genuinely happy for her. "I think that's great."

The next words burst out of Kiera in a little flood. "I'm not sore with you about Chance. We only dated for a couple of weeks after all. And anyway I've been dating someone else that makes me a lot happier."

Jenny smiled, encouraging her to keep going.

"His name is Dirk. He works for the M Rocking B Ranch so you probably know him."

Jenny felt a little shock that someone as young and vulnerable as Kiera was dating a jerk like Dirk. However she decided to keep her mouth shut so she didn't rain on Kiera's parade.

"I'm happy for you. Hey, I've been meaning to call you. I just moved back to Montana too and all of my friends have moved away. I was wondering if you'd like to go to a movie or something with me."

Kiera's face lit up. "That would be great. How about Friday."

"Sure," Jenny said.

"Should we make it a double date?" Kiera asked rather uncertainly.

"No, forget the guys, It's more fun to go on a date with a girlfriend."

Kiera looked relieved at not having to see Chance and awed at being referred to as a 'girlfriend.'

Jenny continued. "Let's do Chinese food beforehand."

They made the date for 6:00 and Jenny took her coffee 'to go' wondering what had possessed her. She supposed that it was protectiveness. Chance had broken Kiera's heart and Jenny felt responsible. Finding out Kiera was dating Dirk, someone who was bound to use and hurt her, made Jenny even more protective. Girls should take care of other girls.

By noon Jenny was at The Feed Store with Judd. "I have drawn a plan for a commercial kitchen in the back. We will have a long set of steel cabinets, two double sinks, a walk in refrigerator and pantry and stoves and baking ovens on one side. There needs to be a wall down the middle. In the other room will be assembly cabinets that will include overhead dispensers and cabinets for packaging with a little conveyor belt to our mail cart. I plan on having four employees working here and two in the front once we have regular orders coming in. The bathroom needs to work for both the front room customers and employees and should be handicapped accessible."

"For now I'm leaving the front room as it is to save money. Besides it has the old oak floor and cabinets and the ancient antique cash register they used at The Feed Store. I'm putting a bunch of antiques and big plants there and some shelves to show off my products. I am going to need the shelves built. Something simple and open. The only change I see is to refinish the floor, reseal the windows and change the overhead light fixtures. The porch might need some small repairs too if any of the boards or loose or anything is sagging."

"What do you think?"

Judd replied, "Have you already ordered your cabinets, sinks and appliances?"

"No, but I've picked them out. They are only a couple of weeks out."

Judd asked, "What do you plan to do about your office in the back."

"Someday I'd like to have a big window and door that opens into the back of the property. I'm going to plant grass and make the back lot a community meeting place. I thought I'd put benches by the creek, a pathway and some picnic tables. It will be like a little unofficial park area downtown."

Judd smiled. "That is mighty generous of you. You know all the kids will be hanging out there since it's close to the bus stop."

"Fine by me."

Judd asked if he could borrow her magazine to get some copies. "Have you laid any of this out to see if it will work in your spaces?"

Jenny whipped out a drawing. "Yes." Also, I'd like this wall to be replaced with drywall painted white and this wall to be replaced with corkboard that can be used for pinning up schedules. The floor is going to be grey industrial tile and we will be putting down some rubber mats so people don't slip. Can you start right away?"

"Do you have your funds now?"

"Yes I am planning on $35,000. The equipment is 10K and I'm hoping your changes won't be more than 25k."

Judd looked at it again. Installing tile, building one wall, fixing some floorboards, installing equipment and setting one large window. "We can easily do it if you wait on the window and door in your office."

Jenny thought about it. "How much more to do that too."

"Probably another 2500."

"Then lets do the whole thing. I would like to be operating in a month."

Judd thought about it. "I have a crew of three now. We could put Chance on it too and should be able to knock it out pretty fast."

"Do you mind if I drag a desk in here and start working in the office?"

"It's your prerogative."

As soon as Judd left carrying a copy of her key with him Jenny dragged a little folding table and folding chair out of her car and pulled out her notebook computer to look at her 'to do' list.

After checking item number one. She got back in the car to go get the power and phone turned on.

She was back by 1:30 and was studying her list again.

She needed to purchase a good computer, copy machine, and paper.

As Jenny made each decision and took something off her list another item got added on. She needed to decide whether there should be outlets for computer ports throughout the building, and if she should get a networked computer system or go with Ipads for everyone and one master apple desktop iMac. She decided on the Apple. She and Bricca were both most familiar with that format and

Bricca would be working for her a couple of days a week on her marketing campaign. What she needed now was at least one employee. The bulletin board at the diner was the place to advertise for employees. Jenny wrote out an ad. She would start with one employee, make samples of her treats and then find a couple of local markets for them before she began a large Internet campaign.

Next Jenny went to the car and unloaded the business license that she had proudly framed, tacking it on the wall behind her makeshift desk. Then she started a search for an accountant.

It surprised her to see that one of her friends from high school was working as the town CPA. Danny still looked like he was sixteen but he had a pile of folders on his desk and head down when she knocked on the door and came in.

"Hey Danny."

"Jenny, long time no see. What's up?"

"You know I'm starting a business here and I'm going to need an accountant."

"How big a business.

"Eight employees, S Corp"

"Do you need payroll done too?"

"To start I'm going to do the day-to-day bookkeeping and then eventually I'll hirer someone in-house. I just need someone now to file taxes, set us up as an S-Corp and give me advice."

"Then I'm your man. If you decide you want a bookkeeper I'd recommend Marge Nelson. She does the books for a couple of local business and is very professional and affordable."

Jenny hesitated for a moment more and then decided now was as good a time as any to get some advice.

"Are you completely confidential."

"Yes, I never say a word outside of here."

"My real father left me an inheritance. The will was just read because I wasn't to receive the trust until I was 21. Ned's family is very influential in Chicago and they have hired a large firm to contest the will. They are very determined, powerful and greedy. I have decided to fight them and have no idea how to go about that."

"Hmm," Danny said. "You need a good estate lawyer who won't back down under pressure and some money to pay him. You can always get someone who will agree to work for a portion of the amount he gets you. How much is the inheritance?"

Jenny gulped. "I'd rather not say right now."

Danny looked more interested. "Well if it is over a million it puts you in a different tax bracket and there will also be inheritance tax. It would be better to keep that pretty quiet. There are lots of dishonest sharks that are willing to scam you. The best estate lawyer I know is Ian Abbott. His credentials are Harvard and he comes from an influential family. He understands corporate law and he has plenty of money himself. His family has a fourth home here and he decided to settle in Paradise Valley because he loves the mountains. I don't think he can be bribed or bought off. You could do a little research on him to make sure there is no conflict of interest. You never know how far the good ole boy system stretches."

Jenny sighed in relief, glad she had confided in Danny. "Do you remember what happened to my dad?"

"Jenny, It is urban legend around here."

"So, you know he had connections to the mob. I don't know how deep that goes and what the Tavery family is willing to do to get even."

"I'd expect the worse, that way if it doesn't happen you just feel relieved and if it does happen, you're prepared."

"That's what I'm thinking. I'll call Ian and do some reading about him on the Internet. What do I owe you for your consultation?"

"Nothing. But if you decide to hire me as your CPA my going rate is $80.00 an hour."

Jenny and Danny shook hands and she left feeling much better. As soon as she got back to The Feed Store, Jenny started a search on Ian Abbott.

His background looked impressive. He had graduated from Harvard and then worked on some Civil Right's cases before focusing on Estate Planning. His two brothers were also lawyers and his mother had been a lawyer so it ran in the family. He was married with two children and served as the treasurer of the Livingston Arts Council. In his spare time he was a Boy Scout leader and advocate for Green pathways.

The family didn't seem to have any connection to Chicago.

Jenny wondered where she could get another recommendation and then thought of Cissy Harlon. She was married to Harlow Harlon the owner of the extravagant Lazy Joker Ranch on the north end of Paradise Valley. Cissy knew everyone around. She was a good friend of Lily and always said it like it was.

Jenny gave her a call and was surprised when Cissy immediately picked up the phone.

"Did you recognize my number?" Jenny asked.

"No, but I don't screen calls. If someone calls that I don't want to talk to I give them hell so they don't call back again."

Jenny laughed. "Hey, I was calling to get a confidential recommendation. Do you know anything about Ian Abbott? I mean is he a good, clean top notch lawyer?"

Cissy took her time answering. "He's represented a few friends of mine. He was professional and knowledgeable and didn't overcharge. One woman had to fight an estate battle and he built a good case for her. She lost it anyway, but maybe because it was going to go that way no matter who represented her. The other friend of mine half fell in love with him but he didn't bite. He's loyal to his wife. So I'd say that goes a long way. He's tall and good-looking and comes from a whole family of brothers who all look like Roman gods. They have huge tracks of land out east where land is like gold. All-in-all I'd say he'd be a lot of fun to have as a lawyer."

Jenny laughed. She could always count on an honest answer from Cissy who had married a wealthy Texan for his money, big cowboy belt, and love.

"Are you still designing clothing?" Jenny asked.

"Gave that up long time ago, but I recently designed the most amazing wedding dress. She used her mother's wedding dress as a lace slip underneath and then we did an exquisite low back overdress of soft doeskin leather. She was too beautiful for words. You'll have to let me design *your* dress. Word is that you and Chance are back together. Do I hear wedding bells?"

Jenny laughed. "I'd never say. It would get broadcast up and down the valley."

Cissy laughed. "You know me too well. But I do have a great idea for a dress for you. Not leather, you are too old-fashioned for that, but something loose, summery and romantic with a tiny bit of a train, and itty-bitty thin straps. It would be a simple design with little roses all the way around the bottom, one on each shoulder. Then around your waist a belt of real tiny white flowers that are in your hair too. I think you'd wear it long with some loose curls."

Jenny caught her breath. "Why Cissy, you are describing the dress that I picked out when I was twelve and pasted onto the wall of my bedroom."

"I have a gift," Cissy said smugly. "Say Hi to your mamma for me and ask her why we haven't been out dancing in too long. Oh, and have you heard from Ellie Bell. I miss her. She was the best employee I've ever had, she had a real knack for clothing design."

"Well she still does, but she's doing it as a clothing model."

"I'll be. Let me know if Ian Abbott works out for you," Cissy said.

Jenny went back and forth for a while with pros and cons and then called and left a message for Ian Abbott. It wouldn't hurt to have one consultation with him.

Jenny was back at the store going through her computer files when she got a phone call from Lily. Lily sounded upset.

"Jenny, Sophie just called me. She and grandpa have decided to leave Chicago and spend another year in Europe. Sheila's granddaughter is going to live in their house while their gone and they are leaving in two weeks. I tried to talk her out of it but you know how stubborn Sophie can be."

Jenny felt a little panicked flutter. "I'll call her now. There is no way they can do something this reckless at their age. What is something happens to one of them over there? They'd be too far away for us to get to them."

Jenny called feeling determined to stop them and met a stony wall of resistance. Sophie just said over and over. "Jenny Bunny, we will be fine. We've lived a lot of years, made a lot of decisions and taken care of ourselves for a long time. We want to do this now before we are too old. The decision is made and there is no changing our minds."

Finally Jenny tried her last card. "But I need you. Ned gave me an inheritance and the Tavery family is contesting the will. As part of the inheritance I'm 1/3 owner of their business. I'm going to have to come to Chicago and face them down. They are scary people. I need Grandpa to help me."

Sophie seemed to relent a little but held firm. She knew that if Drew were on the phone he would have given in. "If something happens grandpa can always fly back to help. What you need is a good lawyer, not Grandpa. You are stronger than you think. I know you can handle this."

Jenny stamped her foot but hung up. Well, good grief. Who saw *that* coming? She really meant what she had said to Sophie. She was scared to death about facing down the Tavery family in Chicago.

That night Dirk drove up to the gate again, his lights out, and parked out of sight behind some shrub. The moon was waxing and the night clear so it was easy to pick his way in the dark without a flashlight. He'd gotten the gate code after watching her a second time.

When he got to the guesthouse he slowed down making sure not to crack any twigs or set off a motion sensor light. It was a good thing she didn't have a dog. Working his way around the side of the building he saw that the house didn't have curtains, only blinds that were partially up. He could see right into Jenny's room.

Jenny was pulling a shirt over her head and undoing her bra and Dirk started to get a hard on. Just then Chance walked up behind her and cupped her breasts in his hands kissing her neck and pushing her into the bathroom toward the Jacuzzi tub. Dirk was panting now. He hadn't expected to get a show.

Sneaking around to the bathroom window a little twig cracked and he stood as still as possible. Unfortunately the window for the bathroom sat high on the wall and the ground was sloping down there. Dirk couldn't see anything.

Dirk sat and thought for a minute. What would a crazy, unstable woman do? Kill her boyfriend? Set fire to the Princeton's house? Run a few kids off the road with her car? Sell drugs to the kids at school? Dirk started to get excited at the possibilities.

Leaving the window he prowled around the main house and thought about the best way to frame her. Then he got an idea. He couldn't do it until he got everything ready. But by this weekend Jennifer Bridger-Mead would be sitting in a jail cell.

Twelve

❧
Bricca and Will

Bricca pulled her big brimmed hat over her eyes and picked up the colorful mimosa. There was a soft breeze blowing over the Mediterranean carrying the smell of olive flowers and orange blossoms. Her skin was being gently caressed by the thin white shift she was wearing and she had been barefoot for two days.

Will walked up behind her to give her a hug and ran his hands through her hair. "Have I told you that you look like a goddess?"

Bricca giggled. "Twice in the last hour. I think I've died and gone to heaven. I've missed you so much and now here we are: exotic birds, walking under trellises of flowers, bathing in roman baths and strolling down cobblestone streets."

Will put his hand over his eyes. "When I think about how close I was to loosing you I panic. I want it to be different when we go home."

"It will be. We'll get help with the kids. You can get a partner for your practice. We will have a regular date night and weekends like normal couples get."

Will picked up Bricca's hand and then reached in his pocket for a diamond band set in platinum and slipped it on her finger next to her silver band.

"This a symbol of my commitment. I want you to marry me again while we are here, " Will said.

"What?"

"We shouldn't have eloped the first time to Vegas. It was a non-wedding. I want to get married under an arbor of roses with the ocean only one hundred feet away. I found a Father who is willing to perform the ceremony tomorrow morning. Will you marry me?"

Bricca smiled. "Yes, I will marry you. William Beaux Bridger-Mead, Jr. I will marry you again and again and again. However many times you want."

The rest of the day was spent eating, making love and reading Italian poetry. It had been idyllic for the past week and Bricca wished it would never end.

That night as Bricca laid in bed the ocean pulled at her. She felt like she was floating in warm water, then she slipped into a dream that wasn't a dream.

A young woman who looked like Jenny was standing at the end of the bed. She was wearing a wedding dress with a high collar and long sleeves. The full skirt trailed out behind her and in her hand was a bouquet of white narcissus.

Gwenn Anne said, "I'm carrying the narcissus for Benjamin. I have his locket tucked at my waist and a tiny piece of the confederate flag hidden beneath the sole of my shoe. And next to my heart, tucked under my petticoat is a dagger just in case I decide to kill myself or kill Captain Stoddard. Can you get a message to Benjamin to let him know?"

"You mean to let him know that you are only getting married because you have to? That it is only to save the life of your servants and family, the horses and the plantation?"

Gwenn Anne looked forlorn. A single tear slid slowly down one cheek. "You understand, but I'm afraid he doesn't. I need to get him a message."

Bricca got ready to break the bad news to Gwenn Anne that she was dead. But before she could speak the apparition had disappeared and Bricca fell into a troubled sleep.

The next morning she told Will about the dream. This was the second time that Gwenn Anne had visited her. Will didn't doubt Bricca's psychic ability. He'd seen it too many times.

"Something needs to be resolved. It will all work itself out somehow. Maybe we need to figure out where Benjamin Thomas' family live and pay them a visit."

After a blissful morning spent making love and eating an exquisite breakfast, Bricca dressed in the nicest dress she had brought, a white floor-length gown with a little diamond clasp that gathered the material off one shoulder. She left her waist length hair down and Will pinned a small jasmine flower in it and put another jasmine flower in the pocket of his black tuxedo. He presented her with a bouquet of perfect white roses to carry. Father Renaldo was a tiny old man who had brought a small crowd of villagers with him to witness the ceremony. Bricca found a tourist who agreed to film the whole celebration for her. The vows were ancient, the solemnity of it perfect, and Will's kiss tender. Afterwards Father Renaldo invited them to a celebration of wine, pasta and fruit that the villagers had prepared. Someone was playing a gypsy violin. Children ran in circles and the small crowd spoke excitedly in Italian. When it was time for them to leave the crowd threw flower petals. The women gathered around Bricca and the men lifted Will on their shoulders sending them back to their Villa.

That night Bricca played back a little of the video. It was an excellent recording of the whole ceremony and celebration. The videographer had a nice eye and had gotten close-ups of things that Bricca hadn't seen in her excitement. Children kissing each other. An old woman and man holding hands. And even a shot of the sun shining down through the trellis as they had said their vows. Bricca played it back a few times. She was sure she could see Gwenn Anne floating above the Trellis offering her blessing.

The next day Bricca got a text from Lily. Sophie and Drew were moving to Europe for a year and would be overlapping with Bricca on the last week of their stay if they wanted to see them in Ireland.

Bricca was thrilled and sent an enthusiastic message to Sophie congratulating her for making such a brave decision. They made a plan to spend a day together out in the moor in the cottage that Sophie had stayed in when she wrote her last book, *An Unusual Beauty: Starfire*.

The next day Bricca sent Will out on a fishing boat for the day and got on the Internet searching for her Dad's family, the O'Briens and while she was at it Benjamin Thomas McBride's family in Ireland.

The O'Briens were easy to locate. All it took was a phone call home to her Dad and she had addresses and instructions about how to get there. The McBride's were more of a challenge. There were three areas of Ireland that the McBride Clan had come from. Benjamin Thomas was a popular name and Bricca found twenty Irishmen living in southern Ireland alone named Benjamin Thomas McBride.

Bricca's began to make phone calls asking if any of those families had settled in Georgia and had a son named McBride that was a confederate in the Civil War.

Bricca hit pay dirt on the 12th Call. The woman on the phone was ancient and gnarled. Her hands were hooked and frozen into claws; her eyes were hidden by deep wrinkles. She said her name was Minnie McBride.

"How old are you?" Bricca couldn't help asking.

"I'm not exactly sure. My parents don't remember the day I was born. But we figure I'm somewhere around 105."

"Do you remember any McBride's who moved to America and settled in Georgia? They had a son named Benjamin Thomas who served in the confederate army."

That would have been my grandmother. She had a brother named Benjamin Thomas that served.

"Do you know what happened to him?"

"Why do you ask?"

"He was the beaux or fiancé of my great, great, great grandmother Gwenn Anne Stoddard. I have love letters that she wrote him when he went off to war. Unfortunately to save the plantation and the life of her family she was forced to marry a Union Soldier. Her greatest sorrow was that she couldn't get a message to Benjamin to tell him why she was being forced to marry."

Minnie sucked her gums and shook her head. "That might be why it happened. Benjamin Thomas McBride shot himself on May 25th, 1888. I remember the date because he's buried in a cemetery here. He was apparently disillusioned in some way. The family story is that he saw his horse being ridden by a Union Officer. The Horse was a stallion out of the finest stock in Ireland named Heather

Down. It broke his heart. He had already lost his land and he didn't have anything left so he took his life."

Bricca started to vibrate. "My great, great, great grandmother owned Heather Down and carried his line forward. She was a well-known horse-breeder. I was named after his fourth generations sire Bricca Down. I own Bricca Down Starfire and my sister just got another colt from his line called Bricca Down Starborn. We own a horse-breeding farm in Montana called Bricca Down West.

Minnie McBride gasped. "That can't be a coincidence. Well it all started on a horse stolen from our family. Fortunately Heather Down's Sire, Down Dandy, had a full brother who never went to America. My Niece's grandson is still breeding horses out of his line here in Ireland."

Bricca found herself tearing up. "Remember that Gwenn Anne and Benjamin loved each other. She was forced to marry and it probably saved that horse's life. The plantations were being burned to the ground then and horses shot."

Minnie McBride suddenly sounded determined. "You need to meet the grandson. I think he still has pictures of Benjamin Thomas since he was his great, great grandfather. You see Benjamin committed suicide but he left behind a small family. He married a year after the Civil War and had two children. They lost the farm after struggling for years. His wife Mary had his body cremated and brought his ashes back home to Ireland with their two children. There is a whole clan here now that that is related to him.

When Bricca got off the phone she called Jenny and relayed everything that she had learned. Jenny called Lily to relay the story forward. It was all a bit shocking and disturbing. Something had to be done to make amends to this family. Gwenn Anne was determined.

When Will got back sunburned and happy, Bricca told the story again. Will was flabbergasted. "So what next?" He asked. "We go see Sophie's cottage on the moor, visit the O'Brien's and then make a trip to see the McBride family all in the last week that we have left?"

Bricca came him a hug. "It will be wonderful. Can you imagine getting to see Sophie in Ireland? It is like a dream come true. The O'Brien's will be easy. Lots of eating and drinking. It's the McBride's that I'm a bit worried about."

Will grinned. "I can't believe the trouble you get me into. You know who I miss?"

"Who?" Bricca asked.

"My old horse Trip. I'll never forget the night you set a record on him barrel racing. It is hard to believe he has already been gone two years."

"He should still be out in our pasture getting to spend his old age eating grass," Bricca said.

"Well, at least he died doing something he loved up in the mountains." Will said.

"I'd still don't believe Dirk couldn't save him. I distrust the guy. Jace should have fired him for taking Trip on such a grueling trail. Trip was the most sure-footed horse I know. Why would he slide off the trail and break his leg. I think Dirk got drunk and shot him for fun. I think he is a sadistic pig!"

Will looked a little shocked. "How come you never said anything like this before?"

"Well I always felt it. There is something evil about that guy and you should tell Jace to fire him. Soon."

Will took Bricca's hand but she wasn't ready to calm down. She started to sob and she couldn't stop. Bricca was crying for Trip. She was crying for Heather Down and Benjamin Thomas and Gwenn Anne. She was crying for Sophie who had lost Lizbeth after spending a winter with her on the moors of Ireland. She was crying that Sophie was old now. She was crying that she had four children and didn't want to go home.

Will just patted her back waiting for her to talk to him.

"I'm scared to go home. I'm not even looking forward to seeing our kids. I'm afraid I'll get lost again and lose you. Also there is something dark hanging over us right now. I'm not sure what it is but I feel it every day. I'm scared for our family. Especially Jenny and Chance. It feels like the day that the sniper tried to kill Lily and Jace. It is a kind of dread that is hanging over everything. And because I can't see what is causing it I can't stop it. I only know a few things. One is that I need you now more then ever. The second is that we need to be careful."

Thirteen

∾

Lily rushed back from the barn trying to remember what she had gotten for supper and whether or not she had fed Tootsie. They'd just have to eat grill cheese sandwiches tonight.

Lily had been finding herself spending more and more time at the barn. With the birth of Starborn and with Bricca gone she gotten the bug again to be with the horses and help Musty do the chores.

Jace couldn't quite understand why she was suddenly obsessed with the horses again until he met Starborn.

"He's a replica of Thunder and Starfire."

"He was born as a star was shooting across the sky. There is something about him. He's special." Lily said.

Jace gave her a hug. "Have you noticed that Bricca's kids seem to be settling down and behaving themselves?"

"Yes, they have completely stopped screaming and whining. Did you see Bern playing with them the other day? He even brought Jack home with him and they are hanging out together again. Jack is on the debate club and he has convinced Bern to join. Before Bern thought that was stupid stuff. I have to tell you I'm relieved. I was getting really worried that he was being influenced by some bad kids."

Jace gave Lily another hug. "It is like going through the eye of the needle, trying to get them through the teenage years without them hurting themselves or getting into serious trouble."

Lily pulled Jace into a chair in the living room and sat on his lap. I have something exciting to tell you. I had a long talk with Jenny. Bricca called her from Europe."

Lily proceeded to tell Jace the whole story while his eyes got bigger and bigger.

Jace summarized when she was done. "So the bottom line is Heather Down was stolen from Benjamin during the Civil War along with his childhood sweetheart. He married someone else and had two kids but was never happy and when his farm went bust he killed himself. His wife took the two kids back to Ireland where other generations of McBride's continue to thrive breeding Down Dandy's full brother. Meanwhile Gwenn Anne's ghost keeps showing up because she wants to make amends to Benjamin. Bricca is going to go visit the McBride's to figure out how to do it."

Lily cuddled down close. "That's about it. Let me say here that I'm not giving up Starborn or any of my horses to make amends. But I would be willing to let them have a foal or filly out of Starfire or even Starborn when he grows up."

Lily continued, musing, "I wonder if I saw one of the McBride's if it would be a weird kind of love at first sight since our families were star-crossed lovers."

Jace frowned. "I wouldn't put anything past this family. I still can't believe Will and I married sisters because you guys moved next door in the middle of nowhere and out of the blue."

Lily grabbed ahold of the idea. "I never asked how it was that my uncle ended up with the 240 acres I inherited here."

"Actually it is thanks to Judd and Della's family." Jace answered. "Originally your property belonged to my family. This is also true of the cabin at Spotted Horse Draw and a lot of the other land around here and in White Cloud. My great Uncle William Bridger-Mead inherited half of the ranch along with his brother, my father Beaux. William sold off parcels of his land after World War II because he came back with one leg and couldn't ranch it. Also during those years the stockmarket crashed and things had to be liquidated everywhere.

Della's mother and father, Glenna and Tom O'Reilly were original homesteaders in the valley. They had moved to White Cloud in the 1930s and started the mercantile. They bought the 240 acres that is now Bricca Down West intending to ranch on it. But they couldn't hold onto the land because of inflation in the early 80s. The property taxes were so high they decided to sell. While my father was willing to buy the land back, Tom O'Reilly said he had already found a buyer living in Virginia who had originally known Della's family before they came to Montana. That man was your uncle Henry Applewhite. We were told that he was purchasing the property with the intention of starting a horse operation but he never did anything with it. Twenty-five years later you inherited it and made a success of it."

Lily could feel herself getting excited. "This could all be fate! What if Glenna O'Reilly was a McBride? That would explain how she knew my Great Uncle Applewhite. Both families would have been neighbors in Georgia."

"That would be pretty far-fetched but it might be worth getting out the genealogy books."

Lily shuddered, "Well this thing with Gwenn Anne is spooky to me and I hate it when Jenny and Bricca both start having visions and getting premonitions. They almost always come true."

Tootsie chose that moment to bark twice and Lily and Jace both laughed. It sounded like he was agreeing.

Dirk was almost ready. He'd gotten the gasoline and made sure there were no prints on the can. Then he'd stolen a pair of Jenny's riding gloves from the barn and a sweater off the clothesline next to the ranch house. The damn dog had nipped his leg when he'd done it. If he became a problem Dirk would just kill the mutt.

Next he'd managed to get into her computer notebook on a day she was out riding with the kids and Tootsie. He snuck in web article on arson. In another file he'd written a to-do list of things she'd need to buy to do the deed. Finally he'd written a fake journal entry for her that sounded pretty crazy and fucked up. In it she'd written about how her father had left her with nothing and she hated working for rich bastards like the Princetons. She'd talked about how much fun she had starting little fires and about how much fun it would have been to see Bricca's barn burn. How she should finish what her Dad had started.

Dirk had typed it all and then just closed the file. He doubted Jenny would find it by tomorrow night.

For one last piece of incriminating evidence Dirk had put a gasoline soaked rag in the back of her truck and spilled a little gas on the floorboard.

Now all he had to do was wait for Saturday night when Jenny and Chance were home. If he could lock them in, maybe they'd end up burning too. That would probably be worth a huge bonus from

Sandra. He was planning to up the anti-soon. He deserved more money for sticking his neck out and now that Sandra was hooked on him he had lots of other things to blackmail her with. For now he'd rather she give him the money willingly. Dirk even imagined her leaving that worthless husband of hers and marrying him. Then he'd be a millionaire, just like he'd always planned.

The week had been going well for Jenny. Judd was making good progress and every day Jenny saw something else accomplished towards setting up her business. Jenny had even made a few inroads on her vision for a better town plan. She'd made a few phone calls to the town fathers and enthusiastically detailed her vision to them. They had been polite but dismissive. Jenny knew that things would change when she donated land for her part of the pathway and started a petition asking others to create a corridor next to the creek. It just took someone to start and spearhead the project.

While Jenny kept busy in the daytime, night times were difficult. Jenny had had a few panic attacks out of the blue and had insisted that Chance stay with her at the Princeton's house. She had also insisted that he answer his phone messages from her because she felt scared often and needed his reassurance. Jenny didn't like being alone at the caretaker house. Every night she had begun to feel more and more unsafe until she was ready to move and was considering quitting the caretaking job just because the house spooked her.

It started when Jenny began hearing noises at night. She wouldn't be able to sleep all night when that happened. On Friday night lying next to Chance's warm body she had though she heard a clanging sound. But after lying very still to listen she hadn't heard anything again. She had dozed off only to wake to a lucid dream. Gwenn Anne was standing in front of her wearing a long wool coat and carrying an old fashioned basket.

"Jenny," she whispered. "Wake up they are coming."

"Who are coming, the Yankees?" Jenny asked.

"The enemy. They set fires and set traps. They poison people's minds with lies. Beware they are coming."

Jenny sat up in bed.

Gwenn Anne was starting to fade out. "Are you warning me? Is someone trying to hurt me?" Jenny cried.

Her cries woke Chance who looked alarmed at the terror on Jenny's face. He'd had about enough of it.

"Tomorrow you are staying with me at my house. We'll go on a date to Livingston have a nice meal, then sleep at my house so you aren't woken up by nightmares."

Jenny had to admit, it sounded good.

Saturday night came and Dirk was prepared. All he had to do was strike the match and Jenny's life would go up in flames.

As usual he hid his car and walked up the path to the house. The moon was almost full tonight. Jenny's truck was parked in the driveway. She must be already sleeping. Then he saw a little light float through her darkened house. Was she carrying a flashlight or a candle as she walked into the bedroom? It didn't matter; it was proof she was home.

Dirk light the match along the base of the logs at the big house and then dumped gasoline so the fire would spread toward the caretaker house too. The fire exploded and he ran. He'd be long gone before they found Jenny's charred body in the house.

A couple of kids out necking on the Eagle Rock Road saw the flame and the truck speeding out along the road with his lights out. They immediately called the police and the fire brigade was at the house within 10 minutes. The grass around the house and a big tree had caught fire but the logs hadn't taken yet. Judd was on the crew and panicked thinking Chance or Jenny might be trapped. He broke the door down to the caretaker house to find the place empty. That's when the police found the gas can, the gloves and sweater and the gasoline in the back of Jenny's truck. They were on their way to question her for arson when news came that Jenny and Chance had been at dinner and a movie in Livingston.

Who could have set the fire and driven down the road? After interrogating the teenagers they were no farther ahead. It had been too dark and the headlights had been turned off. All they knew was that it was a truck.

Jenny and Chance spent the evening sitting in the sheriff's office trying to piece together what had happened.

The sheriff was pretty clear on what he thought. "We know you didn't start that fire and can't think of any reason you'd leave your gloves and sweater there if you did. Clearly someone was trying to frame you for this. The thing is, the line of gas lead toward the caretaker cabin and they had put sticks in the door so you couldn't open them. I think whoever did this was hoping you'd burn too."

Jenny shivered and asked a few questions.

"Was there any damage to the big house?"

"Not much," said the Sheriff as he leaned back in his chair with a pipe that he didn't light. "A little smoke damage to some of the logs. I don't think the Princeton's are going to be too happy with it though and rightly so."

Jenny shivered again and Chance put his arm around her.

"Do you have any enemies?"

Jenny looked the sheriff in the eyes. "Can this be confidential?"

The sheriff looked a little miffed. "Jenny you know how things are around here. Everyone in town already knows what happened because the whole fire brigade was there and they all are going to know the same thing that we know here."

Jenny looked at Chance apologetically. She hadn't even told *him* yet.

"My Father, Ned Tavery had a will which was read when I turned 21. In it I'm given 1/3 ownership of the Tavery Business assets and other monies that he put in a trust for me. The Tavery family is contesting the will."

"So they could have sent someone to either kill you or make you appear like the fire bug that your Dad was to discredit you?"

Jenny flushed not liking the way that he said that and noticed that Chance looked hurt that he hadn't known such an important thing about her life.

"Who would have access to your gloves, clothes, your truck and your house? Have you noticed anything else strange?"

"Just that I remember my computer being moved one day when I was home."

"You'd better check it while we are here."

Jenny opened up her notebook. She was uber organized so it wasn't hard to see that she had three files that weren't organized into file folders. Opening them she gasped.

"There is a to do list that lists stuff for setting the fires. A crazy journal entry basically planning it and some kind of Internet article on how to set a building on fire. All the files are dated yesterday during the middle of the day when I was out riding horses with the kids. Someone came into the ranch house to do this."

The Sheriff patted her arm and tried to calm her down.

"The more important thing is that they didn't succeed and now we know that you are being targeted. You can use this in court if you need to against the Tavery's if we can find out who did this."

Jenny had started to shake and Chance wrapped a coat around her. Nothing was helping. Her teeth began to chatter and the sheriff looked alarmed. "I think you might be going into some kind of delayed shock. I'm going to have a nurse come and give you a valium to help you relax and then I'll call your Dad and Mom and fill them in on what happened for you so you don't have to go through it again."

Jenny tried to say thank you but suddenly she couldn't breath and she thought she was blacking out. Chance helped her up and made her walk up and down the hallway until the feeling went away.

"You are coming home with me tonight."

Jenny gripped his arm gratefully. He was already leading her down the steps toward his truck.

Fourteen

Dirk couldn't believe his bad fortune. Jenny and Chance hadn't even been there and two kids had seen the flames moments after the fire started. Shit, the fire hadn't even spread that much. Now on top of everything else, everyone would be a suspect at the ranch and Jenny had already let it be known that she didn't like him.

He wasn't willing to go to jail for the Tavery family and was ready to give them their money back.

Then it struck him that he'd made another mistake. He'd just deposited the 20K in his checking account without even trying to hide it. Shit! If they checked his account he was fucked.

Sandra kept calling him and he didn't answer. He didn't quite know what to say to her yet to save face.

Besides these Chicago people were crazy fucks. Word was they had had Ned killed. Maybe it had been Sandra that had made sure the trigger was pulled.

Dirk felt a little sick. The sticks in the doors had been a bad idea. If they caught him it would be attempted murder. It might be time to just take the money and split before it all blew up in his face.

He had volunteered with Reese to go up into the high country with the cattle. Maybe things would cool down and no one would even question him. And if they started to come down on everyone at the ranch he'd hear about it from the other wranglers and just split. He could ride his horse off through the mountains and they would never find him. Then he'd just go somewhere new with a new name and start again.

Dirk checked his phone. Fuck. Six calls from Sandra and twelve from Kiera. That bitch Kiera was a stalker, that's what she was and not even good in bed. He'd only gone out with her for a way to get in a little closer to Chance.

After thinking about it for a moment he called Sandra back.

"What is going on there?" were the first words that she'd screamed at him. "The police have contacted us for questioning. It seems someone tried to burn down Jenny's house and frame her for it and completely botched it up. What did you do with the money that I sent you? They are going to be following every lead. You didn't do something stupid like just deposit in your bank account did you?"

Dirk flushed and tried to get control of the conversation again.

"First of all, nothing will lead this to you because I didn't do anything. This had nothing to do with you or me at all. Jenny must have other enemies and probably they'll get flushed out soon. Secondly, I'm happy to send the money back to you, but that is even more stupid now. I just kept the check in a sock. So I can just burn it if you prefer. Finally, I don't appreciate being blamed for someone else's stupidity and I'm not willing to be spoken to like some kind of underling."

Sandra paused. No one in her life talked back to her. Her husband was a wimp and she was the dominatrix of everyone else around her.

Immediately she felt a little flush of attraction again for Dirk.

"I'm sorry, I jumped to conclusions."

"You're damn right you did," Dirk said. "I'm on my way up to the high country with some cattle. I'll be out of touch for two weeks. Don't contact me again. I'll contact you when I'm back."

Now Sandra was feeling a little sad. "It's just that they're breathing down our neck. My mother is scary. I never know what she is going to do."

Yeah, Dirk thought, *Like put a bullet in someone*!

"Okay, just don't do it again," Dirk said and rang off.

Fuck, he needed to close the bank account or somehow come up with a good reason that he'd just gotten a check for $20K. While it was dangerous to get anyone else involved Dirk decided that what he needed was an alibi. For that he needed Kiera.

The next call was to her. "Hey babe why did you stand me up last night?"

"What do you mean?" her voice was shaky.

"I thought we agreed to meet at the dam to do a little night fishing. I waited there from 9 to 11 for you."

"Oh, Dirk, I'm so sorry."

"Now things are sticky cause someone tried to set fire to Jenny's place. I was there waiting the whole time for you but no one saw me there."

Kiera hesitated for just a second. "I'll tell them I was there with you the whole time. I'm so sorry."

"Okay, well if someone calls, you tell them that. I wanted to tell you about a special surprise that I have for you."

Kiera held her breath, Was he going to propose to her?

"I borrowed $20,000 from my kid brother so that we can buy a house together."

Kiera gasped. "Oh, Dirk, how wonderful."

"I'm going to write you a check for the $20K and then I want you to just go look for something and buy it. I have to go up to the high country for two weeks and we can move in when I get back."

Kiera seemed beside herself.

Next Dirk called his brother, Vic.

"Hey Bro, I need a huge favor and I'll owe you. In fact I'll give you $2,000 for doing this favor for me."

"Sure, man, what is it."

"If the police call just tell them that you loaned me $20,000 so I could buy a house to move into with my girlfriend. If they ask you how you got it just say you don't believe in banks and you've been saving under your bed for a while. Tell them I promised to pay you interest so it seemed like a good investment."

Vic coughed nervously. "Is this going to get me in a lot of trouble?"

"None at all, it is just an easy way to make $2,000.

"Okay sure, no problem."

Dirk sighed with relief. First he drove to Livingston and wrote Kiera a check feeling a little disgusted with how she clung to him. Next he drove up to the dam and threw out a few empty coke cans, his brand of cigarettes and put a piece of a phone bill with his name on it in the fire pit, smearing it with ashes. Then he left some stinky bait sitting on a rock. Next he put the 2,000 in an envelope and mailed it to his brother. Finally he took a couple of saddles down in the shed and started cleaning them then left the mess unfinished. If he needed, that would have to be his alibi for the afternoon he wrote in Jenny's computer. Packing his bags he headed up to the high country taking one of the sturdier horses that he knew could make it through the mountains if he had to run.

Fifteen

Ireland

Bricca and Will headed out over the moors in a little rental car. The wind was blowing and it carried the smell of thyme and salty sea air. They passed an old castle and a few sheep walking down the road with a boy and his dog but nothing else for miles. Bricca took a deep breath and felt the pureness of the countryside that stretched deep green around her, big and empty. She couldn't wait to see Sophie. There was something about Sophie that was as big as this countryside. She was a woman who could be alone with herself. Sophie was quiet and calm without over absorbing others. Bricca guessed that she could best describe her as a professional observer, or maybe a sage.

Will rolled down the window enjoying the open view too. After years of being pinned to an office and a schedule he had missed the light of the mountains and the fierce life force of nature. Here everything felt raw and illuminated, full of untamed energy. Following Bricca's GPS they drove through a quaint but isolated town, turn right at a four way stop in the middle of nowhere and wound down an even narrower road to a little cottage.

It was summer so the cottage was surrounded with flowers that also spilled out of two window boxes. Another small rental car was parked in front on the gravel driveway. Bricca hauled out her bag looking at the peat roof with a little bit of awe.

Suddenly Bricca was swung around and enfolded in Drew's warm hug, Sophie was close behind giving Will a warm hug too. They had already lit a little fire in the stove and pulled out a teapot, picking up groceries on their way of eggs, milk, cheese and bread. Bricca and Will had brought wine, salami, dried fish and olives. Both women had thought of chocolate. Sophie giggled at the feast.

"All we need is our red shoes," she said and Bricca laughed to.

"How about this instead," Bricca fished a package out of car. It was a gift for Sophie, Murano glass from Italy shaped in a perfect small deep crimson red high heel. It was a private joke between her and Sophie that also was tied to heartbreak. Lizbeth's last words to Sophie had been, "When you see a pair of red shoes, think of me."

Will and David were already engaged in conversation and Bricca checked out the sleeping quarters. Thick down quilts covered the beds. It was very charming. Bricca had always wanted to come to Ireland and she was finally fulfilling a lifelong dream.

A little gale shook the shingles outside and the rafters rattled. Bricca heard the sound of sheep bells and looked out the window. The afternoon sun was just breaking through the clouds.

"Are you up for a brisk walk?" Bricca said.

Sophie grabbed her favorite gray sweater and wrapped a scarf over her hair. Bricca just slipped on a muck coat that was hanging on a rack by the door. The ground felt marshy and soft, but the breeze still cool. It was perfect.

Sophie broached the subject first just to get it out of the way. "We heard about what happened to Jenny."

Bricca looked alarmed. "What happened? We've had a dead phone for two days. Our charger isn't working."

Sophie filled Bricca in and Bricca shuddered. "I have been feeling this coming. I told Will two days ago I had a premonition of something dark. Thank god they weren't hurt. I hope they come down hard on the Tavery family for this."

"Apparently they can't find a link to them and all the people they have questioned have had alibis."

"Even Dirk."

"Even Dirk."

"The main thing is that Jenny just has to stay strong and not let this intimidate her." Sophie pulled her scarf off and let her hair go out of the tight rubber band. It flew out like a flag behind her and she and Bricca laughed.

"I can see why you loved this cottage. It's charming and so isolated."

"Believe me it was completely different in the winter, freezing."

Bricca twirled around and began to run.

"I haven't gotten to stretch my legs all day. I'll just run down to the ocean and back up."

Sophie waved her off and stopped to pick a wildflower to put in her hair. That's how the men saw her when they walked up. For a moment Will saw her as a young woman. She would have been beautiful. Clearly Drew still saw her that way because he walked up and immediately put his arms around her. Will trotted off looking for Bricca. She was running back and forth on the beach, dancing so her feet wouldn't get wet with the waves. Will watched her for a moment and without knowing it could happen again fell completely in love with her in a way that was deeper than young love. This was like loving a peach when it is perfectly ripe. Or like opening a pomegranate for the first time. Will felt like his heart had suddenly gotten thicker and heavier and that there were tears just behind his eyes. He wanted to hold onto the feeling forever.

Sophie and Drew came up behind him and Sophie hooked her arm around both men's elbows.

"She's beautiful isn't she. Bricca has always been special. There was only one other person that I've ever known who had her vivaciousness. Her mom. When I see Bricca I get to see Lizbeth again and I'm so grateful."

That night over crusty bread with salami and olives, Will and Bricca told the story of Gwenn Anne and Benjamin Thomas.

Sophie looked at Bricca. "I hope you are planning to write this?"

"Yes, that's the idea. We are leaving tomorrow to go see the O'Brien's for two days and then we are spending two days with the McBride's. I'll certainly be able to write about this first hand."

Sophie smiled. "You should just loosen up and write the way that you talk. I loved how you wrote for the Atlanta Sun. It was funny, smart and you naturally knew how to tie up an idea and keep the reader interested. There are lots of historical romances out there. The difference about this is that this is a true story and includes everything you love...the south, horses, Ireland, and a brave and loyal woman."

Bricca nodded. "That is if I don't get caught up only in the grief behind the story. It all seems like such a shame. They didn't get the love they deserved. He committed suicide, and she is still roaming the spirit world looking for redemption from her terrible guilt and loss."

Sophie interrupted. "Look at the bright side. You are here because of her. The horses you raised are here because of her. Your children and Lily and everyone you love owe their existence to her because she was brave and did a hard thing. She was like your mother. She sacrificed what she wanted so that her family, the servants and the horses could live. It seems to be a reoccurring theme in your family. Lizbeth, Gwenn Anne, Lily and now Jenny. There is an enemy who attacks and then the need to triumph over the attack, even turning it into good fortune and finally triumph. Whatever this is about, you get to heal it, to go to the root cause of all of this karma once and for all and make amends for Gwenn Anne. Okay enough of my telling you what to do. Pour me another glass of wine."

The next morning they shared a large meal in the breakfast nook waiting for the sun to warm everything up. Bricca and Sophie seemed to be soaking each other up. Bricca only knew that she had longed to be here with Sophie with an odd intensity. She felt a kind of frail but numinous joy and could automatically read Sophie's mind. The men seemed to be enjoying their company with each other too. Sophie reached out and stroked the flame of Bricca's hair taming its wildness just a little.

"I can see that you needed this. The last time I saw you you looked faded. Tired, like a caged animal needing freedom. Now you look transparently beautiful and natural. Like you're back in your clement again."

Bricca nodded. "You are describing it perfectly. I'm afraid of losing this when I'm back taking care of four kids."

"But you love being a mom too?"

"Yes, I do."

"So what didn't you love?"

"Not having Will. Doing it all alone."

"It looks like you've fixed that problem.

Bricca watched the peat crack and sizzle in the fireplace.

"Yes I think we have. I think we have."

Sophie was quiet again, remembering Lizbeth. How she had made her feel complete inside. How Sophie had needed Lizbeth so she could cook her soup, sit with her, laugh, write her books.

"I know that feeling that you are speaking of. There is a kind of closeness that nothing can separate. That even change can't destroy. It is a miracle when you get to experience that with someone."

Bricca grinned. "You had that with Lizbeth, your mom, and now with Drew. You've been lucky. I've had it with Will, my kids, my dad, Lily, Jenny, you and Starfire. I've been *super* lucky."

Sophie's eyes teared up. "I had that with my surrogate mom Betty too. She once wrote this for our women's writing group."

The wind has come up and blown me away.
I can feel it ripping through every thing I thought solid.
As if all those solid things were made up of wind, anyway.
But when it came to rip me from you
There was no place for it to go
We were both solidly the wind together.

Bricca laughed with joy. "That's amazing!" Then Bricca got serious. "I'm worried about Jenny. Nedra Tavery is a dangerous woman. Someone close to Jenny just tried to kill her and could have succeeded. I need to go home."

Sophie nodded. "Yes you do."

Late that afternoon Will and Bricca gathered their things and loaded their tiny car. Sophie and Drew were standing close together by the door. Bricca watched them and waved until she couldn't see them anymore. The farther they got away the more she saw that Sophie and Drew were one person instead of two.

Bricca wasn't sad anymore. Sophie was having a great time and riding the wake of change instead of resisting it. To do that she had come back to the place where she had written a book about the wind and now Sophie and Drew were "solidly the wind, together."

Bricca turned around in her seat and consulted the map. We are only two hours away from the O'Brien's. We'll be there in time for supper.

Sixteen

Jenny made herself open her notebook and work again on a "to do" list while Judd's crew banged away in the other room. Every once a while Chance would stick his head in the door to check on her.

"How's it going?"

"Slow, I need my computer."

"Sheriff Russell said you'd get it back today. You could walk over to his office."

Jenny sighed. "I wonder if it will be okay then to delete those three bogus files."

"Probably, I bet they just downloaded your whole hard drive."

"Even that feels like a violation of privacy. All of my emails to friends when I was in school are in there, even some racy things to my boyfriend. I feel like my recipes, business plan and finances are being perused by the whole of White Cloud.

"Boyfriend?"

"Don't worry, it was an overnight wonder."

Chance squeezed Jenny's arm. "I trust Sheriff Russell. He's not going to let anyone read the files on your computer. Plus all of this is to help them catch the guy. They needed to dust it for fingerprints and save the letters as evidence."

Jenny sighed again. "This is such a nightmare. Maybe I should write the Tavery family and say I don't want the inheritance.

Then it will all be over. How can I even interact with them after being violated like this? I'm sure they hired someone to do this that botched it up. My strongest suspect would be Dirk. I don't trust him."

"Didn't you go to a movie with Kiera, Friday?"

"Yeah and she is head over heels with Dirk. I feel like I should warn her."

"But Kiera says Dirk and she were at the dam together Saturday night. I know Kiera. She isn't the kind of person to lie. You may not like Dirk, but he didn't do it."

Jenny set her jaw. "I would like to question Kiera myself but she hasn't answered my phone calls for the past two days. I'm thinking about driving to Livingston to make sure she is at work and not laying somewhere bludgeoned by Dirk."

Chance shook his head. "Now you're getting dramatic."

Jenny stood up and paced nervously back and forth. "They could start *this* building on fire. The Princeton's have kicked me out as a caretaker and I have to move my furniture by next weekend and I'm still being watched by somebody! That is NOT me being dramatic!"

Chance put his arms around Jenny and his chin on top her head. "We will get through this, honey. You are surrounded now by a battalion of soldiers protecting you. All of White Cloud is on duty. You aren't ever alone, now."

Jenny let one tiny tear leak out then straightened her shoulders.

"I'm going to drive to Livingston and see Ian Abbott the estate lawyer. We already had an appointment before this happened and I'm not going to break it. Then I am stopping by the coffee shop to talk to Kiera. I'll call mom to see if she can come with me. If not, I'm just going to drive by myself in my truck."

Chance stood up a little straighter. "I'll take you."

"You need to work."

"We have a big crew here. They won't even miss me."

"Okay," Jenny said. "We need to leave in an hour."

While Chance went to finish the sheetrock he was hanging, Jenny put in a call to Sheriff Russell. He answered the phone himself and got right to the point with her. "You must be wanting your computer. I'll bring it over for you in the morning. Forensics is almost done. In case you are worried we haven't looked at anything but those three letters. If you think there is anything else on there you should okay us to do a search."

"No," Jenny said. "I prefer some privacy. If I find anything I'll let you know."

The sheriff continued. "We haven't been able to pick up prints off of anything. Whoever did this wasn't a professional arsonist. He didn't even know how to start the fire. All of the wranglers at the ranch had an alibi so we have to figure out how someone got down to the M Rocking B and into the ranch house without being seen. We've found a place near Princeton's house where someone had been parking every night and picked up some tire tracks. Unfortunately while they are truck tracks, the tires are generic tires commonly used around here and the ground was pretty dry so it didn't leave deep prints. I wish I had more to tell you."

"What about Dirk, did you check out his alibi?"

"Well I ought to fine him for littering. He'd left a bait can, cigarette butts and empty coke cans on the dike. We knew they were his because of an envelope from his phone bill that was used to start a little fire. Besides he was with Kiera Paige there. His alibi is airtight."

Jenny sighed again. "Thank you for all your hard work."

Sheriff Russell cleared his throat. "Jenny, we are going to find this snake. We are pursuing the Tavery family and have a warrant to look through their phone records and bank account. If they paid someone to do this, we'll find out. They are the only ones with motive and the PD in Chicago has been helpful. They would love to catch them on something that would stick. They've long suspected Sandra of giving kickbacks to politicians and fraudulent practices with her shareholders. It is just a matter of time before they get caught with their hand in the cookie jar. In the meantime I want you to stay with your family or someone you trust all the time."

Jenny felt a little better when Chance and she were on the road with the window rolled down and a cool breeze blowing through the truck. Every once in a while she looked behind her to make sure no one was following. If they were, they were experts because the road looked empty.

Ian Abbott's office was unassuming but still professional. His one concession to formality was a huge rosewood desk. The top of it was clear except for a picture of his family. There was an oil painting of Snow Mountain on one wall and of Mammoth Hot Springs on another wall. The chair in front of his desk was comfortable and Ian moved to the other desk chair so that there was only a small table between them.

Ian's huge body took up a lot of space. He looked like a pro football player, probably 6'5" and everything about him seemed oversized. His hands were huge but his voice well modulated, and polite. When he started to speak Jenny was impressed by his complex thinking and obvious intelligence.

"So Jenny or do you prefer Jennifer, what can I help you with?"

Jenny started from the beginning giving Ian a brief synopsis of what had happened with her father and then his will. By the time she had gotten to the part about Saturday night's attempted murder Ian was sitting up straight and being very attentive.

"What is the name of the corporation that the Tavery Family owns?"

Jenny shook her head. "I don't actually know."

Ian took a moment to think. "We need to find out more about this corporation. Is it in the red or black? Who are the officers and board members and what do they produce? How many shares would 33% ownership be and what is their current value if you sell them? Also we need to do some research on this family and see if they actually have connections with the Chicago mob. Was it Ned who made those connections or the whole family? Can you give me any names?

Jenny was surprised she knew so little. She only knew Nedra, Sandra and Edward's names. "Here is the copy of the will that Pincer and Pincer sent me."

Ian read through it and jotted down another note to himself.

"I recognize the name Nedra Tavery. She is my own father's age and used to attend some of the same fundraisers. She was married to a man named Joseph Tavery who was rumored to be a crook. Joseph was prosecuted for tax evasion but beat the rap and was never sent to prison. He had a stroke when he was in his sixties and Nedra took over the business. I remember meeting them both once. My father didn't have any business dealings with them at all. Will this be a conflict of interest for you?" Ian asked.

"No, more of a confirmation you are the person that needs to be researching this for me," Jenny said, and then continued. "Before we go any farther I need to talk about payment. I don't have the money now to pay you. However, as you can see, I have the possibility of a large inheritance. I'm wondering if you would be willing to work for a percentage of the monies you are able to win up to an agreed upon maximum. Let me warn you they are contesting the will so that might be nothing if we lose the case."

Ian smiled. "They already played their hand and did it poorly. If it was the Tavery family who arranged for the fire to be started they not only didn't cover their tracks they pointed blame toward themselves. This could go a long way with a jury even it is never proven that the Tavery family did it. They won't get another chance to try to discredit you. Right now they are probably scared that they are going to get caught for the first blunder. The only other strategy they would have is to try to discredit the firm that wrote your father's will or discredit your father as being insane and incompetent when he signed the will. My guess is that this is how they will build their case. We will need to build a different case."

Jenny saw for a moment how painful this was going to be. Everything about her Dad and her relationship would be questioned and exposed. Lily would be dragged through the mud too.

"What do you think I should do?"

Ian didn't hesitate. "Fight. This is your money by law willed to you by your father who wanted you to have it. I am impressed by the last sentence that he wrote over his signature. He wanted you to take this money and free him from some bad decisions he had made in his life. The stock in a corporation this big could be worth multi-millions. You can do a lot of good deeds with millions of dollars."

"I'd say the Tavery family has played their hand rather stupidly. It would be suicide for them to try something with you again. That doesn't mean you may not still be in danger. Right now

I'd think the person that started the fires is in more danger with them than you."

Jenny felt stronger and more confident when she left Ian's office. She had retained his services with a $1,000 check and a contract to pay him a percentage of his winnings up to a maximum of $300,000. They would meet again next week after Ian had done some research and decide what documents he wanted subpoenaed from the Tavery family and their corporation.

Jenny filled Chance in as they drove to the coffee shop. "Maybe I should stay in the car for this meeting, too." Chance said.

Chance parked the truck around a corner and Jenny walked to the coffee shop. Kiera was working and Jenny could tell she was flustered to see her.

"Hi," Jenny said. "I've been trying to reach you. I've had a miserable few days."

"Oh," Kiera said. "I'm sorry I can't talk now, we're pretty busy."

Jenny let her face drop. "I could use a friend right now."

Kiera looked even more flustered then took off her apron and dropped to the seat next to her.

"Dirk, filled me in on what happened. You must have been scared to death." Kiera said.

Jenny asked casually. "Where is Dirk now?"

"You should ask Jace, he's some where up in the high mountain camp for a couple of weeks. He's going to be so excited to see what I found for us when he gets back."

"Found, what do you mean?"

"Dirk borrowed $20K from his brother so that we can buy a house to live in together. He's already given me the money and just trusted me to find a place. I found the cutest little two-bedroom house that has a little front and back yard. It is right near the river, too in a quiet neighborhood, 215 Hickory Drive. The people were in a hurry to sell cheap so I gave them the money as a down payment and they will take a contract for the balance. My dad is going to sign it with me so Dirk won't even have to worry about that part."

Jenny had started to shake a little inside. "Where does Dirk's brother live?"

"I don't know. They must be close for him to do something so nice for Dirk."

Jenny decided now was a time to go for broke.

"Kiera, I need to know something important. A lot rests on this including your own safety. Were you really at the dam Saturday night with Dirk? It is critically important that you tell me the truth."

Kiera flushed bright red and her bottom lip started to tremble. "Yes, Yes I was. Jenny, I love Dirk. You already took away my other boyfriend, you can't take away Dirk too."

Jenny reached out to touch Kiera's hand. "I'm saying this because I'm your friend. I have no desire to be with Dirk. But, if you are lying about this, Dirk could be the one that started the fire. That means he probably got that $20,000 from someone other than his brother. This also implicates you. You are in danger. Someone that would do that isn't someone you want to be with. He is using you. What if he tried to hurt your family, your sister or your Dad? He could have killed me."

Kiera set her jaw stubbornly. "I'm sure you'll find he got the money from his brother just like he said. You are being mean and unfair to a wonderful person. Just because you're family has money doesn't mean they should put down their employees."

Jenny could see she wasn't going to get anywhere today.

"Okay Kiera," Jenny said, "But promise me you'll call me if anything happens. I can come get you. Besides we might want to go to another movie together sometime. Still friends?"

Kiera didn't respond. She was still angry. "I need to get back to work."

Jenny was shaking when she got back in the truck to tell Chance. "It was Dirk, I know it. He gave Kiera $20,000 that he said was from his brother to buy a house. There is no way Dirk wants to buy a house with Kiera. Also she turned bright red and almost broke down when I questioned her. She is lying. We need to tell Sheriff Russell about the brother and the money. Maybe he can come down hard enough on the brother that he breaks."

Jenny couldn't drive fast enough on her way back to White Cloud. Sheriff Russell seemed impressed with her little bit of sleuthing. "I'll check it out. But you stay away from Kiera now. She is bound to tell Dirk about you questioning her and he has a lot to lose if he *is* guilty. This is our job, not yours."

Dirk had started to relax. The heat during the days and being on his horse all day didn't allow him to worry much. This was his favorite job on the ranch. He could relax this high up on the mountain. He'd drink enough to get drowsy out of his flask then sleep like the dead until the birds woke him singing in the dark of dawn.

The one thing he'd done right with his life was to be a cowboy. He wasn't proud of some things: slipping date drugs to girls, killing that damn horse, Trip, for bucking him off, stealing from his mother's stash: but he was proud that he was a damn good cowboy. He could ride like a pro, knew everything about cattle, and had good sense in the mountains. He'd seen some beautiful sunsets and ridden though fields of wildflowers. He'd eaten tasty meals around the fire. The more he thought about it the more he realized leaving might be the best thing. There was always room on another ranch for a good cowboy.

Dirk went out in the dark to find a tree, relieving himself before he crawled into his bag as was his habit. All he heard was a snap of twig and a little rush of adrenaline before the world went black.

It wasn't until morning that the guys realized Dirk hadn't made it to his sleeping bag. It was Reese who found him at the bottom of a steep drop of rocks. He was hanging dead over the shrubs, his neck broken by the fall. Reese radioed down the sad news then started to organize the men to recover his body.

Jace told him to wait and not touch anything. The next voice on the radio was Sheriff Russell. "Nobody was to touch anything or go near the body. They would need to make a wide perimeter around the scene including the camp. The Sheriff would appreciate everyone finding a place to sit down while he got a helicopter to send some men up.

Jenny got the call by 8:00 from Lily. An hour later she got a call from Kiera. "It's your fault," Kiera cried hysterically. "You got him killed." There was no consoling her and no talking to her so

Jenny just went back to waiting for news. Jace had ridden up on the helicopter with the Sheriff and his men. Jenny wanted to go with him but had been given a firm "no". This wasn't anything for her to do but wait in White Cloud for news.

When the helicopter landed Reese ran up to shake Jace's hand and then filled him and the Sheriff in. The men were all down the draw a bit waiting in the shade. Nobody had had breakfast yet and everything had been left undisturbed in camp. Dirk was right where they had found him.

The Sheriff took a quick look and radioed for a coroner sending the helicopter back down to town while they unloaded crime scene tape and worked to secure the area.

The Sheriff had brought along White Feather aka Bennie Bud an expert tracker from the Shoshone tribe. Bennie was often used by the police to find people in search and rescue missions. This was the first time that he'd been called to help with a death. White Feather examined the tracks and came up with a theory within 15 minutes bringing everyone over to see what he had found.

"See here. This is Dirk's bag. You can see that he must have drunk from his flask and then walked over to this bush to pee. Smells of urine. There is a faint print in the mud behind him and then a little drag mark. My guess, murdered. The killer broke his neck and then slung him over his shoulder and carried him. See here, the little swirl in the dirt and now the prints are much deeper even though the ground isn't wetter. From a hiking boot with a deep tread, probably new."

"The deeper prints and a few snapped twigs and turned over rocks lead directly to the cliff edge. When he dropped him off his shoulder you see another heel and drag mark. Dirk was heavy so it was probably a guy not a girl who did this. Had to lift 170 pounds. The prints are around a size 9 so not a big guy, probably stocky though. Also it probably wasn't a cowboy cause the boots were some name brand like Merrill by the print. I'd say new 'cause he's leaning off his big toe in almost every step. Probably a blister breakin' in the new boots. After he tossed Dirk over the cliff he headed north. I think if we backtrack on the trail from camp we'll see that he came in from the north too. I say we follow the trail as far as it takes us. It would be easier if we had a dog for this."

Jace and Sheriff Russell were impressed. Jace said what they were all thinking. "How in the hell would some stranger find the guys up here?"

Another younger Deputy named Frank Grover had the answer. "That's easy. You have a satellite phone for the guys up here. Right? They send out a signal that any small plane can pick up. That is how they are used for rescues. Perp flew over and found the coordinates, and then he hiked in from the north. The nearest road due north is only five miles as the crow flies" Frank picked up his phone and looked at a Google map. "Big C Creek road. We should question people there and see where the nearest small airport is."

Russell slapped the younger man on the back and put him in charge of that while they went back to question the cowboys and radio to see if a search dog could come in with the coroner. The helicopter could then fly Frank out to Big C Creek Road.

The cowboys were grumpy, hungry and feeling spooked. Since they had been the only people they knew of on the mountain they were also worried they would somehow be blamed. When they heard about the boot prints they were skeptical not really believing anyone could just sneak up on camp without someone hearing them.

"Are you sure some he weren't running from some grizzly late at night when he went out to take a piss or somethin'."

"Pretty sure," said the Sheriff." "Now show me what boots you each brought with you. Down to one they all had cowboy boots. The last guy had brought some tennis shoes too.

Russell addressed them after the search. "The camp is still off limits but I'll have someone bring you guys food and some water."

"What about our horses? They need fed and we ought to go check the cattle. Maybe this crazy guy killed some of them too."

Sheriff Russell looked at their worried faces. "I'll go get Jace and he can come tell you what to do. Maybe we'll have him and Reese ride out and check everything. Be patient. It'll only be four or five hours at the most."

By the time the search dog was there Jace had checked the cattle and was ready to ride behind the dog and Bennie. The coroner after an examination announced that Dirk had a broken neck and some bruising around his neck that could be thumbprints.

They were getting ready to move the body and put it in a body bag. Photographs had been take of all the evidence.

A radio call came in from Deputy Frank Grover at Big C Creek Road. "A local rancher here says that there was an unmarked black sedan parked on his road when he drove home last night and that it was gone when he went back out early in the morning. He didn't see anyone in the car and he slowed down to look in because he didn't like the look of the car. The nearest airport is a strip only twenty miles away. They had a small private plane ask to land there two days before. The plane was registered to someone named Dudley Dirkham. You can probably bet this is a play on something about Dirk. The single pilot had a driver's license with that name on it. The license looked legit. The guy was stocky, Hispanic, and had a crew cut with hair grease on it. Had a tattoo of a dagger on his neck. He was wearing a maroon jacket, new hiking boots and dark glasses. This morning without filing a flight plan he jumped the locked fence and flew the plane out. We've found the black sedan abandoned near the airport. The sedan looks stripped. No vin, fake plates, no registration. I'm betting no prints, but we are having it dusted now.

Sheriff Russell shook his head with frustration and went back to the group of cowboys. "You're all free to go. Jace will tell you what he wants you to do."

In Chicago a private cell phone rang. The voice said only two words then hung up. "It's done."

With a little smile the recipient of the call wiped crumbs off the table and poured another cup of tea. *Now, what to do about the girl.*

Seventeen

Ireland

Bricca sat surrounded by children who each wanted to touch her or play with her hair. The meal of thick vegetable soup and crusty bread had been eaten around a heavy wood table on a stone floor. The women were still in the kitchen putting things away and visiting. Bricca realized she couldn't make out a word of their thick Irish brogue.

Will had been pulled outside with the men to have a shot of whiskey and a smoke and the older women sat in the living room knitting. Across the thick beam of the mantle were at least 20 framed pictures of family outings, fishing trips, a favorite horse, or school graduations. Above the mantle was a large ornate cross and a Madonna.

Bricca was worn out. She only wanted to sleep somewhere where she could hear the slap of the ocean and the killdeer on the moor. The oldest of the O'Brien's sat by the fire knitting. She whispered to one of the kids and crooked a finger toward Bricca and someone was leading Bricca up to a big straw bed with a down cover.

A rosy-cheeked woman turned the bed back. "Here's a warm brick from the fire. Twill take the nip out. Tis never quite warm here, even in the summer time. You'll to be sleepin' in on the morrow. We've no hurry ta eat til the sun be over the hill."

Bricca was so tired she started thinking she might be in some kind of dream. The stone walls and old wood beams made it seem that she was caught somewhere back in time. Feeling safe she drifted down into oblivion.

Suddenly Gwenn Anne was standing at the foot of the bed.

This time she was dressed as if for mourning in black with an armband. "They're almost home. Only a few more days and they'll be home."

Bricca tried to talk to the apparition. "We are going to go see the McBride's and find Benjamin Thomas McBride's kin and make it up to them. We are going to make amends for you."

Gwenn Anne looked sad. "I wrote to him, but he never got my letters. They came back unopened. He didn't know. Give him my letter."

The next morning Bricca made an effort to get a signal and call home. Jenny answered filling Bricca in on Dirk's death.

"How frightening. Can they trace something like this back to Nedra and Sandra?"

"Follow the money. They have to prove they paid for Dirk to set the fire and then paid someone to kill him when he screwed-up."

"Oh, my God. These people are vipers. I have been so afraid for you. I'll be glad to get home. I don't like being this far away when bad stuff is happening."

"

"You are going forward with your lawyer, like you should. They might continue to retaliate. We'll be home in four days. Be very careful and watch my kids too to make sure they're safe."

"I will Bricca."

Bricca seemed to take a deep breath to shake everything off and Jenny tried to lighten the conversation.

"Tell me about your trip," Jenny asked.

Bricca did and then described the dream she had had last night. "There is some letter they she wants me to give them. I wish now that I had brought them with me."

Jenny pulled out the box.

"What day did the Civil War end? You said she was wearing black with an armband. That might have been for the day the Confederate army surrendered."

Jenny opened a few more letters and put them according to date.

"Here it is. This must be this letter. Listen to this."

June 2, 1885

My Darling Benjamin Thomas,

At last we can be together. The war is finally over and I know that you will be coming home soon. I write this letter in fear for my life. I have been forced to marry Officer Stoddard. When the Yankees invaded only those of us who opened our homes saved them. I was responsible for my servants and ailing mother and father. We heard reports that they were burning and shooting their way through the valley. All of the horses were shot and refugees filled the roads pulling their possessions in carts.

I made a plan with our women's auxiliary. We met the soldiers on the road bringing them refreshments and invitations to stay in our homes to rest. Captain Stoddard picked my home. Thank goodness I still had the youth and beauty to be chosen. Other women didn't fair as well.

I had no choice. Without this sacrifice everything would have been lost.

But now that I know you are free, we can make plans.

I am still married to you in my heart. We will steal away and take our horses and family with us in the night. Perhaps we can sell my jewels and go west. I have always wanted to see the Mississippi.

I haven't received any word from you since I started writing. Please, please let me know that you have received this letter. For I am always yours in my heart and soul,

Gwenn Anne

Bricca voice rose with excitement. "Can you take a picture of that and text me the picture?"

"Sure," Jenny.

"This is what I needed. I need to read this letter to the McBride family."

Jenny started to get excited too. "Would you take pictures of everything for me or have Will videotape them and their horses. I also want to see where your staying and I hope you took photos of Sophie's cottage.

"Yes to that all, and even better I have videotape of Will and I renewing our vows in a catholic marriage ceremony in Italy."

Jenny whooped with joy. "Way to go, that's wonderful. Did you tell mom?"

"Lily doesn't know yet. We'll show the tape to ya'll when we get back."

Bricca's voice turned serious, "Stay vigilant. I feel a release of pressure, like the danger has passed but like another storm is coming."

Jenny didn't pull any punches. "Well the shit will hit the fan when they get the subpoenas from my lawyer and we will be doing that next week."

Eighteen

Lily stroked Starborn gentling him for a moment then slipped a halter for a yearling on him and snugged the buckle up. He tossed his head around and tried to rub it off then picked up his hind feet and ran in a little tight circle around the pen.

Lily laughed and crooned at him and he came back to suck on her fingers and butt his head against her. "Your quite the beauty aren't you."

Musty walked up to watch them and smiled too. "He's really gotten his legs under him after only a couple of weeks."

Lily laughed. "We've had a lot of babies here. I have loved them all. In the past 16 years we've had over 90 horses come out of our mares and find good homes. That is four generations now of ribbon holders and winners. I've decided to map it all out on our next issue of the Blog. Our horses have been at the top in most of the championships and I've decided we need to up our prices again. It seems like each new crop is better than the one before it. But I'm sure Starborn is more than a champion. He's a super horse. I just wish we had someone riding now."

"Bricca is pure talent but after watching her kids for her I can see that there is no way for her to go back on the circuit. Jenny never had the bug. She is a great rider but she has always been a businesswoman. Lizzy is going to go a long way but she is still too young. Starborn will be ready to go out in two years and be competing in three. We will blink our eyes and the time will come."

"I can do the training, but we need to be training an equestrian too to represent Bricca Down West."

Musty stroked his chin and didn't say anything. Sometimes it didn't do to say too much when women were thinking out loud. He'd found that to be true of Bricca. "It must be exciting riding in competition," he offered.

"You wouldn't believe how exciting. You have to be as athletic as your horse and ready mentally to perform under pressure. Your horse depends on you to stay calm and see the win. A lot of riders can't take the intensity because they are too young and inexperienced. In the international competition and Olympic competitions the youngest riders are in their early 20s. I remember it well. Trigger and I were right on the brink of going to nationals when I got pregnant. I'd never give Jenny up but it is one of the few things in my life that I regret, not going all the way."

"I guess you *could* on a horse like this." Musty said.

"Not me, I'm 47 now, way to old."

"Hmmm," Musty commented.

"But I do ride every day. I teach and jump regularly. I'm probably in as good of shape as I was in my twenties. I don't know why I always tell myself I can't do it. The fact is I'm probably as capable of taking him international as Bricca was. She was like a meteor, a rising star, with just had plain old talent from the moment she got on a horse. I'm more like an aged wine. It's possible I've been getting better or better or I might be already past my prime."

"I guess you never know until you open the bottle."

Lily laughed at the analogy. "You're right. My kids are almost grown. Bern will be in college. I should start preparing to ride and then we'll see what happens when I go to my first competition. I'll either fold or find I'm as good or better than I was before."

"Sounds like a plan."

Lily's face had lit up like a beacon and Musty thought again about how young she looked and shook his head. These women were a mystery to him. Sophie had looked younger last time he saw her too. They aged backwards.

When Lily got back to the ranch she was beaming and barely able to contain her excitement. Jace was just riding in and saw her before she saw him. She looked about twelve years old and she was doing a little boogey around the vegetable patch, throwing her hands over her head and then bumping hips with some invisible dancer.

Jace jumped off his horse and in a few long strides had picked her up and was swinging her around.

"What has gotten into you?"

"I made an important decision today that I'm excited about."

"And what was that?"

"I'm going to train to take Starborn out into competition. I want to ride him to the nationals and then international."

Jace's mouth fell open and he frowned. "What?"

"Bern will be 18 then and starting college. I want to be starting something myself. I don't want to have any regrets. The only thing I didn't finish was riding in the Olympics and internationally. I had the talent but life interrupted me. I want to try to go all the way."

"But you'll be almost 50 then."

"People ride in the internationals at all ages."

"But it would mean traveling all over the place and being gone for months at a time."

"You could join me and we could travel together."

"*Me*, leave the ranch, you've got to be kidding!"

"Jace, just stop it. Don't act so heavy-handed about this. Don't you want me to challenge myself? Just making the decision makes me feel younger, happier, and more capable. I want to believe in myself. I'm more than a mother, more than your partner, more than a businesswoman. I've always been a damn good equestrian."

"I never said you weren't and it seems anything I say now is going to get me in trouble."

"Yeah, it will, so just be happy for me. You'll have plenty of time to adjust to the idea. For now I'll just be increasing my riding schedule to an hour a day and I'm going to want to set up some jumps and eventually find someone who can coach me."

"Just as long as you are careful. I don't understand why you would risk getting physically hurt when you are getting older."

Lily never let herself forget that Jace's mom had died falling off a stallion when he was only 13. "I'll be very careful, I promise."

Jace found himself stomping into the house. Why couldn't things just get easier? Jenny comes homes and then someone is trying to kill her. Turns out it is one of his own men who has betrayed him. Will and Bricca almost break up and he didn't even see it coming. His son starts running with the wrong crowd and smoking pot and the harder he tries to get him to work on the ranch or follow the rules, the more he rebels. Now it's Lily. She's ready to change everything between them and risk her life jumping to prove something to herself. Even Sophie threw him a curveball by taking off for Europe.

Not to mention that his Dad just up and died out of the blue while doing chores and the next day he had to make the decisions for everyone on a 20,000 acre ranch with 2500 cattle. Jace couldn't remember anything but having responsibility and now it looked like he hadn't been doing a very good job at it.

Jace threw his gloves down on the hutch and caught a look at himself in the mirror. He looked old. His hair was grey now and decades of being in the sun all day had turned his skin into tanned leather. There were deep wrinkles between his eyes and age spots on his hands. And even though he could still ride all day long, it hurt. In fact Jace realized he hurt all the time. His body was a machine that fixed things, loaded hay and carried five gallon buckets. And the machine was wearing out a little more every year. Had he ever had any other dreams?

When Jace walked into the kitchen he saw that Lily was still bouncing off the walls with excitement as she moved between the table and the fridge frying up some sirloin tips for supper. The only plan Jace had ever had was Lily. She made him more than force, more than will. She had made him feel love and sentimentality. Lily was the only thing that he couldn't lose and survive.

Jace gave her a long hug that had a little bit of desperation in it and Lily looked in his eyes and tried to read what was going on. It only took a few moments before she got the whole thing. She'd always been able to understand him.

"Jace you are my center. Everything turns around you. When I spin in my own orbit whether it is with the kids or the horses, that orbit still circles around you. That is never, never, never going to change! Never!"

Jace felt her words sink into him and he smiled. "Okay!"

Nineteen

Jenny and Chance had a lot of work to do loading all of her furniture and boxing back up her house. Jenny looked around feeling sad. It had been such a great deal caretaking this house. The cabin had been luxurious and huge. Her stuff had just fit. Now she needed to take some stuff to her office and store the rest unless Chance would let her move it into his place. For some reason Jenny didn't really want to ask him. She had never wanted to live with a man before she got married. It was an old-fashioned idea, but then Jenny had grown up pinning pictures of wedding dresses on her wall and playing house. She had watched her parents worship each other and always wanted her life to be like them.

Jenny stopped for a moment and stretched her back then tied her hair off her neck.

"Chance, you don't need to help with all of this. I can work on it more slowly and then just rent a U-Haul again and pay a couple of kids to help me."

Chance stopped what he was doing and just looked at her in his quiet way. "What is going on?"

"I'm feeling weird about you having to spend so much time helping me, protecting me, and letting me stay at your house. I'm not usually the dependent kind of woman and I feel like I'm forcing myself on you."

"Did I ever do anything to give you that impression?"

"No, never. But you can't help feeling that way."

"Believe me Jenny when I say that I don't feel put out, AT ALL. I've missed you these last four years. Being around each other makes everything feel like it is place again. And you know me. I've always been the kind of guy who helped people move. Why wouldn't I want to do that for you?"

"I think that is the very trait that made me back off, though, and wonder if we would be good together. I wondered if you would always be there to support other people or if you would have your *own* thing. Don't you want to start your own business instead of working for your Dad? Wouldn't it be a drag for you to just help me with my business without having your own?

Chance pulled Jenny over to the couch and made her look at him.

"What you're really saying is it bothers you that your motivated and I'm not. That I'm willing to eat my mom's food, live in a caretaking cabin and work for my dad while you went off and got a degree in Business Management and a grant to start your own business."

"Well, yeah. But that sounds a lot more snotty than I feel."

"Do you know what is important to me?" Chance asked.

Lily thought about it. "I'm pretty self-obsessed. I get so involved in doing my own thing that all I can think of is what is important to me. A lot of the time I assume what matters to me should be on the top of your list too. I'm ashamed to say I don't really know the answer to that."

Chance laid his head back on the couch and tried to find words. Words weren't his strong suit. He did better with action.

"I'm busy all of the time, just like you are."

"Oh," Jenny asked, "How?"

"I eat my mom's food so that I can visit with her a little every day. She is worried about Ellie Bell and has been seeing the doctor because she had some abnormal test results on her last physical. I work for my dad because he is fair, kind and wants me to. We share little moments all day long working together that we wouldn't have had otherwise. I care take because I don't want the pressure of a mortgage when I can live free and also help out an older woman who needs someone around her that she can trust, especially since she has been forgetting things. I help you because I like soaking up the essence of you, even the part that is obsessive-compulsive or a little judgmental of me."

"What is important to me is how I connect to people, not some arbitrary idea of getting ahead in life. I didn't go to college because I was learning something every single day from my dad. There are other kinds of colleges. I don't plan to buy a house, start a business and move to the city. If that's what you want you've got the wrong guy."

The more he talked the worse Jenny felt. She had been judging him for a long time without trying to understand him.

Jenny took Chance's hand. "How can you be so good and what did I do to deserve you?"

Chance laughed. "The better question to ask is why did you feel uncomfortable telling me about your inheritance?"

Jenny groaned. "I knew we were going to have to talk about that."

"Well?"

"I didn't tell *anybody* if that helps. It just felt weirdly unreal. Like getting a diagnosis that you have cancer. I didn't believe that it was happening. I felt deflated by getting the inheritance when I had set out so hard to prove myself by trying to start my business on nothing. I've always measured my value more on the amount of effort I was willing to give to something."

"How do *you* feel about me getting that much money?" Jenny asked.

"Like it will be a pain in the butt that will change our life forever by making things complicated instead of simple. It will hang over us needing to be managed or donated or used all the time. People will use you and they are already abusing you because you have that kind of money. You'll spend half your life trying to invest it." Chance said.

"Hmm, seeing it from your point of view it doesn't look too good."

"No."

"I've been thinking though. If I do get this money, I want to use it to do something good in the world. But I want a simple life. I imagine buying Halls farm or something like that. But that's a long way off, how are we going to get through this?" Jenny asked.

"How about a nice ride and a little run down to the creek?"

"That sounds perfect. And then we'll load the rest of the truck and take the evening off. We still have two more days to get the stuff. For now I'll just load things I can take to The Feed Store."

The ride to the creek pulled out all of Jenny's tension and soon she was lost in the sound of the frogs and the bliss of the light filtering through the pine trees. She wondered why she had ever let herself loose her priorities. Loving Chance was a priority. But after an hour she found herself checking her watch. They still had a lot to do.

For an answer Chance just gripped her hair and went for her vulnerable spot. Jenny loved having her neck kissed. Soon they were lying down next to the creek and the load of furniture was forgotten.

Chance held Jenny down when she tried to scramble up an hour later. "Jenny, will you marry me?"

"What?"

"Soon, in the next month. Marry me."

"Everything is unsettled. There is this big legal fight on the horizon. I don't even have a place to live."

"I don't care about all of that. There will always be something that needs to be done or is unfinished or pending."

Jenny quit struggling and lay back on Chance's arm instead noticing how the light was hitting the top of the grass and shining through little may flies and pollen making the filtered air look like a golden shower in the after glow.

"Yes!"

Chance whooped and pulled her on top of him.

"What about the ring, did you think of that?" Jenny jibed playfully.

Chance shocked her by getting his jacket and opening a pocket. Inside was an old-fashioned ring box. "This was my great great great grandmother's ring on my mother's side. She emigrated here from Ireland with a sister and a brother just before the civil war. The brother and sister both died but she stayed and eventually married and moved west. This ring came with her from Europe. It has a diamond and the family crest."

Jenny looked at the ring with wonder.

"How long have you been carrying this in your pocket?"

"All week long. I'm giving it to you with my mom's blessing."

Jenny started to cry then, great big gulping sobs.

"It is the most beautiful thing I've ever seen and to have all that history. I'm so grateful and so humbled and so…"

Chance interrupted her, "Jenny, It's just a ring. The important thing is being together after all of this time."

Twenty

❦

Sandra was not only furious with her mother she was scared. Sometimes she looked in her mother's eyes and thought she was seeing someone that was mentally ill. Nedra's eyes could look vacant and mean. Sandra had long ago stopped expecting recognition, encouragement or pride.

Today was worse than most days. The drapes were pulled in the parlor and the room looked almost dark. Her mom and been just sitting in her chair all day, barely moving. Her food tray looked untouched beside her and Sandra noticed even her fingernails looked a little bit dirty like she hadn't taken a bath for a few days.

Sandra tried to get through. "Mom, are you okay? Would you like me to order you something else to eat?"

"Stop fawning over me, Sandra." came the sharp retort. "I'm just thinking. I have to do all of the thinking for both of us because apparently you've been thinking with your skirts up over your head."

Sandra gasped at the insult. Her mom seemed to enjoy turning the knife and seem to take pleasure in her next announcement.

"Dirk is dead."

"What, no I just talked to him yesterday. He was going up into the mountains to do a round up. You must be mistaken."

The police just called. "He was murdered by someone who flew in and hiked to their camp and broke his neck then threw him down a cliff."

Sandra's heart started beating hard. "You couldn't have…"

"I could have but I didn't. That leaves you…."

Sandra started to feel dizzy.

This couldn't be happening. "Of course I didn't kill him, he was helping us out."

"Apparently all he did was botch things up like a bumbling idiot."

"That wasn't him, mother. Someone else has it out for Jenny. Also he hadn't even cashed our check. He offered to send it back."

"The check went through my auxiliary bank today."

"What?"

"Yes, and thank goodness I used a bank account that is in the Cayman Islands or they would be able to trace it back to me if they get suspicious. Apparently Dirk and another woman were buying a house together and he gave the money to her."

Sandra felt a little spurt of dark jealously. Maybe Dirk had been playing her.

"There's more. We were just subpoenaed for information on the corporation. Jenny got a lawyer named Ian Abbott who is fighting us. Unfortunately he happens to be a good lawyer who I won't be able to buy off. His whole family are wealthy do-gooders that I've always despised. We could threaten his family but the farther we go with this, the more likely it is that this is all going to lead to the attempted murder of Jenny and the murder of Dirk."

Sandra gasped with shock. When Nedra spoke the shock was half because of the venom and half the fact that what she was saying was true. Sandra had always prided herself on doing nasty things in a nice way, or at least a way that looked nice. This had become her worst nightmare.

Sandra also felt sadness. Dirk had been the first man in decades to give her attention. Now he was dead just like Ned was dead, just like her life felt suddenly dead.

Nedra turned now with a bitter twist of her mouth and Sandra shuddered.

"I've made a decision. We aren't going to contest the will. If we have an enemy it will be better to have her close to us. We will invite Jenny to come to the corporate meetings and participate as a full 1/3 member. We'll welcome her into our family. And then when the right time comes and all of the other dangers have blown over we'll strike. Chicago is a dangerous city. The members of this corporation are powerful people that don't like to be crossed. I'm sure she'll make her own bed and then have to lie in it."

Sandra tried to protest. "But don't you see that you'll have a witness to any back room meetings. It is like having a mole in the house."

Nedra shook her head. "Not if she's never invited behind the curtain to private meetings. Chances are though she won't be able curb her curiosity. The sooner she blows it, the sooner we are rid of her without getting our hands dirty. Someone is already out there raising Cain and we don't know who it is."

Nedra contacted Ian Abbott through her lawyers that same day and by the next day Jenny was sitting in Ian's office feeling discombobulated.

"They what?"

"They have decided not to contest the will. The lawyers said Nedra would like to get to know her granddaughter since she is old before she dies. They would like you to meet your family and participate in decisions of the corporation.

"You've got to be kidding me."

"No I'm not. Unfortunately I don't trust this all very much myself. You need to walk carefully. I haven't had time to really investigate what this corporation has been doing and whether they are involved in illegal activities."

Jenny sat down hard. "I'd like you to keep working for me doing that very thing if you don't mind."

Ian nodded. "Of course I will not be charging you a percentage of your winnings now as there is not going to be a trial. I'll be charging you my normal rate of $350.00 an hour."

Jenny gulped and Ian smiled. "Don't worry, that is an average rate for any lawyer and you can afford it."

Twenty-one

☙

Ireland

Bricca was nervous as they drove down the long drive to the McBride stables. There was fencing on each side and acres of deep green grass. The road was gravel and they drove slowly in order to check things out. At the turn out was a large sign. McBride Family Farm. Under that was a by-line. Home of Champion Rosemary Down, Since 1763. Beneath that was the family crest. Bricca took pictures of the sign and the mares grazing out in the pastures and squeezed Will's hand.

"Okay, here it goes."

Minnie McBride had already given them an introduction and Nathan McBride had agreed to meet them at the farm to show them around and hear the story directly from them. Bricca had brought pictures of Bricca Down and Bricca Down Thunder, their website address, a copy of Gwenn Anne's last letter and her camera. She hoped this man was as nice as Minnie had been.

When they drove up to the barns Bricca saw a girl in a paddock wearing breeches, jodhpurs and a helmet who was taking a lesson in English riding and jumping. The jump had been set low and the girl looked accomplished but green. Her instructor was calling out constant instruction. Legs under. Look ahead. More collection. You lost your gait.

Bricca remembered what it had been like when she was first learning. There was so much to keep track of at the same time. In the end it came down to how well the horse was doing.

She stood at the fence quietly until the lesson had ended and waited to greet the man that she assumed was Nathan McBride.

When he turned Bricca had a little flash of recognition, wondering when she had seen him before. He had a pleasant square face and a muscular body and was obviously an athlete. When he smiled she saw a row of perfectly white teeth and friendly green eyes.

Bricca congratulated the girl on a good lesson and Nathan's eyes sparkled with a little challenge. "I'm for thinkin' twould be a fair thing if ye be willin' ta ride wi' me 'round the McBride. Ye ken to it now?"

Bricca looked over at Will who nodded and she lit up. "I'd love to ride. We've been traveling for four weeks and I've been missing my horses."

Nathan went back into the shed and came walking out with a horse that was the spitting image of Starfire. Bricca almost fell backwards. "Oh, my God. He's the match of our horse. Look." Bricca brought over her Ipad and called up their website with the first pictures of Bricca Down Thunder, then Bricca Down Starfire along with some pictures of him with his blue ribbons and his main and tail braided in competition.

"Gimmini" Nathan said. "I wasn't really for believin' it, but who ken be blind 'ta wha' 'afore 'ta eyes."

Bricca pulled her boots out of the trunk of her car and tucked her hair up and walked up to her mount.

"So who is this beauty?"

"Dapper Down"

Bricca mounted and took him a few paces around the arena until her seat felt comfortable. "Does he jump?"

"Mightily."

Bricca laughed and caught the fun of the moment. "Do you have an outdoor course?"

"Eye that we do."

"Then let's go."

Will felt a little curl of jealousy as he watched them ride off together but didn't have time to think about it because he was mobbed by a group of four redheaded children who claimed Nathan was their father and a milky-skinned beauty that arrived with cookies and lemonade. From where they sat enjoying the last bit of sunshine he could see Nathan and Bricca jumping the course and the woman's interest. "She's a good seat on 'er."

Will just smiled. That was an understatement.

Within 20 minutes Bricca and Nathan were back laughing like old friends. Bricca was hugging Dapper Down like she did Starfire and Will and Megan McBride had become good friends. Megan was impressed that Will was a vet as well as an American Rancher and had lots of questions to ask about cowboys and Indians. Nathan was quizzing Bricca on their breeding program. When they got off a groomsman came to curry the horses and put them away and Bricca began to tell the story of Gwenn Anne and Benjamin Thomas.

Megan cried when Bricca read them the letter and Nathan looked solemn.

"Would ya' be wantin' to see a likeness of 'em?" Nathan asked.

Bricca was enthusiastic. "Wonderful. Also I'd love to take some photographs too for my family. Would you mind me getting pictures of you also as well as the horses for my sister and niece?"

Nathan brought out a picture of Benjamin that was an old tintype of him in his confederate uniform. He looked young and handsome and again, Bricca thought, familiar. Bricca took a picture of the tintype. Then Nathan pulled out another unexpected photo. It was a picture of Benjamin with Down Dandy. On the other side of the horse was a young girl who looked just like Jenny. Bricca was struck by the photo and convinced of her hypothesis.

At the end of the lovely evening Bricca got to her point. "Gwenn Anne will not rest until she has made amends to Benjamin. Maybe meeting you and reading you the letter was enough. However, Lily and I would like to give you a colt off of Starfire for your breeding line. When he is born I'll contact you and we'll work out shipping. We usually keep the colts until they are 10 month old to give them extra time with their mothers and then a few months for some simple training. I've never shipped a horse oversees but I know people send horses on airplanes all the time."

Nathan looked a little overwhelmed. "That is a large investment for ye to be makin'."

Bricca looked him right in the eyes. "Heather Down was originally your horse. It is only right that we give him back to you. I'll make sure that we are sending you a horse that follows the original line. We have a mare that only picks up the stud."

Nathan and Megan were so grateful they searched the house looking for a gift for Bricca. "Here be our clan's crest sewn by me own gran on a blanket for Dapper Down to wear during festival days. Take it with our blessin'."

As Bricca and Will drove away Bricca could hear Gwenn Anne sighing. "Finally, I can rest."

Bricca couldn't wait to contact her family and send the photographs. She sent the pictures to Jenny with little captions describing the visit. The caption of the photos with Benjamin said, 'Who do you think this looks like?!'

When Jenny got the file she also got a shock. Nathan looked exactly like Chance and so did Benjamin Thomas. She gasped when she saw a photo of them standing at age 17 on either side of Downs Dandy, next to a photo of the McBride family crest."

Jenny called Chance right away. What is your mother's Irish clan name?

"McBride, why."

"Chance, you are related to Benjamin Thomas! He was a McBride! You have an uncle in Ireland who looks just like you and they have a photo of Benjamin Thomas that could *be* you, same build, same green eyes, brown hair with square faces and a row of straight shiny teeth in a square jaw. It is unmistakable."

That night Jenny and Chance fixed supper at the ranch for their parents, Bern and Lizzy, Paddy, Tonka and Charlotte. Chance grilled steaks and Jenny made a chocolate cake as well as Sophie's scalloped potato recipe and orange Jell-O with grated carrots. Jenny made a special little steak for Tootsie that was medium rare.

They set the table with flowers and right before desert made their announcement. They were getting married. After tears and hugs, they showed Lily the pictures that Bricca had sent and showed everyone how Lily's engagement ring, an heirloom from Della, was the McBride crest.

Lily shared the information she had just learned from Jace about how they had ended up with land in White Cloud because Della's mom and dad had known her Uncle Applewhite from when they both lived in the Deep South together.

Chance and Lily were a bit overwhelmed by the whole idea. "We are the star-crossed lovers finally finding each other again?"

Lily said, "Yes you are. You are both starborn.

Lily was in a state of shock herself. She couldn't get over one part of the story that was shaking her up a bit.

"Bricca told them we would *give* them one of Starfire colts off of Dilly and *send it to Ireland*?"

Twenty-Two

❧

The Feed Store was finished. Judd and his crew had finished the remodel in two weeks and it had taken her another two weeks to unpack and make a few samples of her product line. Jenny was having her opening party tonight and she was running around trying to finish last minute details. Bricca and Will had gotten home yesterday and would be coming to the party along with half of the valley.

Bricca's antiques were attractively decorating the front room along with her large plants and some modern art. Large bouquets of fresh Sunflowers and purple delphiniums were strategically placed in each room. There were shelves with the first batch of dog and cat treats attractively displayed and a guest book sitting on the front counter as well as plates of grapes, cheese and little finger foods. Jenny had made everything herself to save money, freezing little quiches and puff pastries so that she could give them another pop in the oven before putting them on platters. It helped to have a commercial kitchen at her disposal. Lily had helped her make the floral arrangements, picking everything from her own gardens.

Thanks to Bern's ingenuity, Jazz music was playing over the speaker system that connected the two rooms and the back yard.

Yellow and purple balloons were tied to the front porch along with a cooler full of soda water, coke and beer.

The back room was scrubbed and polished with all of the new equipment in place and gleaming. Jenny had ordered an oversized banner of her logo and pinned it to the bulletin board wall and strategically placed other appetizers on all of the cabinets. The bathrooms were scented, decorated and stocked with extra toilet paper and there was a picnic table in the back of the building for those people who would rather hang out outside. Jenny had made a path down to the creek with LED lamps and set folding chairs borrowed from the church in conversation groups. She had also strung a square of twinkle lights around the backyard and across the front porch.

Jenny checked everything again to make sure she had her gold napkins and dark purple paper plates where they needed to be. Then snapped a few photos of how pretty it all was.

Jenny had invited everyone in White Cloud, most of the people who lived in Paradise Valley and put flyers out in Livingston. She didn't have enough products to sell tonight but her new employee Amy would be helping her take orders. She had printed 200 color brochures using Adobe InDesign and Internet printing.

Chance had watch this whirlwind of activity with a little alarm.

Jenny had the ability to set a goal for herself and then work against her own self-imposed deadline. She had only been in business one month and she had a store, an employee, product, and marketing material and was getting orders.

In order to thank the Brinton Foundation again for their 'Golden Grant' Bern was in charge of making a dynamite video of the whole night that they could send to the board. It would include her verbal thank you for their support in a little speech she had planned.

Jenny was wearing what she thought of as her power suit. It was a dress with a little jacket over it with matching shoes. She had kept her hair and jewelry casual.

Lily and Jace were the first to arrive. Jace looked uncomfortable in new jeans and Lily looked a little nervous for Jenny. "What can we do? We came early to help."

Jenny looked around. "Perhaps open some bottles of wine and set them out on the counters with glasses. Jenny slapped Bern's hands when he grabbed a whole plate of chicken satay sticks and tried to walk out with them. "What are you doing, you animal."

Jace patted Bern on the back and laughed. "Let's men go out in back and have us a coke."

Lily had Jenny turn around. "You look perfect but I snipped off a little string that was hanging off your hem. It looks like you've got a lot of food here. Do you really think that many people will come?"

"Yes, If only because everyone will be curious about what kind of party I can throw."

"You made all of the appetizers yourself?"

"Hopefully they won't all know that. I couldn't afford a fancy caterer."

"Cooking is something to be proud of," Lily said, "You've been in the big city too long."

The door opened and the first guests came in, walking around to view the antiques and get something to eat. People seemed impressed when they saw the state of the art kitchen and picked up brochures. By twenty after the room was packed and Jenny had turned up the stereo. Bern was wandering around eating and filming and Jenny pronounced the evening a complete success.

After an hour Jenny got everyone's attention and called Chance so they were standing together while she said thank you to Chance, Judd, her family, the community of White Cloud and to the Brinton Foundation.

Someone from the audience called out. "Is that an engagement ring we see on your left hand?" Jenny smiled and took Chance's hand.

"You might as well know. Chance and I are engaged to be married!" There was loud cheering and some catcalling to tease them so Chance swept her up off her feet and Jenny gave him a big kiss.

By the time everyone left she had 150 orders for cat and dog treats and 38 people had signed up for her monthly shipments. Jenny did a fast calculation. The profits tonight more than paid for her open house party. It was a great start.

Jenny was exhausted but not willing to leave a mess so she started to pick up. Before she knew it Amy, Bricca, Will, Jace, Lily and all the kids were helping too. Paddy and Tonka made a game out of running to get as many cups as possible and aiming to dunk them in the large trashcan. Some of the wine was ending up flung around the room.

Jenny felt so supported and happy she didn't even look at who was on the line when she picked up her phone.

"Hello," she said happily.

"This is your grandmother." Came an imperious voice. "It sounds like you are at a party."

"I am with my family cleaning up after the opening celebration for my new business The Feed Store. I manufacture and sell gourmet animal treats."

Nedra just humphed as if a little disgusted by the idea. "There is a board meeting next week on Wednesday at 7:00 pm in the Chicago Tower penthouse. You are expected to be there. We will introduce you. So don't be late. The attire is formal for men and a conservative dress for women. Most of the women wear black or dark blue. No loud colors."

Jenny thought about it for a moment. "I'm expected to fly to Chicago for one board meeting?"

"The board only meets four times a year. So yes, that is the expectation."

Jenny clamped her jaw shut to keep from saying something rude.

"I'll be there."

Twenty-three

❧

Chicago

Chance was furious that Jenny had agreed to go to Chicago. It was a week where he couldn't go. He and his dad, Judd were finishing a house for a difficult client who had a nonnegotiable deadline. Chance insisted that Jenny at least go with Lily or her dad. But Lily was teaching a workshop and Jace was short a man with Dirk gone. He had already gone up to the mountain camp to relieve one of the other guys whose wife was having surgery. Bricca and Will were just back after being gone for four weeks. Jenny didn't see any choice but to go alone. She told Chance that she could stay with Sheila and would contact Alexander and Nina. She'd have to face the old dragon Nedra sometime and it might as well be now.

What really made Jenny angry was only getting a few days notice for booking her plane fare. The extra fare could have gone towards her new business. As of now she had no access to the monies in her trust and she had no idea when that might happen. Her new role as board member was turning out to be expensive. At the last second Jenny bought a dark blue dress but dressed it up with a crimson scarf with bright flowers on it. She didn't care what her grandmother said; it was okay to look nice.

Jenny brushed up a little on corporate law and boardroom procedure just to be prepared. She was grateful to have a degree in Business Management. She had been the president of plenty of boards so she was familiar with Roberts Rules of Order.

At the last second before leaving for the airport Jenny ran back and got her locket that had a little piece of her childhood stuffed Bunny in it. She might need it for support.

There was no one to meet her at O'Hare airport so Jenny took the subway and then a cab to Sheila's house. Sheila was thrilled to see her, hugging her and holding on tightly. Sheila was feeling lonely and emotional.

"I can't believe how much I miss Sophie and you and Max right now. It is as if you all flew away at the same time and figured I'd be just fine visiting with my grandkids. Actually it makes me a bit angry. I've been trying to figure out something that I could do to make some kind of difference in the world again.

Jenny questioned her carefully. "Have you ever thought of starting a business or creating something or traveling?"

Sheila had an immediate answer. "I've always wanted a flower shop. I've learned a lot about gardening over the years and I have some of my own ideas. I'd like to plan and design theme gardens for people. You know, round gardens, gnome gardens, oriental gardens, water gardens. I think there is a place for something like that in Chicago. The thing is how do you begin?"

Jenny knew just what to tell her since she loved making business plans. Impulsively she volunteered to help with more than the business plan. "I'm supposed to be getting an inheritance at some point. I'll stake you as your financial partner for your start-up money."

Sheila looked a little overwhelmed. "Really? Is this a good idea? You don't want people asking you for stuff like that do you? You might be setting a bad precedent doing it for me."

Jenny hugged Sheila. "We will keep it confidential. And you're not 'people' you're my nana."

Sheila and Jenny stayed up until late coming up with idea after idea Tuesday night. Jenny slept in late Wednesday. It felt wonderful to lay in bed after working so hard on the start-up and opening party of The Feed Store. But she wished she were here on vacation. Today was going to be a dreadful day.

At noon Jenny was surprised to see she had a text from her ex-boyfriend Kelly. Kelly had been working for Sandra Tavery's real estate firm. He explained that he had overheard Sandra say that Jenny was coming to town today and he was hoping that they could have a late lunch. Say 1:00.

Jenny texted back that she'd meet him at their regular hangout and then hurried to shower and dress. It was muggy and hot so she just threw on a pair of shorts and a tank top and called it good. Sheila was fine with Jenny borrowing her car.

Kelly stood up when she walked in. He was wearing a suit and a tie and looked uncomfortably hot, especially sitting in a burger joint. As soon as he saw her he grinned and pealed off his tie and rolled up his sleeves.

Jenny was genuinely glad to see him and gave him a big hug before ordering a raspberry ice and a deluxe hamburger with everything on it.

"How's the job going?" Jenny asked.

"Weird but lucrative. Sandra likes to have me run errands for her. Sometimes I end up picking up dry cleaning or getting a gift for a client. I thought I would be a bookkeeper but I'm kind of a glorified assistant. When she wants numbers crunched on some deal I'm supposed to be a numbers whiz. I never know what I'm going to be asked to do next."

Kelly sat forward and lowered his voice, "Listen, this is what I wanted to talk to you about. I hear things. I'm invisible to Sandra so she doesn't hold her tongue around me. She doesn't know that we dated and I haven't told her after hearing that they were contesting a will with you. Then I hear they've changed their mind and your invited to come to the board meeting now."

"The thing is, don't trust these people. They are vipers. They probably are having you followed right now and I'm getting into hot water just by seeing you." Kelly looked around him nervously.

Jenny sat forward. "Is Sandra into anything shady. Is her family corporation connected to mafia or laundering schemes?"

Kelly broke out into a sweat. "Sandra regularly has luncheons with politicians. She wheels and deals to get special deals regarding zoning and permits. She has a few politicians in her pocket just because she flirts with them or strokes their ego. The mob family that is ruling Chicago now is the Tetrazonni family. Sandra just bought an elaborate pair of diamond earrings for Tony Tetrazonni's daughter's 18th birthday party. Sandra was super nervous about looking perfect when she went to the party. The next week she was sent a couple of clients of his that were looking to buy big buildings. Sandra gave them a deal under the asking price but told the sellers some smoke about them needing to lower the price because of the market. This just happened recently. I don't know what other kinds of deals have been made over the years."

Jenny asked, "What about their corporation?"

"I just know that the Board of Directors rubber stamps everything put in front of them. Edward is CEO and prepares the budget and packets the Board gets. Sandra doesn't even read the stuff and in the past Nedra didn't go to the meetings. Everyone is all-uptight because you are going to be there today so they are being ultra cautious. Nedra is going so they can present a united front in case you vote against anything."

"What do they buy, make or sale?"

"They buy companies that are having financial difficulties, fire all the employees and file bankruptcy. Then they re-organize and make deals to keep the company operational, manufacturing the same product and negotiating down debt to creditors. Now they pay half the salary to the employees and make the product with cheaper materials and lowered environmental standards. If the company had a good reputation to begin with it will begin to make a profit. Soon, however they start getting bad consumer reviews or boycotts. Then they sell the company and find another company to do the same thing. We are talking huge numbers and dozens of companies."

"Is this legal?" Jenny asked.

"Yes but they are pretty cold-hearted and unethical. It is a rotten way to do business."

"Thank you for telling me all of this. I've been a wreck not knowing what to expect. I suppose you heard that someone tried to burn down the house I was staying in and incriminate me as an arsonist. The trail led to a wrangler who worked for my father who was paid $20,000 by someone. He bungled the job. A few days later he died of a broken neck. The Sheriff was able to prove it was murder. Whoever did it flew out to Montana in a small private plane, drove a dark sedan and then disappeared. He was described as

Hispanic or Latin, short and stocky with a greased crew cut and a tattoo on his neck of a dagger.

Kelly leaned forward almost whispering now. "That sounds like a gang tattoo. What was the wrangler's name who died?"

"Dirk."

Kelly turned a little pale. "A couple of times I heard Sandra talking to cowboy. She sounded very attracted to him."

Kelly continued, "I think you should stay away from these people. If you cross them or worse one of their business associates you might end up tied to a concrete block. The mob never lets anything implicate them. If Sandra screws up the same would go for her. She's playing with fire to do business with them or try to court their favor."

Jenny started to feel nervous. "I'm worried about you, Kelly. What if they find out we dated, or what if they hired you in the first place because of that in order to influence me at some point in the future. You shouldn't be there at all. You've got a bright future ahead of you in business. Quit and find a better job somewhere else."

"Can't, I'm in over my head now with an expensive car and a lease on a fancy flat. I've been dating a hot chick who expects champagne not hamburgers. I've dug myself in."

"Well you can dig yourself out easily enough. Sell the car, leave the flat and break up with the girl. If she cared about you she wouldn't want you working for someone like Sandra."

"I'll think about it. It's hard. I like getting $100,000 for running a few errands as long as I'm not being asked to do something illegal."

Kelly threw down his napkin and sucked down the rest of his coke quickly. "I'd better get back. I'm supposed to be doing some shopping right now for a gift basket for each of the board members for tonight."

Jenny made herself lie down when she got home and then dress slowly and carefully for the board meeting. She was too nervous to eat anything but she made sure she had a bottle of water in her purse and her phone set to tape record the meeting. She decided to take a cab so she wouldn't have to negotiate downtown traffic.

The Chicago Towers were impressive and the penthouse had a living area for everyone to socialize in before meeting at a long solid wood table with windows that overlooked Chicago and Lake Michigan. The air conditioning was set on high and Jenny was glad she was wearing a scarf.

No one came to say hello to her as she walked into the room of visiting men and women. Jenny figured she must be a dangerous person for them to ally with. Jenny moved over to the drink table and got herself a glass of sparkling punch and a strawberry. At five minutes until seven Sandra walked imperiously into the room followed by Edward who trailed behind her. Nedra was wheeled in by an attendant in a chair then helped to the table by the staff. Immediately everyone sat down and was handed a packet of information.

Jenny reached in her purse and turned on her tape recorder just as Edward started the meeting. He briefly introduced Jenny without giving any background about her and Jenny wondered if the board members even knew that she was his niece.

Jenny began to quickly scan the information she had been given wondering why the packet hadn't been given to everyone in advance so they would have time to read it.

Edward stood up.

"We'll start with old business. Do I have a motion to approve the corporate expenses and income statement?"

Jenny couldn't help it, she didn't like being pushed and she'd never taken orders well. She said politely, "Could we please have five more minutes to look them over. Perhaps everyone else had this packet mailed to them in advance but this is the first time I have seen it."

There was a little gasp in the room and Edward's cheeks turned red.

Jenny ignored him and studied the income and expense sheet carefully. "Can you clarify line item 25 please?" Edward looked flustered and turned to Sandra for guidance. She just sat stony faced and he was forced to address the question. "It is $25,000 for guest expenses."

"Who was the guest?"

"The president of the United Trade Union."

"He accepted $25,000 in gifts?"

"No in expenses, he was flown here, housed, wined and dined, taken to a gala event with his wife and children, they both played golf, and he was given a lifetime membership in our corporate club."

"All of this expense was for one guest?

Edward was getting angry now and even Sandra was starting to lose her cool.

Jenny stood her ground. "I'm asking these questions for a reason. If a Union leader or Federal employee accepts corporate gifts he is violating Business Codes. By law he is liable for fines and even a jail term for accepting bribes related to his position. The person offering the monies is equally liable. The board shouldn't agree to a line item like that. I suggest that you ask the President of the United Trade Union to reimburse us $25,000.00 so that he is not breaking the law unless you can think of another way to solve this problem.

Edward was sputtering and Nedra's eyes were glittering with triumph. Her plan was working. Jenny was going to dig herself a deep hole. When the vote was taken the board still rubber stamped Edward's budget. Jenny voted against and asked that her discussion be recorded in the board minutes and they went on to the next item of business.

Here things got worse if that were possible. Edward had listed the purchase of a number of companies. Since Jenny already had a heads up that they only purchased companies in trouble she was curious why they were purchasing two multi-million dollar companies that were still making a 6% profit without significant debt. On another sheet he showed both corporations scheduled for Chapter 11 bankruptcy proceedings. Something didn't look right. Jenny pointed out that 6% was considered an average profit margin for a large corporation. Why was this corporation also listed as scheduled for bankruptcy? Was this a mistake?

Again the board members kept quiet. Only this time things turned in Jenny's favor. Nedra started asking questions too.

"What were the allowable parameters for bankruptcy? Why were they considering purchasing these two companies?"

Unfortunately Edward didn't know the answer and another board member answered the question for him. He was loosing control of the meeting. A conversation began among the board members as to what the bankruptcy laws were and to clarify they called in the corporate lawyer who was waiting on retainer in the penthouse. He was surprised to see these two corporations scheduled for bankruptcy and recommended they be promptly taken off the list.

Edward was seething and suddenly Jenny wondered if she had stepped into a hornet's nest.

Before the discussion closed, Jenny asked the loaded question no one else was willing to ask.

"Who owns both of these companies?"

Edward was forced to answer while Sandra dropped her eyes and froze like a deer caught in the cross rays of a powerful rifle.

"The Tetrazonni family."

There was a little collective gasp as the board members looked at Edward and then Sandra. Edward and Sandra had assumed the board would rubber stamp something that was going to cost the corporation millions and benefit the Tetrazonni family by millions.

Nedra was livid. Not at Jenny now but at Sandra and Edward.

Nedra and Jenny voted against the purchases and slowly the nervous board members joined her vote. Edward and Sandra turned a sick shade of green. They had made promises in exchange for favors and now they couldn't keep their end of the bargain.

Jenny had had enough. She stood up and walked out of the meeting feeling disgusted. She didn't want to be a part of any of this. If Edward and Sandra were running things and they were going to practice unethical business practices Jenny wouldn't agree to any ownership in the corporation. She would ask them to buy her out and leave them to rot in their own waste.

As she was walking towards the elevator a man in a black suit rushed out of the room and caught her arm.

"Your grandmother would like to speak with you. I'll bring her into the sitting room."

Jenny waited impatiently while Nedra was wheeled in.

Nedra got right to the point. "I want you to consider staying on the board and being more involved in our corporation. Without you here today we would have made a deal that I wouldn't have wanted. Believe me I don't want to have anything to do with the Tetrazonni family. I believe they are responsible for Ned's death. I also blame you and Lily for what happened to Ned. I still think Lily drove Ned the actions that he took. But, I'm afraid I have been trusting Edward and Sandra and have had the wool pulled over my eyes. I have no idea what they have been doing behind my back for the last ten years."

Jenny shook her head, ready to say no but she was softhearted. "I would recommend you hire someone to audit all of the corporate books. Make sure that it is someone that you trust. Then you need to hire a new Chief Operating Executive for your company and fire Edward. I would only be involved with this corporation if you set your company on a better path. Buying failing companies and putting them into bankruptcy edges on dirty business practices. I would recommend buying companies you believe in. Look for companies that offer good services that are ecologically sound with a view toward future trends that are healthy and positive. To do anything else is to invite scum in like the people that killed your son and my father. Whether you believe it or not I loved my father. But Ned abused my mother then attempted to murder her. He made his own bed. You shouldn't let your bitterness lead you to do the same thing."

Nedra was flabbergasted to be spoken to in such a way. If Jenny had looked back when she walked away she would have noticed that she also looked sad.

Nedra had just lost her daughter, her son-in-law and maybe her only granddaughter. But Nedra had a plan to win Jenny back and it included giving her everything she was asking for.

Jenny went down to the Chicago Tower bar and bought a couple of martinis to relax and come down from the tension of the botched board meeting. There were only a few people in the bar and she was happy to just sit quietly in a corner thinking things through. She checked her tape recorder. It had picked up both the board meeting and the conversation afterwards with Nedra. Jenny saved the file and considered. She was pulling out of everything tomorrow. She definitely didn't want anything to do with the Tavery family.

Feeling tipsy from drinking on an empty stomach, Jenny called for a taxi surprised that it was already after 9:00 pm. While Jenny was crossing Chicago in the Taxi her phone rang. It was Kelly on FaceTime talking from a bathroom at a whisper.

"Jenny, I stayed late at work to finish some letters. Sandra and Edward are here and she left her office door open. Sandra is on a rampage. She just got a call from Buddy Tetrazonni and a threat that she make good on their agreement. She screamed at Edward for ten minutes about him stupidly blowing the board meeting. She's talking to a lawyer about declaring Nedra mentally incompetent and continuing to contest the will in order to keep you out of the family business."

Kelly continued, "Edward looks like death warmed over. I guess Nedra came back into the board meeting after you left and said that she wanted Edward to be fired for incompetence and for misrepresenting information to the board. She said she had your vote by proxy and the majority of the board backed her. They fired Edward and made Larry White, one of the CPAs on the board acting director until they hirer someone to replace Edward. Edward's been on the phone whispering to someone while Sandra pulls her hair out. I have a bad feeling that you are in danger. You need to get out of town and then watch your back. I'm going to take your advice and quit this job. I think I'm in over my head too."

"Thank you, Kelly," Jenny said. "More than I can tell you. Be careful."

Jenny reached for her locket compulsively and then made a quick decision saying to the Taxi driver, "Take me to the airport, now!" Jenny didn't even stop to get her bag at Sheila's house. Instead she texted Sheila.

"I've had a change of plans and needed to leave. I'll call tomorrow to explain everything."

Once at the airport Jenny realized there wasn't a flight to Missoula until the next morning. The next flight out was a red-eye to New York City that had room for stand by passengers. Being in 'fight or flight' mode Jenny bought a stand-by ticket. It looked like she would be spending a few days with Ellie Bell in New York City.

Once on the plane, Jenny collapsed. The martinis had been too much for her. She almost never drank. Now the day and the alcohol kicked in and she fell into a drugged and dreamless sleep."

Had Jenny gone to Sheila's house, she would have been intercepted. There was a dark sedan waiting to pick her up. The driver had instructions to just scare her this time, to let her know that it was in her families best interest to support Sandra and Edward's business plan.

Jenny spent her taxi ride into New York City calling her family. Chance was worried and ready to fly out but Jenny talked him out of it. I'm completely safe right now. Just be careful if you see any strangers in White Cloud. I'll be home by Saturday. Then Jenny called Ian Abbott to fill him in on all of the details.

By noon the next day Ian Abbott received signed documents that some heavy hitting lawyers were contesting the will again, this time at the behest of Sandra Tavery. The same day Nedra received a notice that she was being taken to court. Sandra and Edward were contesting her vote at the board and questioning her mental competency. The vote would not be valid until there had been a hearing with a judge.

Sandra was already working to find the right judge who had the right connections.

Sandra realized this was the first time in years that she had felt truly happy. She was out from under her mother's thumb. She hated Nedra. She wasn't going to try to please her anymore or accept her criticism and control. Sandra was going to win this because she was going to prove that it was her mother who had had Dirk killed. Sandra knew that *she* hadn't done it and that left Nedra. Nedra's own mis-steps would hang her, high and dry. Sandra called a private investigator and then went to spend the day at the salon. All of this stress was making her look gray and wrinkled. She needed her skin conditioned, her hair colored again and a pedicure.

Nedra opened her little hidden desk drawer and took out the file with pictures of Jenny. She studied the young man that was with her, Kelly Walker. Nedra had asked Samuel Swift to hire him and had suggested he be Sandra's assistant. For the right amount of money Nedra was sure that Kelly would keep her informed about Sandra's plans.

Nedra was shaking now, a little tremor that wouldn't stop. When she held her hand against her lap she could still feel the tremor. The doctor had told her she would loose her coordination, find it difficult to walk and eventually not be able to stop the violent hand tremors. It might be five years or ten but eventually she would have dementia. She was terminally ill. Nedra picked up a pen and tried to write without the line weaving all over the page. It was more difficult than she thought it would be. If Sandra wanted to declare her incompetent she could use this against her. It was only a matter of time before Sandra found out that she had been diagnosed with Parkinsons Disease.

Nedra decided she needed to convince Jenny to come to Chicago and work for the corporation. She could offer her the CEO position or maybe it would be better to offer it to her boyfriend, Kelly. She could always have her own man there pulling all the strings behind things. Nedra wished now she had taken enough time to learn more about her granddaughter and what made her tick.

A little bit of panic came up when she tried to sign her name and had to try it twice. The worst part of this now was the depression. Why had it been her fate to lose everyone: her only son and now her ungrateful and scheming daughter. Joseph her husband had disgraced her too, both by not paying their taxes and then becoming an invalid for five years. Nedra wondered if it was the curse. Her mother, Marina, had been a devoted Catholic. She had believed the Tavery family was cursed because her brother had broken into the church as a teenager and stolen the sacrament. Nedra had hated her mother's superstition and portents of evil. Now she wondered if there was something to it.

Perhaps something needed to be made right with God.

Twenty-four

New York City

Jenny looked again at her GPS and gave Della's instructions to the cab driver. She hadn't been able to reach Ellie Bell on her phone line, but it was early. She was probably still asleep.

The address was in an industrial area turned sheik. Factory floors had been converted to high-end flats. Charming coffee shops, bookstores and unique clothing stores were housed on the ground floors. The noise and litter alarmed Jenny. She hadn't expected to see so much trash everywhere. She was also surprised at the wall of people walking everywhere as they drove down streets filled with cabdrivers, city trucks and limousines.

The cab driver dropped her off it at a flower shop with a metal door to the left of it that opened to stairs leading to the flats above. Jenny knocked on door 2B and then waited. Nothing. She knocked again this time louder and called out seeing the peephole open and hearing a number of dead locks turn. Jenny hadn't seen Ellie Bell in four years. This probably wasn't the best way to do it, dropping in on her unexpectedly at 8:00 on a Thursday morning.

When the door opened, Jenny gasped. It was Ellie but not the Ellie that she remembered. First she was wearing lingerie that matched. The long black gown was covered by another long robe that had a lace inset showing off the low back of the sexy gown. She had a sleep mask over her curls and a pair of earplugs hooked around her neck. Her finger nails were buffed clear and French manicured, her face looked like she had just had a facial and her hair was long with layers of streaking in shades of honey gold, light brown and copper. What was alarming was how thin she was. She looked like a size 2 or 4 and she was a 5 foot 10 inch girl with big feet and big hands.

Jenny rushed forward and gave her a hug while Ellie tried to semi-fend her off.

"Jenny, what are you doing here?"

Jenny ignored the irritation in Ellie Bell's voice. "Let me in you dwerb and I'll tell you all about it."

Ellie seemed to crack a little at the familiar teasing.

"Why am *I* the dwerb when you just showed up at my house without calling at 8:00 in the morning after flying here from Montana."

"Chicago," Jenny corrected. "You're out of the loop. You have been gone too long."

"What if Nicky Demetra had been here?"

"Well. Is there a Greek Adonis lounging in your bed?" Jenny tried to peer around Ellie.

"No but he could have been, he's here every other night."

"You'll have to tell me all about it.

"Not until more sleep, coffee, and a shower."

This time Jenny agreed. "I'm with you on that. I'm bushed. I've been flying all night. I could use your couch for a couple of hours before I fall down."

Ellie let her in and motioned her toward a long contemporary red leather couch. I'll get you a blanket. Use one of the throw pillows. They are down so they work pretty well for a sleep pillow.

Jenny looked around. The throws were large squares covered with African patterns of black and white geometric shapes. The lamps looked like works of metal art. There were only a few pieces of furniture in the whole apartment and they all looked Designer. The apartment itself was small consisting of an open living room/kitchen with industrial tiles on the floor and one bedroom which looked only big enough for a bed. One entire side of the living room was windows that had heavy gray mechanical blinds on them. A simple blue vase with peonies in it sat on the lacquered black coffee table on top of a square thick shag rug that was off white.

Jenny was impressed. Everything looked so 'New York City' that Jenny didn't have any trouble imagining that Ellie Bell would have a wardrobe to match.

Jenny slipped off her shoes and was asleep before Ellie came back with the blanket.

It was noon before she woke to the smell of a croissant being warmed with imported cheese and spinach. Ellie had picked up fresh orange juice. She sat on her yoga mat eating one boiled egg and half a grapefruit. The tangerine colored yoga mat was spread out in sunshine that filtered through the blinds. Elle was wearing a pair of lacy see-through tights and a stretchy top. The result was that she looked even more skeletal, the bones of her arms standing out and her pelvic bones sticking out along with her collar bone.

Jenny pulled her hair back and tied it in a knot and then came to sit down in a low chair that faced the mat.

Ellie saw she was still in her dress. "Where is your suitcase? Did it get lost?"

"I got scared and ran. I just left it in Chicago?"

"What!" Ellie said sitting forward.

Jenny took a grateful bite of the delicious croissant and sighed, beginning her long story. The farther she got into it the more alarmed Ellie looked until she got to the last details."

Ellie's mouth fell open. "You walked out of the board meeting, talked Nedra into firing the acting CEO and are now afraid of the Chicago mafia retaliating? How do you get yourself in these messes? Couldn't you just keep your mouth shut for one board meeting and then quit without wrecking havoc and pulling it all down on top of you?"

Jenny looked sheepish. "I was never good at following orders."

Ellie Bell scoffed, "The understatement of the year."

"So now what? What do you plan to do besides this crazy stunt of taking the red-eye on the first plane out-of-town."

"I wasn't thinking clearly. I had had two martinis and you know I'm a lightweight when it comes to alcohol. I think I suffer from anxiety disorder after what happened to my Dad. Also it was unbelievably creepy having Dirk set fire to my house and having a ghost waking me up at night to warn me that I'm in danger. I've been on edge and burnt out for weeks. I know that I need to go home and let Sandra and Edward make the first move then play out the battle just like you do chess. Only use my lawyer to help me make the moves instead of my impetuousness."

Ellie leaned forward and squeezed Jenny's hand. "I wish I could have seen Sandra and Edward's face when Edward got fired."

Jenny smiled. "I tape recorded the whole meeting. I don't know if any of it can be used later but at least I have some proof Edward was trying to pull the wool over everyone's eyes."

Just then Jenny got a phone call. It was Ian Abbott telling her about the fax that Sandra had just sent. Sandra was contesting the will again as well as asking a judge to rule on Nedra's mental competence. Jenny told Ian she'd be home Saturday and that they could meet then to decide what to do.

"Wow, these guys don't waste time." Jenny said as she hung up the phone. "I bet Nedra has already been notified by Sandra's lawyers too."

"Do you think you should call her?" Ellie Bell asked.

"Not without talking to Ian. She is a bitter and manipulating woman. She also has something wrong with her. She is in a wheel chair but I also noticed she has a constant hand tremor that she can't control. I think she sits at home in the dark because the light hurts her eyes. She looks like she is sick to me."

Ellie immediately became sympathetic.

Jenny shuddered. "It is hard for me to feel to sorry for her. She's like a black widow spider pulling people in around her to do bidding. She is used to controlling everyone. Ned probably didn't have a chance with a mother like that. I'll bet Lily was the only good thing that ever happened to him."

Ellie gripped Jenny's hand. "And *you* obviously or he wouldn't have left you such a large inheritance."

"Yeah, he left me his mess too, his crazy family and some kind of directive to fix it all for him."

Jenny took a good look at Ellie. "Enough about me. How are you Ellie Bell?"

Ellie gestured at her cool apartment, "As you can see New York City fits me."

"How do you get jobs?"

"I have an agent. I have been having good fortunate recently. Bonnie Blue just asked me to represent a new cosmetic line. Starting in September I'll be busy all the time modeling and raking in the moola. I spend a lot of time exercising, in tanning salons and in beauty parlors getting ready for the all-day shoots that are grueling."

"How did you get turned on to this?"

"I was waitressing to help pay the tuition for my fashion design school. I was pouring coffee for a table of hot shot men in suits when one of the men commented I had just the kind of hands he wanted for his magazine ad on a new hand cream. He gave me his card and I was interviewed and chosen for the photos. Someone there saw me on camera and asked if I'd model clothes at a fashion show. It was such good money I just slipped into the business and found out I have a knack. You know what an ugly duckling I felt like growing up because I was so tall and Scandinavian looking. As a model that gives me a unique 'look' that everyone wants. Even my name, which I always thought was ridiculous, sells me. Ellie Bell is going to be the new name of the line of cosmetics I'm representing. My picture will be on posters all over the city and they are going have a few transit bus ads. When all this blows over I'll go back and finish my fashion degree. For now though this is perfect. I'm learning a lot about the business from the other side. Then there is Nicky. It is all great!"

"Can't you eat a little more?" You look way to skinny to be healthy right now."

"The camera puts on 10-20 pounds. I look perfect under camera right now. It is just for a little while. A couple years of being underweight won't kill me."

Jenny shook her head. "I've heard of young women in their 20s dying of anorexia. You need to make sure you are getting all the vitamins, minerals and electrolytes that you need."

Ellie nodded. "Maybe I should have a checkup. This body has to last me for a while. Believe me, I'm not trying to do myself in, just stay competitive. You wouldn't believe what it is like out there. There is always a new and gorgeous new model coming up that is sleeping with the photographer."

Jenny smiled. "Is Nicky a photographer?"

"No, but he is an important agent. He's been introducing me everywhere and I need him."

"Do you love him?"

"Not like you love Chance, but I'm fond of him. Mom told me about your engagement. I see you got the family heirloom for your ring. I might have to protest," Elle Belle teased.

"I can't believe we haven't seen each other for four years. I've missed you!" Jenny said.

Elle nodded, "I feel guilty all the time about not going home but not enough to hear everyone go on and on about how skinny I am while they try to fatten me up."

"Maybe just explain and compromise by letting yourself gain 5-7 more pounds. I think you'd look better even under camera if your bones weren't sticking out."

"They are sticking out?"

"Yes, Don't you want to be your most beautiful for the ads?"

Ellie sighed. "I've been needing someone to tell me the truth.

I think I must have a bad self-image because I always see something else when I look in the mirror, my small breasts or my roman nose, my overly long legs."

"Ellie, those are the unique things about you that make you look stunning. But it is not as stunning to see collarbones and hipbones sticking out and thin boney arms. Trust me on this. I'm not lying to you."

"Okay, I'll increase my calories a bit with some healthy foods. Thanks Jenny."

Jenny looked down at her dress. "I don't suppose anything of yours will fit me anymore. Do you have any sweats I could borrow?"

Elle grinned. "Are you kidding, we are in New York City. You are going shopping."

Jenny resisted. "I have plenty of clothes at home."

Elle laughed. "Do they all look like three piece business suits? You need a new hairstyle, a professional color makeover, and someone like me with more fashion flair then you to break you out of your rut.

Jenny protested. "How much will that cost me? I have some beautiful things, I really do."

Ellie just got up and got a wrap around dress out of her closet. Here you can put on this after you shower and we'll go raid the clothes racks they use for the photo shoots. There are always 3 sizes of everything and tons of free clothes that designers send us in order to get publicity."

"Won't we get in trouble?"

"You forget I'm the celebrity for the day. We might as well take advantage of it."

Jenny had never felt so decadent in her life. First she had her hair streaked with long layers of golden brown, and copper with a sexy new side part.   They did her makeup at the salon using gold eye shadow, a luscious brown eyeliner and apricot blush that was heavenly and almost invisible.   Jenny couldn't believe how glamorous but natural she looked. She also couldn't believe how much money she spent buying all the beauty products. The next stop was a fashion designer that Ellie knew who did Jenny's colors. Jenny had always stuck to light yellow, royal blues and colors with blue tones because of her blond hair. The designer showed her she actually had neutral to warm skin tone that looked better in apricot, pinks, cream, spring greens and periwinkle blue.   It was a bit shocking seeing how her hair and eyes light up under the right color swatches.

From their Ellie took her to the Bonnie Blue offices to meet the fashion designers and get a look at the racks and rack of clothes stored in the stock room.

A fashion designer who was a friend of Ellie named Rodney helped pull clothes in the right size and Ellie insisted Jenny just submit to her choices. Soon Jenny had a new wardrobe of stunning clothes that were in her new radiant colors. The dresses had flared skirts with layers of chiffon and were sleeveless or off the shoulder. Everything had something unique about it that would look good on a woman with a small waist and athletic frame. Ellie insisted she pick shoes to match and a few purses too. And then Rodney gave her a Bonnie Blue travel suitcase to pack it all in.

Afterwards Ellie took Jenny out to her favorite restaurant and they both ate a large meal of Indian green curry and vegetables. Ellie looked so replete when she finished that Jenny laughed for joy.

"I haven't had a regular meal for six months," Ellie said.

"I haven't been so decadent in my whole life," Jenny replied.

"Are you really leaving tomorrow?" Ellie said.

"I have to, I have a bunch of orders to fill with my new manufacturing company. I need to get home and get busy."

"Then we'll have to go to clubs tonight and maybe even a show somewhere so you can see the city that never sleeps. New York City at night is magical."

"Let's take naps," Jenny suggested, "or I won't make it. I get to wear one of my new outfits, don't I?"

"You should wear the glittery top and silk pants. The more glamorous, the better, in New York City. Long gold balls for earrings, 4-inch platform shoes, you can just go for it. I have friends who will let us into some exclusive bars. Maybe we will see Nicky and I can introduce you."

Jenny woke up the next day with a raging hangover and a blurry memory of all of the bars she and Ellie had visited. She had met too many people to remember them all and left when Ellie had hooked up with Nicky around 2:00 in the morning. They had hugged goodbye and Ellie said she'd probably end up spending the rest of the night at Nicky's flat.

Jenny's plane left at 8:00 a.m. and she had to leave for La Guardia by 5:00. Jenny left a note.

I love you, Ellie Bell. Thank you, Thank you, Thank you.

You'll always be my best friend. By the way, Will you be my Maid of Honor at my wedding? Jenny Rabbit

When the plane left the gate Jenny finally got a chance to think about what was coming next.

Twenty-five

࿇

When Chance met Jenny at the airport he was surprised to see Jenny disembark looking like a model from Vogue. She was wearing a backless frothy apricot blouse over a wrap-around-periwinkle skirt with 3 inches platform shoes that laced up bare legs. The skirt had a little ruffle down the front and as she stepped forward her long legs were shown off through the slit in the skirt. Her new makeup including luscious coral lipstick with shiny gloss and gold eye shadow with smoky eyes in subtle shades of taupe and cognac seemed to transform her face making her eyes look huge and her lips irresistible. Long golden curls were cut to appear casually windblown catching the light as her highlights and shiny hair mirrored the sun. Her whole image was playful, free and light-hearted. She radiated feminine power and confidence. Chance saw men stopping to look at her as she walked by and stepped forward possessively.

Jenny bombarded him with questions. "Has Amy been working at the store for me? Did you see any suspicious characters around town? Did dad make it down from the mountains yet? Was another colt born while I was away?

Chance didn't answer. He was tongue-tied. First he was so relieved to see Jenny safe he realized that he was ready to pick her up and carry her out of the airport. Secondly, she was so beautiful he was stunned that she was his fiancé. He resisted the urge to cover her sun top with his jacket and hugged her tightly to his side instead.

"Chance, you can put me down. You are half carrying me to the car."

"That's because you look so good I'm worried another man is going to come grab you."

Jenny grinned and twirled. "You like? Ellie completely redid my wardrobe in one day. I'm going to have a hard time going back to my old clothes."

Chance shuddered. This was going to be like torture, watching men fall under her feet as she walked by.

Even though it was late Chance took Jenny straight to The Feed Store so she could check on everything before going home. She was surprised to find the lights on. Amy, the young woman she had hired to last week, was busy cooking up the last batch of Bodhi Bones and had already made and packaged the 150 orders from the open house. The Jack and Jill Snacks and Bodhi Bones sat neatly organized and ready for ingredient labels and shipping labels.

"Clementine is spending the night with a friend so I came over to work for a few hours so I could get these orders out first thing in the morning," Amy said. Amy had on plastic gloves, her hair in a net and she was wearing a white apron. Jenny was pleased see that she was taking the health requirements that Jenny had put in the employee handbook seriously.

Jenny was also impressed that Amy had done so well following the cooking and preparation instructions. She and Amy had cooked together to get ready for the open house and it appeared Amy was a fast learner who remembered little details. The Bodhi Bones looked perfectly molded and exactly the right texture and density.

Jenny put on an apron and began helping with address labels.

Within an hour everything was packaged and ready to ship out in the morning. Jenny and Amy worked quietly. Amy was shy but liked to be productive. Jenny felt incredibly lucky to have found her and after seeing how self-motivated she was decided immediately that she deserved a $2.00 raise. Amy seemed surprised and excited.

"Thank you for giving me a raise so quickly. Knowing I'm going to make enough to pay my daycare so I can do this was critical for me. I hope you are happy with my work because I really enjoy it. I never thought I'd find work like this in White Cloud."

"Once we are in full operation mode I plan to have four employees in the back, someone at the front desk, Bricca to help with marketing and a bookkeeper. For now as this train gets going it will be just you, Bricca and me. You'll be in charge of production."

Amy typed the last address card into 'Address Book' on the office computer and started to turn everything off while she cleaned the kitchen. Jenny checked to make sure the alarm system was on and her fire sprinkler system was turned on. Everything looked beautiful. Even the sunflowers from the party were still looking fresh and cheerful in their blue vases. When Jenny locked up she didn't notice that there was a soft humming sound coming out of the corner where her sound speakers were. She was unaware that someone had installed a camera and was watching her this very minute ready to report back to his boss.

Chance came back to get Jenny with a car filled with groceries. "I haven't gotten an opportunity to shop all week. We've been working 12 hour days trying to get done and didn't put in the last tile until late this afternoon. I'm glad that project is done. The owner's were impatient and sometimes rude. Dad and I both had a hard time appeasing them. Their kids are coming this weekend so they had people moving in furniture at the same time that the painter was finish the floorboard. The wife was complaining about dust getting on everything and had a group of cleaners there while we were still using a saw to do trim. I don't know why some people have to make everything harder than it needs to be." Chance shook his head.

Jenny squeezed his hand. "What kind of groceries did you get? Anything that will work for supper?"

"Stuff to make a stir-fry. But we could save it until tomorrow if you want. It looks like mom is still at the Diner if you want to stop there to get something to eat."

Jenny checked herself. "I am exhausted, so tired that I don't know if I can even sleep. Way to tired to cook, and too tired to visit with your mom. I think I need to sit in a bathtub and just lay in bed not moving for a while."

Judd grinned. "Well, I also got Captain Crunch so we are set."

"You've got to be kidding me, that is just sugar."

"Every once in a while you need comfort food, right."

"But Captain Crunch?" Jenny smiled and laid her head back on the seat of the truck and promptly fell asleep.

When she woke up Chance was carrying her inside and gentle stripping off her new clothes, sliding her under the covers in her slip and giving her a chaise kiss on the forehead. Jenny snuggled down into the warm covers and curled up. It felt so good to get back into her own bed. She dropped into a deep sleep.

Outside the same man who had planted the camera at The Feed Store was parked in a van down the road. He had planted a bug in the bedroom and hidden a camera in the bedroom and living room.

Right now he could just hear a box opening in the kitchen, the refrigerator being opened and crunching sounds. Then Chance came out in a robe with a bowel of cereal. He turned the TV down low to watch a hockey game.

It looked like it was going to be a long and boring night. The man thought. He had been hoping that he might at least get to see some 'welcome home sex.'

At 1:00 am his cell rang. The instructions were terse and emphatic.

He hung up and checked his revolver. He loaded his silencer and put on his bulletproof vest. *It was a shame really. They were just kids.* He thought about his daughter, she was about the same age as this girl. *But a job is a job. He had bills to pay just like everyone else and this job was going to pay his mortgage for a whole year.*

Slipping out of the van the man circled the house to the backdoor where he had found it easy to pick the lock earlier. *Two minutes and he'd be out and headed home.*

Jenny was sleeping so deeply it irritated her when her dream changed and she saw Gwenn Anne again, this time looking frantic. "Get up, NOW. Hide, NOW!!" The panic in Gwenn Anne's voice shocked Jenny out of her sleep and she grabbed Chance and put her hand over his mouth. He woke up startled and she whispered. "Slide under the bed with me, NOW. Do you still have your handgun in the night drawer?"

"Yes, what is it?

"We need to hide, NOW!"

Quickly Chance grabbed his gun and pulled her instead into the closet with him leaving the door open just a tiny bit. The moon was shining through the window making it easy to see the bed. It was only seconds before they both heard a soft footstep and saw the door open. A large man dressed in black was standing in the doorway with a silencer. He was holding it in front of him at chest level with his hand on the trigger carefully checking the darkened room. Very quietly he moved to stand over the bunched covers on the bed aiming his gun carefully. In the meantime Chance was sighting on him trying to decide if he should kill him or wound him. The intruder was wearing a bulletproof vest. If he shot him in the leg or hip the guy could still turn and shoot them. There wasn't much choice. Chance aimed for the center of his forehead and pulled the trigger. The noise exploded in the room, blood splattering against the wall as the man fell hard and his gun skittered across the floor. Chance stepped out of the closet and kicked the gun away looking at the neat hole going through the center of the man's forehead and the gore where the back of his head had exploded. His head was buzzing and he couldn't quite think straight. Chance had always been a good shot. You had to be if you wanted to hunt elk responsibly. But he had never killed a man and suddenly he wasn't feeling well. He turned back to find Jenny. She was curled in a ball on the floor of the closet.

Chance picked his cell of the bedside table still in an odd state of disassociation. He dialed 911 and got a dispatch operator.

"A man tried to kill me and my fiancé. We shot him and he is dead in our bedroom."

The dispatch officer suddenly sounded a bit panicked herself. Things like this didn't happen in White Cloud and she'd never taken a call this serious.

She read the words straight out of her manual. "Stay where you are please and keep on the line with me. What is your exact location, please and your full name."

Chance recognized that he was talking to Doris Baker. "Doris, this is Chance. I'm up at my caretaking house. Could you get Sheriff Russell here as soon as possible, I don't know if there are other men with guns coming."

Doris broke out of her dispatcher voice. "My God Chance, Make sure the doors are locked and find a basement or bathroom that you can lock yourself in. Someone will be there in 10 minutes. And stay on the phone with me while you do that. Is Jenny Okay?"

"She's fine, just in shock. Should I check to see if the guy I shot has a pulse?"

"No, don't touch the body or go near him. Just get somewhere safe yourself."

Chance went into the closet and lifted Jenny off the floor. She couldn't seem to uncurl herself so he just carried her as she was into a downstairs bathroom. He locked the door and sat on the floor holding Jenny in his lap.

Jenny seemed to be coming out of her frozen shock and now she was shaking in violent tremors. "He was going to kill us. We'd be dead now if I hadn't had the dream."

"What dream?" Chance asked.

"It was Gwenn Anne again, she woke me out of a deep sleep and told me to move, to hide, NOW. That is why I woke you up."

Doris Baker was listening to their conversation over the phone but not quite getting the gist of it.

"Is there someone else in the house with you that needs protection?"

"No," Chance said.

Doris gave them an update. Sheriff Russell just turned town your road. He is only minutes away. Sit tight."

Just then another call beeped in. It was Bricca and she sounded frantic. "Are you guys all right?"

"Yes," Jenny said, "How did you know to call? It's the middle of the night."

"I woke up feeling frightened for you. What happened?"

Jenny started to explain but then told Bricca they would have to call back. The police had just arrived.

Bricca just said, "Will and I are on our way."

Chance and Jenny could see the flashing lights from the bathroom window and quickly went to open the front door.

From there things got even fuzzier. A coroner was called and the man in the bedroom examined. He was dead, wearing no ID and looked to be around 50 years old. Immediately other police officers located the van and surveillance equipment and began a search for the cameras and bug, finding them in the house without difficulty. In the van they also found a cell phone, the cheap throw away kind, binoculars and a sniper rifle.

Sheriff Russell called in a special police task force called SSPD to help him and they began working quickly while Chance and Jenny were wrapped in blankets and taken to Della's diner to get some hot tea. The SSPD were experts at quickly solving cases. They only took high priority cases and were given clearances police officers normally didn't have. They were usually only called in when organized crime or terrorists were suspected.

SSPD put the dead man's face and thumbprint into the system to look for a match. Forensics was able to recover the last call he had received. It was from another throwaway cell phone in Chicago. The call had been made from a place along the Michigan shoreline. The local Chicago PD was sent to look for the phone, finding it within an hour in a dumpster. No prints.

The next lead was the dead man himself. His thumbprint was a match for an ex-con named Jerry Larwood. He had a record for burglary and had served two years for it. Then another short pop for narcotics. Nothing for the past ten years. He was a regular member of a gun club, had a wife and daughter and had a reputation at the gun club as an excellent marksman. The SSPD worked quickly to pull up his bank records. He had been receiving large deposits for the past five years that had enabled him to buy a nice house with a pool in the back yard. The deposits for 25,000 to 50,000 came from Cayman Island or Swedish banks. It appeared to the SSPD that Larwood was a hit man. The next important thing was to determine whom he had been working for.

Clearly Larwood hadn't expected to die tonight. This was supposed to be an easy hit of two kids who would be asleep in bed. He had been careless. There was a note in his car with a phone number and a matchbook from a Chicago Diner as well as a bill for two hamburgers and a shake. An envelope was in the glove compartment full of 100-dollar bills. The SSPD immediately began finger printing the envelope and the money. The phone number turned out to be the number for a pay phone outside of the Chicago B&B Diner. The food had been purchased Wednesday night.

The taskforce sent Chicago PD to the Diner. It was an all night diner and the waitress who had been on that duty Wednesday night recognized a picture of Larwood. The young waitress named

Janie nervously told the police that Larwood had ordered a hamburger and shake and talked to another man at about 2:00 in the morning. The other guy didn't order anything. When asked to describe the other man Janie said, "It was late, I just know it seemed he was older and maybe had money. He was wearing a nice black jacket and had a good quality kind of coat. They pretty much stiffed me on the tip, though."

The taskforce showed the girl pictures of the Tetrazonni family, the Tavery family and some local thugs.

Janie stopped and looked more closely. "That was him, this old guy here. Hey, we have tape that we run every night of the parking lot. We had some problems with vandals throwing rocks at our windows. You might have him on tape coming in."

By 4:00 in the morning the tape had been viewed by the SSPD. Edward Tavery had met with Jerry Larwood at 2:00 in the morning at the B&B Diner on Wednesday night. Then forensics came back with good news. There was a clear print on one of the hundred dollar bills in the envelope. It belonged to Edward Tavery. They had him!

By early morning the police were waiting to break down Edward's door. When they knocked a maid answered who was ushered outside. Within minutes they had pulled Edward out of bed put him on the floor and cuffed his hands behind his back. Sandra was yelling hysterically that she was calling her lawyer. Edward was trying not to throw up.

After four hours of interrogation Edward broke. They had a money trail and videotape showing him meeting with the hit man; they had a strong motive, and fingerprint on the money. They weren't letting him out on bail. A search of Edward's bedroom revealed a hidden drawer at the bottom of his desk. He had pictures of Dirk there and recordings of his wife having phone sex with Dirk. There was a list of numbers that turned out to be members of a Chicago gang. When confronted with the contents of the drawer Edward broke and confessed everything.

"It was Sandra. She was talking to that cowboy Dirk like she was a whore in heat. Sandra hired Dirk to burn Jenny's house, not me. I don't know where she got the money, probably Nedra. I didn't have anything to do with it. She is the one who should be here, not me. And while you are at it arrest Nedra. She probably put Sandra up to everything that she did. That bitch Nedra has been using me for years to make her money then she discards me when Jenny comes along. Someone had to do something and I was the only one with the guts to do it. Sandra was in bed with Buddy Tetrazonni on a deal that she couldn't live up to. He would have burned our house to the ground with her and me in it if I hadn't taken some action. I *had* to kill Dirk; I was the only one with the courage to fix the problem. Just like I was the only one who saw the solution with Jenny. Isn't there some way I can get a plea bargain if I give you some incriminating evidence on the Tetrazonni family?"

At noon the day after the night of terror Jenny and Chance got the call from the SSPD taskforce that Edward had confessed and implicated Sandra and Nedra also. Sandra was now being held without bail and Nedra was under house arrest.

Jenny and Chance were at the Diner surrounded by their whole family when they got the good news. Their family had been arriving in mass all night until the Diner was bursting at the seams. Bricca and Will and arrived first with four sleepy kids in the van. Then Jace and Lily had rushed in with Bern, running to grab Jenny in a close embrace. Jace looked grim and frustrated that he couldn't just go after the Tavery family himself. Lily wrapped Jenny in a blanket and held her while she shivered uncontrollably. Bricca went back to Chance's house and got Lily some warm clothes to wear while Will made a bed for his kids in the backroom of the Diner saying, "They'll probably just sleep through everything."

Della and Judd were pacing back and forth. Della kept trying to feed everyone and Judd couldn't seem to stop touching Chance. Chance's brother Joel arrived soon with his wife and soon Ellie Bell was on the phone crying that she wished that she were there to be with Jenny now. Musty showed up with a couple of Jace's men around four in the morning and by 8:00 a.m. Cissy had arrived with Harlow and Amy had walked over with Clementine and Doris Baker. Della's sister found out and came down with her husband and her kids. At 10:00 Ian Abbott showed up. Everyone was crammed together waiting and sitting things out together as a group.

Jenny had never felt so loved and protected. Tootsie wouldn't leave her side. If she moved, he moved. He seemed to need to stay close. The SSPD gave them updates each time they got a piece of relevant information. In a quiet moment Jenny told everyone about Gwenn Anne waking her, saying, "You need to hide, NOW!" How the dream had saved their lives. Judd held Chance tightly and reassured him he had had no choice but to pull the trigger. Thank God he hadn't missed.

Della made waffles for breakfast and everyone helped her also make eggs and hash browns and pour coffee and big glasses of orange juice for family as well as the police officers. When lunchtime came they formed a line to make potato salad and thick ham sandwiches. Bern took them over to the Sheriff's office, which was the staging area for the SSPD. By 1:00 pm the vigil was over. Jenny was safe and the nightmare was finally over.

The SSPD had moved quickly and efficiently. A cheer went up when Edward was arrested and another cheer when he confessed and Sandra and Nedra were arrested.

The family and friends gathered together for a group prayer. Bricca took the floor praying fervently. "Thank you Gwenn Anne for saving our loved ones. We thank you for coming back to undo past wrongs and to bring healing so that Chance and Jenny can share a long life of love together, the life you never got with Benjamin. We thank you for stamping down darkness, delivering us from enemies and holding up the light. We are so incredibly grateful to you." Bricca choked up and Lily took her hand to support her. "We know that you are an angel sent here from God and we thank God his for loving protection."

Jenny could rest now knowing that there was no one left to hurt her.

Twenty-Six

❧

Sunday afternoon Jenny went to bed and slept a deep dreamless sleep. When she got up she decided to go for a walk. She drove to Deer Creek and took Tootsie with her. The evening was perfect. It was only 70 degrees out with no biting flies or mosquitoes because of the cold nights. The middle of June in Montana was like April everywhere else. Sometimes the heat didn't really hit until after the summer solstice.

Jenny noticed that the flowers were almost waist high from the good rains they had been getting in May. Arrow leaf balsamroot, geranium, wild lupine and cow parsley was thick on each side of the trail. A lone deer had made a track down the trail. Other than a couple of frogs, a bald eagle, two mallard ducks, a song sparrow and a yellow warbler, Jenny was alone. Beaver had made 5 impressive ponds down the canyon where Deer creek ran muddy from the recent rainstorms. Tootsie smelled every leaf on the trail, clearly following an animal trail and Jenny let herself just meander. Every time she hit a shady spot she would stop to let the cool air touch the skin on her legs and arms. A few times she sat down on a rock to drop into a kind of hazy sleepy state. It was the adrenal let down from weeks of anxiety. It was such a relief knowing that all of the culprits had been caught. Jenny couldn't even think what to do next about the Tavery Corporation and her impending inheritance. Making decisions like that seemed like some mirage way in her future.

When it came time to meander back down the trail to her truck the walk was down hill and Jenny made good time. Her truck was parked in the sun and hot so she was glad she had left the windows down. Her purse was flung between the middle console and the back half-seat. She grabbed it and began searching for her keys. Usually she just put them on the dash but this time she couldn't find them anywhere. She started to get nervous opening the truck door to see if she had dropped them when she got out. Tootsie jumped out again and started running around in the grass. At some point he put his nose down and wined to get her attention. He had found them on the ground in deep grass.

Jenny put the key in and turned. The truck didn't start. Oh crap, she had left the lights on and there wasn't any cell reception out here. But she had only been gone for an hour and a half. Just her luck the battery had been low. Jenny grabbed a light wind shirt out of the backseat and prepared to walk home.

If she was lucky she might still get a ride from someone driving into White Cloud from the isolated dirt road that led to Deer Creek. Jenny figured if she didn't see someone she wouldn't be home until dark. What a drag. By the time Jenny dragged herself in the front door after walking most of the way home carrying Tootsie. Chance was pacing the floor. They had only just come down off of a traumatic experience. He was worried something might have happened to her.

Jenny called her parents to let them know she would bring Tootsie home in the morning and went to bed exhausted. She thought she must be more tired than she thought to have gotten so careless with her keys and lights.

The next morning Jenny let Tootsie out to go to the bathroom and she began fixing herself a fried egg and toast. After a few minutes she opened the door and called for Tootsie to come in. No Tootsie.

Jenny walked around the house calling and then went down the road in both directions, still no Tootsie. That was when she started to panic. Maybe Tootsie didn't know this area as well as home. What if she'd wandered off and was lost. Jenny called Chance to come home and began checking every culvert on the dirt road. He can't have gone far, Jenny insisted. There was nothing out here but old Mrs. Stewart's house. Jenny remembered she had heard coyotes yipping last week. What if one of the coyotes and run into the yard and picked Tootsie up when she let him out? Jenny started to shake. They drove up and down the road calling, looking everywhere. Maybe Tootsie had tried to run back home to Lily and Jace's ranch. But that was more than fifteen miles away. Jenny called Lily and broke the bad news to her crying.

"It's okay, honey. She probably just chased a deer or small ground squirrel and she'll show up any moment."

By Monday night Jenny had started to give up hope. Tootsie had vanished without a trace. If a coyote had gotten her there was no trail. Everyone was broken-hearted. Just to make sure, Jenny made posters to put up in town. But town was five miles away. She didn't hold out much hope that Tootsie could make it all the way to town.

Tuesday Jenny slept in a little but decided it was time to go to work like normal people. Chance had jumped her truck for her so she drove it in slowly to town, calling the whole way to work for

Tootsie out her window, still hoping to see her come running out of the trees and willow. She was praying for some kind of intervention from the divine and was willing to make deals, if only she could get Tootsie back.

When Jenny opened the door to The Feed Store she saw paperwork and invoices right where she had left them waiting to be sorted, filed and then inputted in her bookkeeping system. But when she opened the door to the kitchen she was upset to see that the extra bags of 'Bodhi Bones' had been left on the cabinet out of the cooler and that the heat in the room had been turned up, peeling labels off the boxes and breaking the glued seals. What a mess. She didn't even know if she could switch the bones into to new boxes. What if the heat had contaminated some of the ingredients? They were perishable and the instructions said to keep them refrigerated after the box was open.

Disgusted with herself for overlooking something so important Jenny ended up tossing 20 boxes. It would take a whole day to make them again. When Amy arrived Jenny told her the bad news. Amy looked surprised.

"I put everything we hadn't shipped in the cooler. What were they doing on the cabinet?"

Jenny shook her head. "It had to have been me. I'm so tired and fried I've been doing things like loosing my keys and leaving my lights on. I suppose you've heard that Tootsie is missing. I need about a week of sleep and maybe then I'd still be in shock. I must have turned the heat up when I thought I was turning it down."

Amy commiserated. "Well don't worry. I have time to do the new batch. You just work on the books today."

By noon Jenny had proudly reconciled her first bank statements for her business and looked at her expenses and income to date. She had some income and they were doing okay. There was enough to pay Amy, her suppliers and the mortgage but not enough to pay her own self. It would all come around, given time.

That night Jenny drove up and down the road again hoping for some sign of Tootsie.

On Wednesday Jenny got a phone call from the Brinton foundation. The secretary of the foundation sounded irritated.

"We are wondering why we haven't heard back from you yet. The photo shoot and interview is Friday morning. Were you able to arrange to be here for it?"

Jenny questioned the secretary. "What letter? What photo shoot?"

Apparently she had been sent a letter a week ago that there was an important opportunity for the Brinton Foundation to get an article in a nationally recognized magazine. They were willing to fly her to Chicago for the interview and photo shoot and wanted her to make flight arrangements on her end.

Jenny was apologetic. "I'll book a flight now."

Jenny scrambled to try to get a seat and ended up having to make a reservation to leave at 5:00 the next morning. That meant she'd have to leave at 2:00 to make her flight. Jenny couldn't believe that she suddenly had to go to Chicago again. Her last visit there had been terrible.

Chance put his foot down. "This time I'm going with you. You might end up having to do something with the Tavery Corporation while your there. You are currently the only major stockholder who isn't incarcerated. Have you called Ian Abbott about this yet?"

Jenny threw her hands up. "I had no idea this was coming. The letter got lost. I can't find it anywhere. And the secretary I talked to at Brinton's wasn't very nice to me about it."

Jenny started to pack feeling better after she realized she would get to wear some of the beautiful new clothing that Ellie had given her. She opened her closet to chose a few dresses and saw another disaster. Part of the drywall in the ceiling had fallen down and her clothes were covered with drywall dust and plaster. A few of the delicate fabrics looked like they were ruined. There was insulation in her shoes. That couldn't be good. Insulation itched and even had little pieces of glass in it. She had no idea how to get it out other then vacuuming her shoes. In the end Jenny had to dig out some of her old suits to wear. How disappointing. Suddenly Jenny started to cry in loud gulping sobs. That was how Chance found her when he walked in carrying his suitcase to pack.

"Tootsie is gone." Jenny wailed. "My clothes are ruined."

Chance tried to reassure her that somehow it would all work out.

"But Tootsie might come back home while we are in Chicago," Jenny cried, "and we won't be here!" They went to bed sad and upset with the alarm set for 2:00 a.m.

At 2:00 in the morning it was another shock to find that they had a flat tire on his truck and that her truck battery hadn't taken a good charge. How were they going to make their flight? Chance called Judd to give them a last minute ride and everyone was grouchy by the time they had boarded the early morning flight. The good news was that Judd agreed to go back to the house and stay there for the weekend with Della just in case Tootsie came home.

Twenty-Seven

❧

When Jenny and Chance arrived at Sheila's they found the door locked. Nobody was home. Jenny had forgotten to tell Sheila she was coming. It was hot and muggy. The chiggers were hopping out of the grass and cicadas were making a racket in the trees. The heavier flowers of summer like roses and chrysanthemums were in full bloom. Jenny and Chance sat on the hot pavement of the porch sweating and irritated with each other. Neither of them wanted to risk getting covered with chigger bites from the grass.

"Did you call her to let her know we were coming?"

"There was something wrong with my cell phone. I think it must have water damage."

"How could that be? Did you drop it in the sink?"

"I don't know. I found it on my desk with the screen saver all bubbled up and water underneath. I must have spilled something on it in the car without realizing it. I tried to make the call to Sheila and it wouldn't connect. I forgot to try in again because we were in such a rush to pack."

"What if Sheila is gone this weekend?"

"Maybe we need to call Alexander or Nina and find out."

Chance called and left messages with no answer back. "We should probably just call a cab and get a hotel room somewhere. We can keep calling Sheila and maybe meet her for dinner later."

Jenny groaned. "What is going on? Why is this all happening?"

Chance just grinned. "We get to stay in a Motel 6 tonight. I'd call *that* good luck. We'll have a TV, a pool and a big bed."

Jenny laughed and Chance made the call for the taxi.

Once they were settled in their room Jenny put on a swimsuit and went to lay by the pool. It was perfect weather for that. As the sun started to set the air was balmy and the pool was still warmed by the afternoon heat. Chance was right; she needed to make the most of she and Chance having a few days together.

At 6:00 pm Jenny's phone rang but she couldn't pick up the messages because the phone was still acting wonky. Jenny ran upstairs to get Chance's phone to call the number back but got a strange number. It sounded like the call had come from a casino. An hour later she got another strange call. This time she called back and a man answered.

"My phone is out of order, were you trying to reach me."

"Yeah, Babe" the man said. "I got your phone number from the newspaper ad. I like kinky phone sex too. So what are you wearing right now?"

Jenny hung up. Kinky phone sex? An ad in the paper? She called the guy back.

"Hey babe, we must have gotten cut off. I was just thinking about how much fun we are going to have tonight."

Jenny sighed. "I just called back for information. What paper did you see this ad in? The Chicago Tribune personal ads? Are you sure? Could you check the number again? The number is a mistake. Please don't call me again."

Jenny laughed. Oh Brother, now that she looked she had twenty-six calls from Chicago numbers on her phone. She was really popular tonight. How could they have gotten her number by mistake?

When Chance got back with Chinese take-out they had a good laugh together about it and then tried out the king-sized bed. The lumps weren't too bad when you were busy doing other things.

By morning Jenny had a terrible headache from sleeping on a pillow that felt like a brick and on a mattress that sloped down in the middle. Showering quickly she got dressed and left a little note for Chance who was still sleeping.

"The interview is this morning. I'll be back by noon."

When Jenny got to the Brinton building she checked her appearance in the glass window one last time and then slid into the cool lobby. Immediately she was ushered into a lovely sitting room where a photographer and two women sat chatting.

Jenny shook hands and they began. All of their questions were succinct and intelligent. Jenny soon warmed up and was happy to tell them about her why she had gotten into the business of making animal treats. She shared some funny stories from her childhood, got them to talk about their own loved pets and was so engaging one of the ladies asked if she would like to have lunch with them. Jenny borrowed a phone at the desk to call Chance and they morphed into three young women enjoying downtown Chicago. By the time lunch was over Jenny felt like she had made two new friends.

"Please come see me if you are ever in Montana," Jenny said. The older of the two, Priscilla smiled. "I think this is going to be a good article. We might be able to get permission for a follow-up to see how far you get with your business in a year. Our readers like stuff like that. I'll put it in my calendar to call you."

At 2:00 Jenny looked for a payphone and called Chance again getting a busy signal. She waited 15 minutes and called again. The line was still tied up. Finally in frustration she just called a taxi and had it take her back to the motel. She had been hoping maybe Chance could join her to walk around downtown Chicago. It would be fun to see a show or musical production while they were here.

The motel room was empty. Clothes were still scattered all around but there was no sign of Chance. Then she saw his phone lying beside the bed. Chance had made a call that was still connected. He had never hung up. The call was for pizza delivery.

Where was Chance and where was the pizza? Jenny started to sweat and her heart began to beat too fast. What if someone had picked Chance up? What if the mafia family knew they were in town and they had tracked them to the motel? Jenny's imagination went wild. Maybe that was why Sheila wasn't home.

Suddenly Jenny saw the motel door rattle and the door began to open. With a scream she crouched behind the bed afraid to look as a man walked in. It was…...Chance! He saw Jenny crouching petrified behind the bed at the same time that she burst into tears.

"You weren't here. I called and the phone was busy. You left and your phone was still connected. I thought something bad had happened to you."

Chance held the pizza in front of him for her to see. "No, I was just ordering pizza."

Chance sat the pizza down and pulled her into a big hug.

Teeth chattering Jenny said, "I imagined all sorts of things. I worked myself up into believing you and been taken by the Chicago mafia. That they already had Sheila kidnapped somewhere."

"How terrible for you. Eat, you'll feel better."

"I just had lunch downtown."

"Well, I can't wait anymore. I'm starved." Chance sat on the edge of the bed and reached for a slice of hot pepperoni pizza saying around bites. "Sheila called. She and Alexander and Nina are in Duluth at a lake cabin this weekend. There's a baseball playoff today. I got the pizza because I wanted to watch the game. Since I don't have to work today I'm making the most of my vacation."

Jenny socked him on the arm. "I was thinking that maybe we could go to a Broadway musical or something."

Chance didn't look excited.

Jenny put her hands on her hips. "Then let me have your phone. I'm going to call my ex-boyfriend and see what he is up to."

Chance turned down the volume on the TV.

"What?"

"Don't worry, Kelly is just a friend," Jenny said. She was already dialing the number.

Kelly answered on the first ring.

"What's up?" Lily asked.

"Funny you should call. What is up is that I am working my butt off trying to fill in for Sandra here. Samuel Lewis has dropped her files in my lap until they can find another real estate agent to take them over. I've been sitting at her desk since she was arrested. From what I can tell she won't ever be coming back, at least not to this firm. An audit of her files and contracts showed all sorts of unethical business practices and the real estate firm has fired her."

"Meanwhile, about once a day I get a call from Nedra begging me to come work for her for five times what I'm making now. All she wants, she says is for me to do whatever you would want with the corporation. She would like you to come visit her. She is under house arrest and is only allowed approved visitors and calls until the trial."

"Trial?" Jenny asked. "I am completely out of the loop, have they set a date for a trial?"

"Not yet, I'm sure you would have been notified through your lawyer since you'll be one of the key witnesses."

Jenny cringed. She hadn't even thought about what was coming next down the pike.

"Is Larry White still the Acting CEO of the Tavery Corporation?" Jenny asked.

"Yes, I'm sure he would appreciate a call from you as one of the major shareholders. You might want to go see him while you're here in Chicago," Kelly replied.

"Are the Tetrazonni's still hanging around trying to force the issue about buying their corporations?"

"No, I heard through the grapevine they sold them to some other big corporation. They probably don't want anything to do with the Tavery family now that they are being prosecuted."

"How would I get ahold of Larry White?"

"He's in the phone book as a CPA. I'd say he is a pretty decent guy. He is definitely not the kind of guy to be in anybody's pocket. I imagine he is doing a thorough company audit now."

"Thanks for the heads-up on everything, Kelly. You've been wonderful. I'm glad to hear they are giving you some responsibility now. Maybe you'll end up getting advanced in the firm. You must be relieved that Sandra is gone."

"Hey, about drinks tonight and I'll take you dancing."

"I'm here with my fiancé. We'll be going out on the town tonight. But thanks for the invitation."

"Bummer for me. I really it blew it with you."

"Friends?"

"Friends."

Jenny signed off and hung up the phone thoughtfully. She didn't notice that Chance had turned off the TV and was watching her carefully.

Chance said, "So, what do you say we both get dressed up and go out on the town. Instead of a musical let's see if we can find some good jazz music."

Jenny giggled. "I thought you'd never ask."

Jenny called Ian Abbott for advice in the morning. He was adamant that Jenny not contact Nedra.

Ian said, "Nedra is going to trial for her part in attempted murder. She would only be manipulating you to try to get you to drop all the charges against her. The police do not want you to speak with her. However, it is a good idea to contact Larry White. You should find out what he is doing and give him some direction. It's possible that after this trial the corporation may belong solely to you and your heirs. You should be getting involved in its reorganization. It is completely within your rights to do this as you are a major shareholder and Sandra is not in a position to contest the will."

After Jenny got off the phone she called Larry White. He seemed happy to have her input and agreed to meet her at her convenience. Chance went with her and waited in the lobby while Jenny and White had a lengthy meeting. As Kelly had predicted Larry was in the middle of an in-depth audit. He had already found some serious discrepancies that showed that Edward might have been embezzling from the other shareholders.

Jenny shared her business philosophy and preferences for the future with Larry and he looked relieved and pleased. "We are of a like mind on this. I would like to see this company turned around so that we are focusing on forward thinking business philosophies, green products and healthy global trends. I believe that the majority of our shareholders feel the same way."

By the time they had finished the meeting Jenny needed to rush to the airport. Chance ran the baggage through check-in and Jenny grabbed them something to eat at the gate. The ride home was uneventful.

But as soon as they got home they realized something was 'rotten in Denmark.' The refrigerator had come unplugged and all of the meat in the freezer had thawed out and spoiled. Water was flooding the floor and the kitchen stunk of rotting food.

Chance shook his head, bewildered. "Judd or Della must have jostled the fridge when we were getting ready to leave and pulled the plug out of the socket."

For the next few weeks everything got back to normal.

Jenny worked hard every day and Bricca came into the store and gave her some great marketing ideas. They created a website called The EFeed Store and put up pictures of their products along with blogs on animal care and organic foods for dogs. The blogs started getting hits, which encouraged sales of Bodhi Bones. Bricca came up with the idea to have a contest for naming their next product, which was a dog toy. The prize would be a year's supply of doggie treats. The idea took hold and the response was great. Out of it they got a winner who came up with the simple but great name, "Fetch." Bricca helped Jenny design a logo for it that had a picture of Tootsie on it fetching in the back yard. He was running forward with his ears flying behind. Jenny shed a few sad tears when the artwork was finished.

Amy was working fulltime now in production and Jenny was doing most of the mailing as well as working on her wedding.

Jenny wanted to get married on Lily and Jace's anniversary date so that they would always share the same anniversary. August was one of the best months in the mountains anyway. The weather cooled down at night and any bugs died out with the cold nights. Overnight, the air became sweet with the pure scent of sage and fall colors appeared in the undergrowth of the aspen forests.

The first thing that Jenny did was contact Cissy Harlon to make her dream dress. Cissy giggled. "Should we go with the dress I told you about?

"Yes, you have my vision exactly." Jenny said. "As I told you, I've wanted that dress since I was twelve years old."

Jenny surprised her mom and asked if she could be married at the ranch on the same day that Jace and she had been married. Lily began to cry. "Oh, that would be lovely! Amazing! Do you remember our wedding? You were the flower girl."

"I remember everything about it. That's why I want the same thing. I want to have an arch in front of your flower garden with the chairs on the ranch lawn. We'll set up tents in the fields for a BBQ and dance. I'm telling Sophie now to save the date so she and Grandpa can come back for it. Sheila is planning to come too."

Between planning the wedding and working a month flew by.

Cissy had the dress done on August 1st. She brought the beautiful dress to The Feed Store for Jenny to try it on. It was perfect. As she had hoped the tiny straps, simple white dress, and elegant train with sweet details like baby roses, tiny white flowerets and pleats fit Jenny's personality perfectly.

Jenny zipped the dress up in a wardrobe carrier and hung it up in the closet of The Feed Store. She didn't want Chance to mistakenly see it.

ଔ

Time flew with a hundred details to attend to and Jenny woke up and realized it was only three days until her wedding. She had let her mom have full reign with getting chairs, flowers, an arbor and organizing tents for food. Jenny had put Bricca in charge of finding caterers and music that was good dancing music. Amy had addressed invitations and done seating charts for the tables and Della had hosted a rehearsal dinner.

Jenny was having Ellie Bell as maid of honor and Chance had asked Joel. The wedding was taking place at 4:00 pm on Saturday, August 15. On Thursday morning Jenny got out the bag that was protecting her wedding dress. She wanted to try it on again just to make sure she hadn't gained any weight and there were no problems.

When she pulled down the zipper of the bag she gasped. Someone had dumped blue ink down the front of the dress and ripped it from top to bottom. Her dress was ruined.

Jenny didn't know what to do. First of all, she was scared. This was the work of someone who was crazy. It wasn't a kid vandalizing her. It was an act of pure venom.

Jenny wondered how someone had gotten into The Feed Store. It had to be someone who knew where her hidden key was kept. And then Jenny remembered the feeling of sabotage she had experienced a month before: her keys thrown out of her car, her phone dumped in water, a tire punctured, food ruined at the warehouse, their fridge turned off, clothes ruined, the missing letter from Brintons. Whoever did the dirty deed with the dress had probably done the other things, too.

Jenny decided to set a trap that night. She told everyone that she knew that the caterer had stored the wedding cake in the large industrial cooler at The Feed Store, that it was beautiful with tiers and tiers of tiny roses cascading down it. Then she sat in the dark behind a counter and waited.

At 11:00 p.m. the front door opened quietly and Jenny heard footsteps. The door to the kitchen swung open and a flashlight bounced around the room. The intruder went directly to the cooler and opened it as Jenny turned on the lights.

And stood in front of her dressed in black with a hammer in her hand. With her black uncombed hair and white skin with dark bruises under her eyes she looked like a lunatic.

Jenny gasped thinking, *Of course! Kiera! She was the only one who could hate her this much.*

Jenny cried out in distress. "How could you ruin my wedding dress? And I see you're here now to destroy my cake. I know it was you sabotaging me a month ago, too."

Kiera's mouth twisted as spit out, "You have everything, money, a boyfriend a business, why couldn't you just let me have the only man that has ever loved me? It's your fault Dirk is dead."

Jenny backed up from the hammer in Kiera's hand and tried to talk her down.

"Kiera, I didn't do anything. *Dirk* is the one who almost killed me. *Dirk* is the one that accepted money to incriminate me. I didn't kill Dirk. I was your friend. I tried to save you from what Dirk was doing."

Kiera stumbled and almost fell as she came around the desk towards Jenny carrying the hammer.

Jenny changed tactics. "I'm so sad for you. He loved you and now he's gone."

Kiera began to wail. "We were getting married. I was buying a house. He loved me, I know he did."

Jenny carefully reached forward and gently took the hammer and flashlight out of her hands reaching for her phone to call 911. "It is so sad. I'm so sorry that you miss him. Kiera have you been doing things to me to try to get even for a while?"

Kiera wrung her hands and paced back and forth with manic tension. "I saw you driving out to Deer Creek and followed you for the first time that day. It was easy throwing the keys out of the window and turning on your lights. It was harder sneaking into your house. But I'd seen Chance hide a key. It isn't fair that you have beautiful clothes and a beautiful wedding dress when I don't get one. I'm not sorry."

Kiera hunched over and began to keen in a high-pitched wail and rock back and forth. Jenny punched in 911.

Just then the door opened and Mrs. Paige called out. "Kiera, are you here?" She rushed in and put her arms around Kiera taking in the scene of the ruined wedding dress and Jenny poised with a phone in her hand. "I'm so sorry Jenny. Please forgive her. Something in her broke when Dirk was murdered. I have been taking her regularly to see a psychiatrist. It has been helping. Please don't press charges or call the police. I'll buy you a new dress." Mrs. Paige seemed frantic. "I'm taking her home today to live with me. We are moving back to California so that my family can help us. She won't bother you again. I promise."

Jenny hung up the phone. "How sad for you and for Kiera. I won't call the authorities but this can never ever happen again."

"It won't, don't worry." Mrs. Paige led Kiera out of the building and Jenny heard their car drive away.

Jenny felt devastated. First for Kiera, but also for herself. Her wedding dress was ruined and there was only two days before the wedding. Then something struck her so hard her knees got a little bit weak.

She grabbed Kiera's flashlight and ran to her truck. Pealing out she drove Bertha as fast as she dared to Livingston trying to remember Kiera's address. *It was the name of a tree*, she thought. *Elm, Oak, Hawthorne, no Hickory! 215 Hickory.* The little house looked dark and empty as she drove up. Jenny parked, grabbed the flashlight and ran up to the door. It was locked. Not really caring about the consequences, Jenny used the flashlight to break a windowpane so she could open the window latch and climb in.

The house stunk of garbage and filth. There were dirty dishes and clothes everywhere. Kiera clearly had completely lost her mind it in the last month.

Jenny turned on a light. No electricity.

That is when she heard it. A pitiful sound of whining came from a closet. Jenny rushed into the bedroom and shone the light into the dark closet. It was Tootsie. He was lying in his own feces with a food bowel that was empty and no water bowl. Tootsie couldn't get up to greet her. He thumped his tail weakly in greeting.

Jenny grabbed a towel and gently wrapped him in it carrying him into the kitchen to get him some water. Wetting a paper towel and tricking some down his dry throat. Then Bricca called Will to meet her at his Vet office driving as fast as she dared back home.

The lights were on when she got there and Bricca was there too with the kids who had insisted on coming along.

Jenny rushed in with her little bundle and unwrapped Tootsie on the table while Bricca tried to keep the kids back so that Will could check her out.

"Is he going to be okay? Daddy. Is he going to be okay?" Tonka chocked out tearfully.

"Tootsie needs an IV with fluids and some nutrients. Then we'll know more."

Within a half hour of getting fluids Tootsie was acting more normal. Will took a warm wet cloth and began to gently clean his matted and filthy fur. Then he let Lizzy help. She had already made it clear that she wanted to be a Vet when she grew up. Lizzy seemed to have a natural ability to comfort Tootsie while still taking care of him. "Look Dad, he has a big crack on the side of his mouth."

"That's from not getting enough water," Will said. "But he'll be fine now."

Jenny started to cry with relief and Bricca and all the kids clung to each other. Tootsie looked like he wanted off the table so he could join in too.

Jenny couldn't believe it. What if she hadn't gone and looked for Tootsie. Tootsie would have died in that closet. She couldn't believe how close she had come to losing him and how grateful she was to find him again. Jenny would definitely be contacting Mrs. Paige about this. She was going to have a police officer visit them to talk to her and Kiera about animal cruelty.

Lily was ecstatic and Bern got her to drive him down to the clinic so he could see Tootsie too. Will decided Tootsie needed to stay in the hospital for a day so Lizzy insisted she would just stay all day with Tootsie until Lily could take him home.

The next day Jenny had to face another crisis. She was getting married in one day and she didn't have a wedding dress. It was Ellie Bell who came to the rescue. They would take Jenny's measurements over the phone and find something in her size in New York City. There wouldn't be time to do any alterations. Jenny would just have to trust Ellie Bell to pick out something that would suit her.

Jenny agreed and called Cissy to break the bad news about the ruin of the amazing dress that Cissy had created.

Cissy was a good sport about it. "Well your safe and Tootsie is too. A dress is just a dress. If Ellie Bell is bringing you one from New York City you can bet she will find you something extraordinary. I'm sorry though you've had to go through this nightmare with Kiera."

Ellie flew in very late Friday night. Saturday at noon she was rushed out to the ranch. She arrived looking like a goddess, all long legs, shiny hair, and sultry style. For her Maid of Honor dress she had chosen a rose pink off the shoulder dress to wear that had rows of ruffles down the back. It was elegant but fun. Ellie carried a huge dress bag for Jenny and rushed her upstairs to put on her makeup and fix her hair. Lily, Bricca and Sophie were in the room when Ellie unzipped the bag and took out the designer one-of-a-kind bridal gown. The dress was everything Cissy had wanted for Jenny but so much more. The material was chiffon to keep it from being too heavy. Tiny rows of pleats each had baby roses on them. The filmy white material gathered gently at the waist and then billowed out in tier upon tier of ruffles in the back. The dress was simple in the front but backless. A lovely belt was covered with crystals and ended in a unique bow over the long ruffled train. The bottom of the 4-foot train had tiny rosebuds circling the trim. The modest sweet heart top had tiny straps. The dress felt weightless yet it shimmered from the crystals placed throughout the soft fabric. Jenny held her breath. It was beautiful but would it fit. As she stepped into it all the women held their breath. The seamstress had gotten her measurements exactly, the dress fit like a glove.

Lily let out a little sob. "You are so beautiful. You look like an antebellum southern bride. In 1885 your dress would have taken years to make. Every detail of it is perfect for you."

Bricca stepped forward. "I have a surprise for you. It is your 'something old.' I found this locket in one of Gwenn Anne's envelopes." It was a small solid gold locket with a pearl on the face of it. The delicate locket had a simple gold chain. Jenny opened the locket and saw a picture of Benjamin Thomas on one side and a picture of Chance on the other side. "I added the photo of Chance," Bricca said.

Jenny gasped. "My hands are shaking. Can you put it on for me? Oh, My God, Thank you. It is exquisite."

The locket looked perfect with her dress.

Then Lily stepped up. "I have your 'something blue.' It is a tiny piece of cloth that used to be part of your first Bunny, Betty Bun Bun. She was a gift from Grandma Charlotte and you had destroyed her by the time you were two by sucking on her and taking her everywhere. We replaced her with Bobby Bun Bun and later Cindy Bun Bun. I sewed the blue cloth into a little flower to pin to the bottom of your skirt." Jenny gave her mom a huge hug and tried hard to hold back tears.

Then Sophie stepped up. "I have your 'something borrowed.' Here is a little pouch to attach to your bouquet. It has the key in it that belonged to my mother that I never take off. It represents her first love, just like Chance was your first and now your last love." Jenny hugged Sophie enthusiastically.

Finally Lizzy stepped up. "I made you 'something new.' It is a brand new penny sewn into a tiny purse. Look, I embroidered "The Feed Store" on the purse." Everybody laughed and cried and then laughed again.

Bern stuck his head in the door looking a bit nervous to see so many women in one room and his sister looking like a princess.

"Mom, its time for me to escort you to your chair." They could hear the acoustic guitar starting down on the lawn and Lily gave Jenny a final tearful hug and went down with the other women following.

Now it was just Ellie Bell and Jenny upstairs together. Ellie put some finishing touches on Jenny's hair, which had been braided into a loose coronet with Babies Breath in it. She squeezed Jenny's hand and said, "I knew you'd marry my brother the very first time you met each other. You asked if you could play 'dolly' with us. You were three and a half and Chance had just turned five. I remember he took off his hat to greet you and turned bright red. He was stricken the first time he ever saw you. We teased him about it unmercifully. The love never went away in all those years of growing up. You were just meant to be together."

Jenny smiled at the memory. Just then they heard Jace and Joel coming up the stairs to get them. It was finally time.

As Jace walked Jenny into the garden everyone's faces turned towards her and they seemed to glow with love.

Chance was waiting in front in a black tux. In deference to his mother, he was wearing the McBride Tartan over one shoulder and he looked calm and strong. Tootsie was lying on a special pillow near the front with a bow in his hair. Lizzy was sitting next to him stroking him gently so he wouldn't try to run down the aisle to greet Jenny. Sheila, Sophie and Lily were holding hands and crying. Jace and Will were standing tall and proud next to Bern who was looking more like one of the Bridger-Mead men than like a boy.

There was luminescence over the whole scene as the angels watched the final moment of completion. Everything was in its rightful place. Destiny had prevailed.

As Chance and Jenny joined hands Bricca stood up. Jenny had asked her to read a poem that she had written when she turned eighteen. It had been a moment when Bricca had seen a falling star and gotten a hint at what was coming in her future.

FIRE FLIGHT

I'm free tonight.
  My roof infinity.

I see tonight
      a million miles into the past
          a short circle into the future

I drink tonight
  with Pegasus, shining steed
  now Earth bound –
  His cup the Lady
        Sweet Water of Life

I can Be tonight
Wind sculpts and shifts me
        Into *Starfire*

Into *Fire Flight*   -   I am *Starborn*   tonight.

Out in the pasture a little colt ran in circles, on the mountain a doe licked her new faun, and on the lawn as ancient vows were shared, the old passed away and a new future was starborn.

About the Author

Diana Yvonne Walter has written two other novels books in the Fire Flight Series entitled *An Unusual Beauty/Fire Flight and StarFire/ Bricca Down West* that tell of the lives of Sophie and Lizbeth when they meet in a small town in Nebraska as young women. The second book follows the lives of their daughters Lily and Bricca as they follow their dream to raise horses in Montana. Walter is also the author of two other books, *Vulcan and the Golden Teachings*, a romantic metaphysical science fiction and *Dear Grandma*, letters written to her grandmother who passed away at age ninety-nine and a half.

Diana is a licensed marriage and family therapist and licensed professional counselor of thirty years. She also works as an astrologer and a yoga instructor. Her studio, Padma Mountain Studio is located at the foot of the Tetons in Jackson Hole, Wyoming.

When not writing she can be found out riding one her horses, (Dollar, Hayden, or Clover) on a mountain trail.

She can be reached through her website at:

www.opensky111.com

email: opensky111@msn.com

This book was self-published by
OpenSky One Eleven Press
8350 S. Henry Rd.
Jackson, WY 83001
307-739-0888

Starfire: Bricca Down West

One

৯

Jenny was holding on tight to Grandpa Barry's thumb and wouldn't let go. She was whimpering that she didn't want 'gamy and gampa' to go away and David knelt down on the floor of the airport to help her understand.

"Hey Bunny, where's that smile I'm used to seeing? Grandma and I will be gone for a little while but we'll write you and send you pictures of us from over the sea. We can even talk to you over a computer and you can show me how 'Cindy Bun-Bun' is doing." David pointed to Jenny's worn white stuffed rabbit and then looked up to Lily and Sophie for a little help.

They were engrossed in their own sad goodbye. Sophie had written a list of things for Lily to give to the caretaker who would be watching their house in Winnetka, Illinois. Most of the list was details on how to care for each plant in her well-loved garden. She had another paper with an address for Lily to mail the shipping box that contained the things she had decided she couldn't live without on their year long sabbatical to Greece. It felt unreal to be flying all the way to Greece to spend an entire year.

David looked at his watch and gripped Sophie's hand pulling her away from Lily.

"We need to go through security," he said.

Standing next to each other, both over six feet tall, trim and athletic, David and Sophie looked like a royal couple. Sophie wore her long hair in a thick gray and brown braid, and was dressed in jeans and a short-sleeved top with a sweater slung over her shoulder. David looked fit and ready to go wearing a polo shirt and canvas pants. They both looked too young and vibrant to be in their mid-sixties. Lily was amazed at how well they matched each other in every way. Lily was going to miss them. They had always been an example of what it meant to deeply and passionately love your partner. She felt sad that any attempt to model them in her relationship with Ned had failed so miserably.

After the break up with Ned, her father had become a fill-in partner in taking care of Jenny. He had joined the school board and picked Jenny up after pre-school. They had spent weekends at the children's museum and afternoons in Sophie's garden. Jenny was attached to her grandpa the way some kids are attached to their father. It would be hard for them to be separated. During the worst days of her divorce she had stayed in her Dad's guest room. David had made omelets and Sophie had made waffles and fresh-squeezed orange juice. They had insisted that she go for long walks or runs with them along the Michigan Lake shore that was adjacent to their house. The walks included thought-provoking conversations on interesting topics since her parents were both liberals and her mother was a well-known author who also taught workshops for college students.

Lily broke away from her reflection to look around the airport terminal. It was time to say goodbye. She reached for her parents in a group hug, unable to stop the tears that slid down her cheeks, noticing that Sophie and David were crying too. Jenny had started to wail.

"Don't go gampa! Don't go!" She stamped her foot and Lily picked her up to comfort her.

"It's only a year; we'll be back before you know it. By then you'll be fully established in your ranch in Montana. As soon as we get back we'll come out to see you," David said. Lily had set an ambitious goal to move with Jenny to a small town out west where she had decided to build a house and breeding stable on a ranch just outside of White Cloud, Montana.

David grabbed Sophie's hand and pulled her with him towards security for their gate, slipping off his shoes and stacking their belonging in the plastic tubs on the conveyor belt. Lily stood on her tiptoes, wishing she was taller than her 5'6" frame, watching their backs as long as she could. At the last second Sophie turned around and blew her a kiss, and then they were gone.

The airport suddenly felt foreign and deserted. Lily gripped Jenny's tiny hand for support. She was twenty-eight years old but she had never been separated from family. All of her bravado about moving out West felt ridiculous. How could she leave her friends in Chicago when the world felt so empty and lonely now?

Fortunately Lily had another set of stepparents. Her nanny, Sheila, and Sheila's husband Max had been with her since birth. Sheila had been her surrogate mother when her mom had gotten sick and eventually died from melanoma. In the nine years before Sophie and her Dad married, Sheila had treated her as her own child. Lily thought of Sheila's two kids, Alexander and Nina, as her brother and sister.

Sheila and Max had promised to help her pack her furniture into the U-Haul that she had rented. Max had agreed to drive the U-Haul while she drove her horse on the long journey across Wisconsin, Minnesota, South Dakota and Wyoming. Her plan was to take her boxes and furniture to White Cloud and find a place to store it while she put up fencing and built a barn and stable on her property. She would need to find a place with hay to board her horse, 'Trigger,' until the work was done. It was already the third week of July and she wouldn't be in Montana until the beginning of August. The snow could start to fly by the middle of October. That meant she needed to be ready in two-and-a-half months.

When her place was set up, Lily would be moving a champion stallion and six prize-winning dressage and hunter-jumper mares onto the property. Lily knew that the odds were bad for succeeding at a business involving breeding or training horses. Horses are fragile creatures with monumental vet bills. They require a huge amount of time and effort to raise from birth to yearlings. Then it takes years to train them into finished mounts. The investment aside, buyers sometimes spent more money on a saddle than they did on a horse because of supply and demand. There were just too many animals flooding the equine market. But those horses didn't have champion bloodlines and proven talent as Jumpers. Lily was determined to find a niche that could make her venture succeed.

Getting from O'Hare terminal out to the parking lot took more time than she had planned with a three-and-a-half year old on her hip. Jenny was at that awkward stage where she was too heavy to be carried but too small to walk any long distance. Going anywhere with her took a lot of patience and time. It seemed that they were always in a hurry.

Lily tucked Jenny into the back seat of her old Toyota and fastened the seatbelt, digging out a juice cup that she had filled half with water and half with apple juice. Because Jenny seemed especially fussy she found her some crackers and her stuffed rabbit to entertain her and swung out onto the bumper-to-bumper highway traffic on the loop back to Chicago. Once she got close to downtown she headed East, eventually ending up on a suburban side street where her little one-bedroom house stood, tucked in the trees behind a chain-link fenced yard.

The previous owners had built the fence to contain three dogs. Over time the dogs had killed the grass. The house looked rundown too. Lily didn't mind because it had been cheap rent. Bodhi, her golden retriever, rushed around from the side of the house to greet them, almost knocking Jenny over in his excitement to say hello and give them a slobbery kiss. Lily hated leaving him alone at home, but didn't want to take him in the car in the humid summer heat. Last summer she had resorted to having Bodhi shaved to keep him cool but he still had his long coat now since she hadn't been able to afford the groomer. He was certainly going to enjoy their move to the cool mountains of Montana.

"Come on Bodhi. Jenny, you too. In the house. Now! We have packing to do."